Mar 2023

To Josh,
Thanks for always
making me
laugh

The Unstoppable
Nurse Nancy

Best wishes always

Barbara Bradley

The Unstoppable
Nurse Nancy

By Barbara Bradley

ISBN: 978-1-957384-19-1 (Paperback Edition)
ISBN: 978-1-957384-20-7 (Hardcover Edition)
ISBN: 978-1-957384-18-4 (E-book Edition)

Library of Congress Control Number: 2022924036

Book Ordering Information
Phone Number: 929-334-4203 ext. 1000 or 347-349-4971
Email: info@eamediaandpublishing.com
Executive Access Media & Publishing
www.eamediaandpublishing.com

Printed in the United States of America

EA MEDIA & PUBLISHING

Dedication

Dedicated to my friends
Cindy, Pam, Jamella and CTR
And my sister Dee
For their inspiration and encouragement.

Contents

Book One

Prologue

Nancy Calloway. A simple and uncomplicated name for someone who is anything but simple and uncomplicated. A compassionate and extremely competent nurse by day, a scoundrel by night.

Nancy always thought her family was from somewhere in southwest England, considering her name, but was shocked to find at the age of 16 that she had been abandoned at a Saint Louis hospital as a newborn and had been adopted by a loving but inept couple. Although her parents tried to give her everything she needed, she never felt like she belonged. She was different from her schoolmates and was restless most of the time, never knowing why. The other girls teased her because of her tall, skinny frame, jet-black hair, and penetrating turquoise eyes. Later in life, she would be described as stunning, but as an elementary school kid, she wanted to be like all the others… petite, blonde, and popular.

She was born in June, making her a Gemini. True to her astrological sign, as a child, she was hyperactive in school, always wanting to dive into challenging projects and trying something new without finishing most activities before beginning another. She was outgoing and outspoken without thought of her schoolmates' feelings. Occasionally she would be embarrassed by uttering a faux pax but would brush it aside and rapidly change the subject. It was her way of coping. If someone hurt her feelings, she would quickly shrug it off, but the wounds cut deeply. She was not one to forgive and forget.

As she matured, she loved the attention from the boys who complimented her new grown-up body. She used her newfound beauty to manipulate the boys. She learned she could get almost anything by promising a kiss or a peak of some forbidden fruit. She loved the attention she finally received after feeling left out for years. The attention she craved was temporarily satisfied by a boy's adoration. She flirted insatiably and loved it when the girls gave her hateful looks.

Things were innocent until the day she discovered who she was…an abandoned nobody. Despite her adoptive parent's explanations and eventual disciplinary actions when she became uncontrollable, Nancy was a wild child.

She would use and/or be used by a boy until one of them became bored or angry and then went on to the next. She let fate lead her life and found that big and small decisions were challenging to make…so she didn't make them.

Somehow, she graduated from High School without getting pregnant or having a life-threatening disease, and her life changed for the better when she finally decided to join the Army. There she found her way. She learned how to work as an integral member of a team. She developed discipline and discovered that strenuous physical exercise strengthened not only her body but also her mind. She became skilled in combat maneuvers and became an excellent shot with both rifles and handguns. Boot camp gave her confidence and a feeling of accomplishment, something she had never experienced. She was ecstatic when she heard her drill sergeant praise her for a job well done. Positive affirmations for her accomplishments instead of her looks were what she craved.

She thrived in the Army. After Bootcamp, she volunteered to become a combat medic. She excelled at her training and became confident in many skills before being stationed in Afghanistan. There the constant adrenaline and fear helped her focus. Nothing mattered more to her than her patients. It was when she saved the life of a young soldier by dragging him out of harm's way and ministering to his wounds, despite the danger to herself, that she decided to become a nurse. She was awarded a Purple Heart medal when shrapnel tore into her shoulder during a firefight. She healed physically, but the injury required her honorable discharge, which caused her great emotional stress. She had found a home serving her country and floundered when she was a civilian once again.

Finding her way slowly, she enrolled in nursing school. She was adequate academically and outstanding in clinicals. Book learning bored her. She became restless. The only thing that gave her pure enjoyment was dressing up and going to the clubs. The sexier she dressed, the more attention she attracted. The more men she drew, the better she felt about herself. Her old habits and insecurities reappeared without the regimentation of being in the Army. It wasn't unusual for her to pick up two different men on a weekend and go home with them, but never did she take them to her apartment. The wilder the sex, the better she felt. It became an addiction. Every weekend was an opportunity to drink too much, dance until her feet hurt, and find new and different ways to satisfy herself sexually. Sometimes things would get too rough. Her combat training came in handy a few times when her "date" went too far or became abusive. She never seriously injured any of them, although she was capable of significant damage. She just made it clear that she would not be taken advantage of. She was the user, not the used.

After graduation, she was hired by a local hospital, where she learned the ropes while working in the ICU, the Medical Surgery floor, and the surgical recovery department. She especially enjoyed the adrenaline she felt during a trauma in the Emergency Department. Nursing was something she loved and was committed to during the day. She even worked as a flight nurse for a year, transporting ill and severely injured patients to facilities capable of treating life-threatening conditions. This was the closest she came to feeling like she was back on the battlefield. Eventually, though, she became tired of the irregular hours and being on call for weeks at a time. They interfered with her nightlife, so she decided to quit.

She hated wearing scrubs and looking like everyone else in the hospital. Instead, she chose (and was given permission) to wear the formal nurse's uniform from the 1950s, including the white uniform dress, white stockings and shoes, and the white cap she was given during her graduation ceremony. She felt it set her apart and above the others. Dressing immaculately every day was her way of drawing attention to herself in a positive way. "Nurse Nancy" became her nickname. She liked it.

She became very accomplished at compartmentalizing her life. Her personal life never crossed into her professional life. Weekdays were for nursing. Weekends were for partying; the wilder, the better. "Drugs, Sex, and Rock 'n Roll" was her motto. However, no matter what the weekend brought, she was "bright-eyed and bushy-tailed" on Monday morning. Her weekday friends were primarily working acquaintances. Her weekend acquaintances were never friends.

She had tried having a relationship with a man once. It hadn't worked. The love and compassion she showed her patients never crossed over to a romantic relationship. She had even tried some dating sites without success. The "straight" men honestly looking for love bored her. The "naughty" men just amused her. She could find a much wider variety of highly sexed men any weekend night. She did not desire a typical midwestern stable relationship with 2.3 kids, soccer games, or PTA. She wanted more. Much more, and she wasn't going to accept anything less, even though she wasn't sure what "more" was. She figured she would know it when she saw it.

Chapter 1

Nancy woke up to a bright and sunny Monday morning. The weekend was a distant memory to her though she had "partied hardy" as usual. She always stopped the party by noon on Sunday to be in top form by Monday morning when she returned to work. She kept herself strictly disciplined during the week. Early morning alarm followed by a three-mile run. The neighbors teased her and said they could set their clocks by her routine. After her run, she would shower, make a nutritious smoothie for her breakfast, dress and apply her make-up fastidiously before leaving her apartment at precisely 7:30 a.m.

Today was no different. She liked her routine. It helped her control her "bad girl" urges, and she knew she was responsible for giving her all to her patients everyday. They deserved nothing less. She got out of bed, put on her running clothes and shoes, and began her day. She listened to self-help podcasts or sometimes mindless novels to pass the time while she ran. Her favorite fiction was the Janet Evanovich novels with Stephanie Plum as the main character. She admired her "pluck" and loved Lula, Stephanie's sidekick. What a hoot. She is so uninhibited and able to say precisely what is on her mind! Nancy only wished she could eat as much "Cluck in a Bucket" and donuts as Stephanie did and keep her figure like the fictional character. But, alas, that was only fiction. The reality was a crueler beast.

Nancy enjoyed a drink or two, but only on the weekends. Only natural "highs" were allowed during the week to compensate for the unnatural ones on the weekends. Weekends were dedicated to whatever indulgence she desired. Besides a great Manhattan made with Maker's Mark whiskey and Martini and Rossi sweet vermouth, her drug of choice was ecstasy, but only on weekends and only from her supplier, who had never sold her anything but 100% pure product. She wasn't a fan of marijuana. It mellowed her out, and that is the last thing she wanted on weekends. She was known to do cocaine occasionally for the energy it gave her. Opioids were not her thing. She wondered how anybody could like them because they made her nauseated and didn't have much effect. Nancy had never even been close to being addicted to any substance. She was thankful for her ability to take or leave about anything, including caffeine, drugs, and men.

She had tried smoking when she was in the Army but found it disgusting in many ways. She threw away the second pack she had ever purchased and never touched a cigarette again.

Nancy's running route seldom varied. Out her apartment door, to Washington Park, around the Lagoon, and back. Her route took exactly forty-two minutes before returning to her three-story walk-up apartment in an old but well-loved brick building. She had lived there for five years since graduating from nursing school. She liked the location because of its proximity to the University of Chicago, its hospitals, clinics, and the park. It certainly wasn't the nicest part of town, but she wasn't the nicest person. It worked well for her. She never had any problems while jogging or commuting. In pubic she presented an don't-even-try-it attitude; and nobody did. She was also known to carry a Taser, legally, of course.

She arrived back at her apartment building out of breath and sweaty. She pushed particularly hard on Mondays to rid her body of the toxins from the weekend. Taking the stairs two at a time, she was swiftly back at her door. After unlocking the two deadbolts, she slipped into her home and engaged the deadbolts once again. "No sense in asking for trouble," she thought to herself.

Soon Nancy had showered and was standing in front of her closet. She chuckled to herself when she saw the six identical Nurse's uniforms hanging pristinely on their hangers. "Gee, I wonder what I should wear today," she muttered before removing her "Monday" uniform. She never liked to wear the same thing for two days in a row and did her laundry once a week on Sunday evenings.

Before dressing, she applied a light coat of foundation, blush, and mascara, leaving the application of her lipstick until she arrived in the parking lot at work. She had a natural beauty that didn't need make-up, but she never left home without it. It provided her "mask," her protective shield from the world.

She pulled her thick black hair into a loose ponytail and twirled it into a bun on the back of her head. This allowed her to easily attach the nurse's cap to the top of her head. She loved the retro look of her white dress and stockings. Her co-workers didn't understand her obsession with the old-fashioned look but admitted she always looked perfect, even after a long shift. Again, it was part of her "mask," her persona. She loved to dress up, to masquerade her true self. Her uniform in the Army had helped, and now her working uniform did much the same thing.

Arriving at work at precisely 7:55 a.m., she had a quick moment to apply her lipstick and be ready to begin her duties at 8.

"Hey, how's Nurse Nancy this morning?" called her co-worker Connie from her desk.

"Fine, thanks," Nancy replied with a smile. She liked it when her patients and coworkers used her nickname. Getting right down to business, "What is my assignment today?"

Connie proceeded to recite Nancy's schedule. Nancy smiled. She liked doing Hospice nursing. Although she knew her clients/patients would not be with her long, the appreciation they showed her was very satisfying. Nancy tried to make every one of her patients smile or laugh during her visits, which were otherwise quite tricky. IVs with nutrition, pain, and other medications needed checking and adjusting if necessary. Bandages needed replacing. Ostomy bags and catheters required changing. "Whoever said that nursing is a glamourous job was misinformed," mused Nancy as she gently and lovingly shifted a bedridden patient to avoid pressure sores.

An essential part of her job was communicating with the families who were rightfully distressed by their loved ones' conditions. She never hurried. She was patient, listening carefully to the questions, often through tears, with compassion and empathy. She helped in any way possible to ease the transition for her patients and their families. She saw grief every day but never became overwhelmed by or immune to it. This made Nancy the best hospice nurse her agency had ever had. She was loved was dearly loved by her patients and well respected by her coworkers. She did her job efficiently and thoroughly each day while looking forward to Friday nights.

After her last patient was seen for the day, Nancy stopped by the office to drop off the lab samples and charts. As she was about to leave, her supervisor, Maria Hernandez, called her into her office. "Hey Nancy, how did things go today?"

"Nothing unusual. I had to spend extra time with Mrs. Johnson's family today. They are not handling things very well, which is understandable. The siblings are arguing about what kind of end-of-life care their mother needs. Two want to honor their mother's wishes and continue the DNR (do not resuscitate) order. The other two want all possible life-saving procedures to be performed, including CPR, ventilation, and continuing artificial life support, if necessary," Nancy explained. The same two siblings can't or won't understand why their mother isn't getting tested and given all the new treatments for her cancer. I explained that hospice provides support and palliative care, including adequate pain management for a dying patient. They are still hoping for a cure."

"That is why it is so important to have an Advance Directive at least and a Medical Power of Attorney to handle the final decisions. It helps define what a person wants when they cannot communicate for themselves. It takes the decision-making away from the emotionally charged loved ones and has saved many families from arguing at a time they should be bonding," said Maria.

"We both know that people handle death and dying differently, either because of religious beliefs, personal values, or the inability to let their loved ones go. That is why we provide counseling and medical services, including access to a chaplain if requested," Maria continued, sounding like she was reading a brochure.

"You are preaching to the choir on this one," said Nancy, and both women chuckled knowingly.

"To change the subject, I have been meaning to have a chat with you for another reason. An opportunity has arisen, and I think it would be perfect for you. Do you have a passport?" she asked.

"As a matter of fact, I do," replied Nancy. "Why?"

"The regional Bone Marrow Donor office has contacted me. They are looking for someone with your background to become a PRN (as needed) courier. It would mean taking stem cells to wherever they are needed, including international destinations. You would hand carry the special container to the clinic or hospital, get a receipt and then fly home. It would mean going out of the US, possibly once or twice a month. If time permits, you could stay a couple of days at your destination. I know how much you love to travel and experience new cultures and how good you'd be. This would be in addition to your regular job, and we would give you the time needed to do the extra assignments."

"Oh my gosh! It sounds wonderful! But why me?" she asked.

"The dispatcher of the Courier Company, Travis Murphy, called and asked for you by name," explained Maria.

"That's weird," said Nancy, puzzled. "Why would he recommend me when we don't know each other?"

"I guess he had heard about you and was impressed. You don't know it, but you have positively impacted hundreds of lives here in Chicago. Maybe he has a friend or a relative you have cared for. Who knows, but who cares how he found you? Just that he did."

Nancy nodded, still confused. "Are you trying to tell me not to look a gift horse in the mouth? In other words, be happy and don't ask too many questions?"

"I think it could be a marvelous opportunity for you, and I'm willing to cooperate with your schedule. I gave you a glowing recommendation." And after hesitating for a moment, "Promise me that you will not quit this job. We need you!"

"Sure, I have no intention of leaving you. I love this job, and I know I am needed. But when can I begin the courier job!" exclaimed Nancy. She enjoyed her hospice job but had recently secretly longed for something with a little more variety. With this new job, there would be further adventures in exotic nightclubs. New men. New everything. She couldn't wait to get started.

"Your first trip will be in a week. It's to a hospital in Berlin, Germany. You won't need anything more than your passport. In the meantime, they need you to stop by their office and get trained and give them your employee information, which should take only about two hours. The training is mostly learning about customs paperwork specific to each country. Otherwise, it should be a breeze. Can you be ready in a week?" asked Maria.

"Are you kidding? I could be ready tomorrow morning! I am so excited! Thank you so much for thinking about me!" replied Nancy excitedly. "I won't let you down."

"It never occurred to me that you would ever disappoint me. It's not your style," was Maria's simple and sincere response.

The following week was a whirlwind of activities and emotions for Nancy. She had met her new boss Travis, who seemed very interested in her and found the orientation very basic...more like common sense instructions than formal training. Paperwork had never been a problem for Nancy. She knew how to dot the i's and cross the t's on her charts, and this would be no different. The most vital part of her job was to be on time for her flights and to keep the container holding the precious stem cells intact and with her at all times. The styrofoam cooler would fit easily under an airplane seat, so there was no need to place it in the overhead bins. She also needed to be flexible in case of a delay or cancellation of her flights. She had forty-eight hours from collection time to delivery at the final destination. If unsurmountable complications arose, like an airline strike or mechanical issues with the plane, she was to contact her office immediately. Whoever was in the office would give her further advice and orders. "Easy peasy," Nancy thought.

Meanwhile, her daily duties varied little. She saw her patients and explained that someone else might take care of them for a couple of days, and explained the reason. "Nice job if you can get it," one patient replied. Nancy had to agree.

Nancy was very excited about the upcoming adventure and the honor she felt by being chosen to do such an important task. She loved to travel, although she had done little after her Army experiences. She had always read the offers she received on her email account from sites like Travelzoo and Scott's Cheap flights. Her mantra had been "Far away places with the strange calling names are calling, calling me," like the childhood song she remembered so well. Now her dreams were becoming a reality... and she was getting paid to boot! Who could ask for more than that? Of course, she wouldn't spend much time in any one destination. Still, she had arranged to spend the weekend in Berlin since she was leaving Chicago on Thursday and would return on Sunday instead of the regularly scheduled one-day turnaround. She would have time to tour the city and check out a few bars on Friday and Saturday nights. She promised herself that she would only visit them, not partake in illicit activities. Not on her first assignment. Her first time in Germany would be an exploratory expedition. She had to be perfect and perfectly demure, she told herself.

Excitement filled Nancy as she selected the clothes and make-up she would take. She planned carefully. She could only take one roller bag and a purse beside her precious cargo. She had to be able to manage everything herself and not depend on others to assist her either in the airport or on the flight. That meant packing light. A white nurse's uniform was not necessary, nor wanted, for her courier assignments. She would try to look very attractive yet not seductive. Professional but feminine. She might, after all, meet someone sexy and exciting in the airports or on the plane. She wanted to be prepared just in case. She would arrive at the airport early enough to stop by the Lufthansa Club and see what it might offer. And then she would need at least two outfits for her evening adventures. Luckily, they were very skimpy and didn't take up much room in the carry-on bag. She decided not to take any "toys" or special lotions or lubes with her due to TSA regulations. "Oh well," she thought. "It will help me to be a good girl while I'm gone…if that is possible."

Nancy arrived at O'Hare International Airport at noon, at least two hours before recommended check-in for the 4 p.m. departure. It had been a long time since she had been at such a busy and exciting place. Her flirting with the check-in agent (male, of course) didn't get her upgraded from her coach seat to Business Class, but it did get her a better seat in Economy Plus. She smiled at her little coup.

Getting through security was a breeze, and she quickly searched for the Lufthansa Club, which she found close to her departure gate. She paid the daily fee and made herself comfortable at the bar. She ordered a Virgin Mary instead of the more salacious Slow Screw she usually ordered in clubs to get the men's attention. She instinctively knew that consuming alcohol during her assignment would be frowned upon. She wanted to keep an eye out for fun and stay within the company's conduct policies.

Although it was merely noon, a few men were drinking. She started a conversation with a nice-looking forty-something man sitting close to her. He was from Minnesota, going to Munich to sell farming machinery. "No way, thank you," she thought and politely excused herself. Not seeing any hot prospects, she demurely settled into one of the comfortable overstuffed seats that had a nice view of the entire lounge. If anyone interesting appeared, she would be able to scope him out. Nancy quickly learned that post-Covid travel was very different from "the good old days" when flying was an adventure. Post-Covid travelers were harried and hurried. Although she was a little disappointed not to meet a hotty at the beginning of the trip, she was not discouraged. She knew there would be plenty of opportunities once she arrived in Berlin and finished her assignment.

Nancy boarded the plane and had an annoyingly uneventful trip. She had been upgraded to sitting right in the middle of a girls' high school choir on their way to Europe to perform at one of the universities. "Ugh," Nancy sighed. She wasn't interested in making small talk with a bunch of teenagers, so she made herself comfortable and slept through most of the flight. "Thank goodness I can sleep on a flight without any problem," she thought.

Before landing, Nancy went to the lavatory, reapplied her make-up, and brushed her hair and teeth to put her best face forward before leaving the plane. She had a short layover in Munich, which she maneuvered like an old pro and quickly made the connection to Berlin.

She had more luck on the second flight. A very handsome thirty-something man who wore no wedding ring chatted her up. Nancy immediately recognized his beautiful English accent and asked him where he lived. She learned that he was from London, in Berlin for a few days, mostly on business, and was single. "Very promising," she whispered to herself.

Their conversation continued without missing a beat for the entire but short flight. Nancy suggestively asked his advice on the best places in town to sightsee and party, hoping for an invitation. She was not disappointed when he offered her a ride into town.

"I'll have to decline your kind offer," she replied. "I am on strict orders to take my taxi to the Cancer Center. Once my mission is accomplished, though, I am free," she smiled coyly to encourage another invitation.

"Well, I have a meeting this afternoon," he stated. "But how would you like it if I took you out for a nice dinner this evening? I can show you some of the sights at night. We Brits like to eat early, but Berliners don't dine on weekends until at least ten o'clock. So, let's compromise and say nine this evening."

"Thank you, I'd love to," replied Nancy, thinking he seemed like a nice guy. Maybe too nice. He was someone to have dinner with but not to party with through the night. "I'm at the Hilton. I'll meet you in the lobby at nine."

They exchanged numbers and headed for immigration. He pointed to the left across the room. "You go to the other line since you are from the United States. I have already gone through customs today, so there are no formalities for me," he instructed. "Best wishes and I'll see you tonight. My name is Jonathan Harris."

"Mine is Nancy Calloway," she added as he disappeared.

"What a nice way to begin my stay in Berlin," she said to herself. "This should be interesting, at least."

Once Nancy cleared customs and walked out of the terminal, she was all business. She hailed a taxi after asking if the driver spoke English, which he said he did as he introduced himself as Hasan. She instructed him to take her to the Comprehensive Cancer Center on the Humboldt University campus. "Traffic is heavy today. It may take longer than usual to get to your destination."

"That's fine," Nancy said agreeably. "I would like it if you could wait for me while I make my delivery. It shouldn't take long. Then you can drive me to the Hilton Hotel where I am staying," she instructed.

"As you wish," he replied, lifting her bag into the trunk and opening the back door. "Is this your first time in Berlin?"

"Yes," Nancy said simply as she rolled down the window to get a better view. This was the first time she had been almost anywhere outside her Army travels. She was so excited to get out of Chicago; early September was a good time. The weather today was outstanding. The sky was sunny with sufficient clouds to make things interesting without being dreary, and the temperature was probably in the high 70s. It was perfection.

The driver kindly pointed out some of the most famous landmarks as they traveled across the city. "You are too young to remember, but Berlin was divided into two parts when the Berlin Wall was built in 1961 to keep the Eastern Germans from emmigrating to the West. The only way to legally pass from East to West for twenty-eight years was through highly armed checkpoints. There is the most famous one on the right. Checkpoint Charlie. Thousands of Berliners lost their lives trying to escape the oppression. Berlin has a very dark past, especially during World War II. The city was bombed heavily, so you see so many modern buildings. There are memorials and reminders of our horrible past everywhere in the city. Perhaps that is why young people need to celebrate every weekend. Berlin is known as the party capital of the world. One word of advice. If you go out to the clubs, please be very careful. A young and pretty thing like you can find trouble."

Nancy smiled. Yes, she knew that. It is one of the reasons she was so excited to find that her first assignment would be to Berlin! "Good trouble, hopefully," she mumbled to herself.

"You are staying at the Hilton? It is on your left, and the Brandenburg Gate is on your right. It was built in the 1700s to symbolize unity," continued Hasan. "During the Cold War, it symbolized Berlin and German, division. It might surprise you to know that where we are driving right now is behind the Wall. We would have been in East Berlin. So sad!"

Nancy asked Hasan how long he had lived in Berlin and where he was originally from.

"I am from Egypt and have lived here for ten years. My family and I were lucky enough to escape the violence of the Arab Spring. We appreciate the German people and government for welcoming us into their home," he said with conviction.

It made Nancy wonder what it must be like to move your family to another country with totally different customs and language…to start again. She had known nothing but Middle America and had never been exposed to war and the horrible damage and insecurities it causes. She had always taken her freedom and independence for granted.

She had witnessed the horrors of war first-hand during her deployment to Afghanistan. She was too young to remember September 11, 2001. The closest thing she had come to experiencing a war in the United States was during the Chicago riots in May 2020 after George Floyd died in police custody in Minneapolis. The National Guard had to be dispatched to enforce a curfew to stop the senseless looting and vandalism. Buildings were destroyed, cars were set on fire, hundreds of people were injured, and there were twenty-eight known deaths. Nancy understood that was a drop in the bucket compared to an all-out war. She remembered how sad and frightened she and her friends had been during the worst of it and now had a greater appreciation for the people who had the unfortunate fate of being in the wrong place at the wrong time.

"We are here," announced Hasan, interrupting her thoughts. "I will wait for you. I cannot stay here, so look for me when you are finished."

"Thank you. I will be just a few minutes," she replied as she exited the cab.

She was correct. It hadn't taken her more than 20 minutes to deliver the stem cells and have them checked and accepted. "It's a pleasure doing business with you," she commented to the tech as she texted her boss to let the company know the delivery was completed without incident. She made her way back to the taxi. "Mission accomplished," she said with a sigh signifying relief at a job well done.

It was too early to check into her hotel, and Nancy had been warned by her friends about sleeping during the day, causing horrendous jet lag. Hotel check-in time was three o'clock, which would give her time to get to know the city a little. She dropped her bag with the concierge and decided to join a Hop-on Hop-off tour of the city. She figured it would be an excellent way to see the sights and get a lay of the city. Luckily, there was a stop near the hotel, and a bus was about ready to depart. She paid the fare and climbed the steps to the upper level of the open-air bus, finding a seat in the front row.

"Wow, what a view!" Nancy exclaimed to herself.

An hour later, she had seen the city's highlights and was ready to find somewhere to have lunch. She kept seeing lines of people under signs that said Doner on take-away restaurants and thought it would be fun to find out the big attraction. She disembarked the bus shortly after seeing a similar restaurant only a block away and joined the line.

"Oh, it's the German word for Gyro," she noted after giving her order and money to the busy man behind the counter. After taking her first bite, she exclaimed, "But this is nothing like the ones we have in Chicago. This is amazing! I think I'm in heaven."

Nancy spent a few more minutes discovering the numerous small shops on the street before realizing she was getting tired. Hailing a taxi, she hoped her room would be ready and an early check-in possible. She wanted to catch a few hours of sleep before the evening and night activities began. "Screw jet lag," she muttered. "I'll be up all night tonight anyway." She was going to make the most of every minute. "I can sleep when I get home," she said philosophically.

Nancy was in luck. When she arrived at the reception desk, her room had just been cleared for check-in. While walking to the elevator, she glanced around the lobby. She had never seen such a beautiful room with so many lovely people. "I could get used to this," she thought to herself. It didn't take her long to unpack, take a long hot shower and snuggle into the luxurious sheets of the king-size bed. "I'll sleep for two hours," she told herself.

Five hours later, Nancy awoke to a siren passing on the street below and realized that the sky was no longer sunny. Panicked and disoriented, she sat up quickly and switched on the light. The clock said 7:30. Realizing she still had plenty of time to get ready for her date, she allowed herself to linger between sleep and wakefulness for a few more minutes.

Through her groggy state, Nancy arose out of bed and began planning her wardrobe. She was a pro at choosing just the right look for the event. This evening she was having dinner with a nice man. A respectable man who saw her as a friendly and honorable woman. "Boy, is he misguided," giggled Nancy. She would dress appropriately for the evening. Thankfully she had packed for all eventualities. She chose a sleeveless "little black dress" that was demure enough to go to any fancy restaurant and not cause an incident but fit her figure beautifully and had a scalloped scooped neckline just low enough to show a hint of cleavage. The slightly flared skirt bounced when she walked, with the hemline just above her knees. She accessorized her look with pearl drop earrings, a small pearl necklace, black nylon stockings, 3-inch bright red strappy sandals, and a small black cross-body bag, the only one she had brought on the trip.

Alluring but respectable…just the image she wanted to portray for Jonathan. The sexy seductress costume would present itself later tonight.

She had forgotten that her curling iron would not work with European electricity, so she had to be content with blow-drying her hair. This would give her a bit of body and wave but no curls. "It will have to do," she told herself as she looked in the mirror. She had just enough time to apply a light layer of foundation, thin eyeliner with "barely there" eye shadow, two applications of black mascara, and some cherry red lip gloss. She looked in the mirror. "The perfectly befitting ensemble for a first date," she said before slipping on her clothes just before nine o'clock. She looked around to see if she had everything she needed…key, credit card, a small amount of cash, her iPhone, and the Apple Tag she always carried with her just in case she misplaced her purse. She had secured her passport and extras in the little room safe.

Chapter 2

As the elevator doors slid open in the lobby, Nancy saw Jonathan walking confidently through the hotel's revolving door. He looked very handsome in his tailored blue suit, white dress shirt, multi-colored tie, and dress shoes. She was a little taken aback. Unless they were lawyers, men in the United States seldom wore suits, even to fancy restaurants. Here was this gorgeous man dressed up to take her to dinner. "Wow, do men like this exist?" she asked herself. "He looks as if he wants to get to know me, not some sleazy image of me." This touched her in a way she hadn't been before. "This man may really like me."

Jonathan saw Nancy and was equally enamored. "You look stunning," he said as he kissed her on each cheek European style with admiration in his eyes.

But this admiration was different, Nancy thought. She had been told she was stunning thousands of times by strange men. Ravishing, beautiful, sexy, alluring, and seductive had all been used by complete strangers who only wanted to get into her pants. This was different. Jonathan's appreciation was for Nancy, not just her appearance. It was a compliment because he was expressing more than carnal lust. It made Nancy quiver with nervousness. This wasn't just going to be a date for a good dinner and a quick roll in the hay. This could be the beginning of something real. Nancy's first inclination was to turn around and flee from this possible genuine connection. She had always been wary of commitments or any deep feelings. Her deeply rooted distrust of men and her insecurities kept her from feeling anything more than a casual attraction. "I have to be careful," she said to herself. "This guy could be the real thing." What helped calm her nerves was knowing they lived on two different continents and lived separate lives. Nothing serious could become of this. "Just take a deep breath and enjoy the evening," she sighed quietly.

"I have made a reservation at a quiet French bistro about a mile away. I hope you like French food. I like German food, but I find it too heavy for a first date," Jonathan explained with a smile. "It's such a beautiful evening. I thought we could walk if that's OK with you."

"That's fine," she replied. "I love walking whenever I can." She was glad she hadn't worn the six-inch stilettos she had packed. They would have killed her feet before they reached the first crosswalk. They were for looking sexy and dancing, not strolling on cobblestones.

They left the hotel and began their leisurely promenade to dinner. The air was cool and delicious. The company was exhilarating. She had never felt as comfortable and happy to be with someone, even from the first moment she met Jonathan. She noticed that he always kept her on the inside of the sidewalk, away from any traffic danger. "Chivalry is not dead," she thought. She liked it. It made her feel important, influential, and respected. All were new emotions to her.

They arrived at the bistro in what seemed like a heartbeat. "Time does fly when you're having fun," Nancy thought. They were led to a table for two in the window where they could observe Berliners and tourists happily going on their way to wherever. Menus were presented, and Nancy was taken aback when she opened it. "How arrogant of me…but I just figured the menu would be in English," she said to Jonathan and laughed at herself. "I'm just a hick from Chicago, I guess," she added. "I'll need help deciphering this."

"Don't be worried," Jonathan said reassuringly. "It's even more confusing when you have a French restaurant in Germany. There are too many languages to try to translate. We could see if there's a menu in English."

"No, but thanks," Nancy replied. She appreciated Jonathan's willingness to make her feel comfortable when she could have easily been embarrassed.

"What would you like to have?" he asked.

"I eat about anything, but please do not order snails or things that come from the animal's insides," she said. "I want to enjoy my dinner with you; not have you waiting for me while I hurl in the bathroom…or is it called the toilet here?"

Her candor made Jonathan laugh out loud. How refreshing it was to hear someone express themselves without reserve. "All right then, I'll order something I think you'll like. If you don't, we can order something else. Fair enough? Do you prefer red or white wine?"

"Perfect, and red, please," she replied, laughing at herself. She had never been able to laugh at herself before. She had built an insurmountable wall to guard herself against other people so she wouldn't be hurt. "Ironic," she thought. "My wall is crumbling like the Berlin wall just blocks away from here."

Jonathan ordered "safe" dishes for both of them. Chicken for her, duck for him. No tartare or sweetbreads. Just regular food made in the French way. He asked the waiter for his recommendation on an excellent dry red wine and accepted his choice gratefully. He wasn't a wine connoisseur and admitted it freely. He was more of a beer drinker who enjoyed a glass of wine with a nice meal and good company.

"So, tell me about yourself," he began.

Nancy didn't know how much to divulge, so she kept things fairly generic and superficial. "This is my first time out of the United States except when I went to Afghanistan with theU.S.Army. It's all a little overwhelming; the different languages, the different cultures, the old buildings combined with the modern, and money are all so new to me. Chicago is a big city with lots of ethnic neighborhoods, but we pretty much stick to our comfort zones there," she began. "It's just home."

"What brings you to Berlin?" asked Jonathan to keep the conversation progressing.

"Didn't I tell you?" answered Nancy. "At home, I am a Registered Nurse. I've done many nursing jobs, and now I work with hospice patients. Before you look at me with pitying eyes, I find it quite rewarding.even though all of my patients leave me within months. I can make their transition less painful and frightening and give them the dignity they deserve. That doesn't happen all the time. I feel like I am making a positive impact on my patients and their families. It's hard work, but I love it."

Nancy realized she hadn't answered Jonathan's question. "But I have a side job that I just began. I am a courier for a company that transports stem cells to places worldwide. This was my first assignment, and so far, so good. I hand-carry the precious cells wherever they need to go. It's pretty simple. My boss at home knows how much I've wanted to travel, and this is a great way to mix a little pleasure with work, especially over the weekends."

"Well, you're a very busy woman then," Jonathan said. "Now that I know what you do, tell me who you are."

"I'm not sure you want to hear all about that," Nancy said hesitantly. "What about you? What makes you tick?" she tried changing the subject. "What makes you available to have dinner with me this evening? Isn't there a special someone at home?"

"Well, until recently, I was involved with someone. We broke up a couple of months ago, and I've been very busy with work, and to be honest, I just haven't been very interested in making an effort with someone else until we met on the plane."

"What kind of work do you do?" Nancy asked, genuinely interested.

"I can't go into details. Let's just say I deal in international relations. I have meetings to go to all over Europe and have contacts in almost every major city on the continent. They come in handy quite often," he said vaguely.

Nancy noticed the ambiguous answer but was distracted as the waiter poured the wine. Dinner was delicious, and the conversation flowed seamlessly from one topic to the next. Jonathan was intelligent, funny, and an excellent listener. He looked Nancy straight in the eyes when he spoke. And most importantly, he made Nancy feel like she was the most exceptional person in the restaurant. Nancy had never experienced anything like this before. For a few minutes, she forgot about all the hurt and abuse she had taken from all the men in her life. Jonathan was different. She knew it.

Jonathan was also enjoying the dinner immensely. Nancy was a little slow to open up at the beginning of the meal, but by the time the dessert menu was presented and three-quarters of the bottle of wine had been consumed, she was pretty effusive. Jonathan listened and observed. There was a depth to Nancy that was not obvious to the casual observer. A dark side he couldn't understand, but it attracted him. This was not some hick from Chicago, even though she had not traveled. She had experienced much more of life than she would admit to. He would enjoy learning more.

After sharing a crème brulee for dessert, savoring a cup of coffee, and paying the bill, they decided to walk off their dinner and see some sights. The Brandenburg Gate was beautiful at night; all lit up. Jonathan put on his "tour guide cap" and explained a little about the gate's history.

"You may have already heard this, but the Gate has quite a history," he began. "It was built in 1791 and modeled after the Athens Acropolis."

"It's so beautiful and majestic at night with the lights," Nancy said. "I've never been to Athens but have seen pictures of the Acropolis, and I see the resemblance in the columns. They are very impressive."

"What's impressive is how the Gate now symbolizes unity, where not too many years ago it was a strong reminder of the division of Germany and the city," recited Jonathan. "It was your President Reagan in the late eighties who made a very famous speech in front of the gate. He called for Russian President Gorbachev to open the gate and tear down the Wall. The Wall finally fell in 1989. You and I are too young to remember, but my parents tell me stories of the reports on the news. And the Gate is a place for New Year's Eve parties and protests for equality. So, it's much more than a pretty monument!"

Nancy was not only impressed by his knowledge but by the firm conviction in his words. "Did your family have friends caught behind the wall? You seem so passionate about it," she asked.

"No. But I have studied history and the whole Nazi movement. World War II fascinates and disgusts me. Such a waste. I think it's essential we remember, so hopefully, history will not repeat itself!" he said adamantly.

"Let's go see the Parliament building. It's not far."

"With pleasure," smiled Nancy. She was enjoying Jonathan's company. More than any man she could remember…and there had been hundreds. He was different. Was it his manners or his posh-sounding accent? She didn't know. All she knew was that he made her feel very special, not for her sexuality but for herself. But she wondered what he would think if he knew the real her. He would probably abandon her just like every other man.

Jonathan perceived her mood change. "What's wrong?" he asked, sincerely wanting to know.

"You seem so wonderful, and I just can't believe it's true," she explained. "If you knew the real me, you wouldn't give me the time of day."

"I doubt that very much," he replied. "Is that a challenge?" he added, smiling. "In that case, I will accept it and try to get to know the real you tomorrow."

"What? Do you want to see me again? Why?" Nancy asked, sincerely puzzled. No man had wanted to see her more than once. But this had been so different from all her previous encounters.

"Of course!" Jonathan exclaimed. "I find you fascinating and funny and wise beyond your years. Why wouldn't I want to see you? How about tomorrow afternoon? I need to do something early in the morning, which may last a few hours. Would that be all right?"

"Yes, of course," Nancy replied

"Good. Wear something casual. I want to show you the city on a bicycle. Can you ride?" he asked.

"That sounds like such fun!" she exclaimed. "Thank you. About three o'clock?"

"Perfect. Now, I'd better get you back to your hotel. It's getting late, and I have a big day tomorrow," added Jonathan.

When Jonathan walked her to the elevator, took her hands in his, and gave her a light kiss, Nancy was slightly disappointed. But she also felt respected and genuinely liked for the first time in, well, forever.

"Until tomorrow then," he said quietly and quickly turned and departed.

Chapter 3

Nancy couldn't believe her evening. It had been the best date she had ever had. However, it wasn't going to distract her from going out and finding some excitement at the clubs. It was only midnight. The clubs were opening. It would take her some time to switch from "Nurse Nancy" to Dolcé, her nighttime name. She liked that name. It means "sweet" in Italian, but it isn't campy or trashy like Candy or Desiree would be for her. She took on the persona after seeing the old black-and-white movie named "La Dolcé Vita." The sweet life.

She knew she had to start over. Her "Nancy" outfit was unsuitable for the clubs. She had heard that Berlin's most exclusive clubs were challenging to get into. She had never been turned away from any club, but there was always a first time, and she didn't want it to be tonight. Berlin's clubs were famous, or infamous, for unconventional modes of dress and undress. Each club had its signature style. The most famous is Berghain, where the bouncers would nix or allow you in by observing your attitude and your appearance. People would stand in line for four hours to get into the door, only to be turned away. Dolcé certainly didn't want that to happen.

She would go Goth tonight. Black from head to toe. She did her hair and makeup first. She teased her straight black hair and pulled it back into a messy bun. She applied heavy black eye shadow and thick eyeliner that extended half an inch beyond her eyes. Then she used four layers of black mascara, which made her turquoise eyes "pop." Bright red lipstick was then applied to give some contrast. She looked at herself in the mirror. "My own mother wouldn't recognize me in this," she said with a smile. She liked disguising herself when she went out. Dolcé longed for the kind of attention that Nancy would never have tolerated.

Next, the outfit. Nancy had packed as much as she could fit in her carry-on bag, so she had to leave many items (chains, knee-high boots) at home. Just the essentials were available to her tonight. Most important was her black lacey corset, which fit her snugly, giving her curves in all the right places. Next, a black crepe mini-skirt and a tiny bolero jacket with black lace sleeves. Then black patterned nylon stockings and ankle-high black lacey block-heeled boots. She topped the outfit off with a leather spike choker necklace and whatever clunky jewelry she could find.

"It might not be perfect, but I think it will do nicely," she said, looking into the mirror and nodding her head. She grabbed the only coat she had brought, knowing that the nights could get cold, especially if she had to stand in line to get in.

It was 3 a.m. as she left the hotel and hailed a cab. She had heard that the clubs don't open until midnight, and most don't get going until five or 6 a.m. and continue nonstop for the entire weekend. So, 3 a.m. was still early. She instructed the cabbie to take her to Matrix. She may have been a pro at the Chicago clubs, but from what she had heard, Berghain was a little too wild even for her. She wanted to get her feet wet at a great club but not one with a reputation for encouraging people to have sex on the dance floor, and in particular dark rooms. She had heard that Matrix was an excellent way to begin.

Dolcé didn't stand in line long. The bouncer doorman took one look at her and waved her in. She acknowledged the favor but didn't smile at him. Goth was somber, not polite. She paid her ten-euro admission fee, entered the club, and checked her coat. She had seen some good clubs in Chicago, but they paled compared to this. The place was overwhelming. Hundreds of people were dancing and laughing…and that was only on one of the four floors. The music blaring, the lights flashing, the DJ jamming. It was indeed the biggest party she had ever seen. Nancy had promised herself she would be a good girl tonight and not overdo the alcohol or take any drugs offered. They were always provided to her. But Dolcé wanted to experience everything and still be safe!

Dolcé spent the first hour acquainting herself to the atmosphere and scoping out prospects. Most of the guys seemed immature and just plain childish, chugging from their beer mugs. She was looking for something unique, someone a little dangerous. If she didn't find a conquest within three hours, she would try another club. At home, she usually stayed less than two hours, and typically, she did not leave alone. Nancy had been attracted to Jonathan. Dolcé liked him but wanted more excitement tonight.

Many men made eye contact with Dolcé as she made her rounds. Some went up to her and spouted cliché compliments about her beauty or body, which she shunned with a flick of her hand. She had heard that a million times. She knew what she wanted, and seldom was it what he desired. She wanted someone with the class to want her. Someone who stood out amongst the crowd. Someone who was subtle with his approach.

Dolcé wanted to drink a lot and get high. Nancy kept warning her not to. She was alone in a strange city. Who knew how dangerous partying in Berlin could be? "Keep your wits about you," Nancy kept saying. Dolcé only paid mild attention to her warnings.

Dolcé made it a point to only pay for one drink in any club. She didn't need to pay for more. Many men would stand in line for the privilege, whether or not she showed any interest in them. After her third Crown Royal and water, her drink of choice tonight, she settled into the dancing and joined in. The pounding beat of the music was hypnotic. She relaxed, let her body feel the rhythm, and truly began enjoying herself.

This was when the trouble began. Within an hour, she started feeling strange. Someone must have slipped some Ecstasy into her drink when she was dancing. Dolcé knew better than to leave a drink unattended, but she had been careless. She slowly felt the effects of the drug. She was familiar with the stages she would go through soon and was only a bit anxious. She had taken X many times at home, but that was when she was with people she trusted. This was different. Someone wasn't giving her a choice, and it worried her not knowing who that person was.

She made sure to go and drink an entire bottle of water before the drug took effect. She knew there wasn't anything else to do but get to a safe place and enjoy it. At first she felt her heart rate increase. Her skin began to tingle and colors became brighter. Soon a feeling of pure contentment embraced her. All her insecurities and worries melted away into a pure blissful euphoria. She wanted to touch anything soft: people's clothes, hair, and silky skin. The music became a part of her, and she couldn't stop dancing and laughing. She was genuinely experiencing the clubbing vibe. Her inhibitions were gone. So was her ability to judge her company.

During her euphoric state while she danced, a man dressed all in black approached her and started a conversation. She welcomed his advances, continued dancing, and stroked his soft leather knee-length coat. They quickly struck up a conversation. He learned she was from Chicago and would be returning home. It wasn't long before he convinced her to help him by taking a flash drive he had and mailing it to a friend once she got home to the States. It all seemed logical in her altered state of mind. She was happy. Blissful and affectionate to this stranger. Hugs and kisses followed until the stranger eventually melted into the crowd. She quickly forgot about the encounter and began dancing with a new group of revelers.

It was 8 a.m. when Dolcé was finished. She was wiped out and needed sleep. Luckily, she could hail a cab that took her straight to the hotel, where she tore off her clothes and fell into an exhausted sleep. She had set her alarm for 2 p.m. just in case she didn't wake up naturally. She had no inkling that the encounter with the strange man would take her life in a new and dark direction.

Chapter 4

Nancy awoke to the alarm at 2 p.m. Dazed and feeling hungover, it took her a couple of minutes to orient herself to place and time. She at least remembered who she was, although Dolcé was still written in black makeup all over her unwashed face. The five-plus hours she had spent sleeping allowed her enough time to come down from the Ecstasy without the depressed mood and feelings of anxiety she usually felt.

"Oh my gosh," Nancy exclaimed. "I'm getting too old for this," as she surveyed her reflection in the mirror. She only had an hour to make herself presentable and realized she was ravenously hungry. She called room service for a sandwich and was told it would be delivered in twenty minutes. Just enough time to wash last night's activities off her body and out of her system. She felt dehydrated, so before jumping in the shower, she drank a full glass of water. She then stood under the hot pulsating water streaming from the showerhead that enveloped her and soothed her tired aching body.

The sandwich was delivered just as she exited the shower. "Thank goodness they supply robes at this hotel," she murmured and answered the door. After the waiter left, Nancy devoured her first meal in almost eighteen hours in less than five minutes. That still left her twenty minutes to get ready. She couldn't recall any time in the last few years she had been able to get ready for anything in less than forty-five minutes. "Yikes," she exclaimed as she began throwing her clothes from the dresser onto the bed. She had tried to think of every contingency during her short excursion to Berlin, but she hadn't expected to be riding a bike. She chose a pair of jeans, a loose blouse, and a cardigan sweater to wear just in case it got cool. She had no casual shoes, so she chose to wear the Goth boots from last night. They looked pretty stylish with their heels. "Can you ride a bike in heels?" she pondered. "Well, I guess I'll find out the hard way." She looked in the mirror and said to her reflection. "So, what's new? You have always chosen to do things the hard way," she commented philosophically.

The phone rang slightly after three. "I'm running just a bit late. I'll be right down," Nancy explained and finished preparing for her date. She had only brought one handbag with her, so it was the same one she had used yesterday and last night. She slipped the long strap over her head so the purse fit snugly across her body. She had heard that a cross-body bag was the safest when traveling and believed it now.

She quickly looked around the room and ensured she hadn't forgotten anything before opening the door and walking through it. She made sure it closed securely before strolling to the elevator.

Jonathan's face brightened when he saw Nancy disembark the elevator. "Hello. How are you doing? It's good to see you," he greeted her with a quick hug and a kiss on both cheeks.

"Fine, thanks," Nancy said vaguely. "It's good to see you too." And she meant it.

"So, I thought we could go to Tiergarten. It's like Hyde Park in London or Central Park in New York, and it is nearby. There are bikes we can rent and ride around the park. Then we can go to the zoo," Jonathan suggested. "Does that sound good to you, or is it too sedate?"

After yesterday's excursions, Nancy thought it would be good to get some fresh air. "That sounds great. I didn't know Berlin had a zoo."

"Oh yes, it's been here for over 150 years. It's the biggest zoo in Germany and one of the biggest in Europe. And it has an aquarium. Are you game?" he laughed. "Get it? Game…zoo?"

"Yes, very punny," Nancy said while joining in on the fun. She had never been able to tease a man or have a man affectionately tease her. It had always been hurtful before. This felt good. Especially since it was a two-way street, she could give and take.

"We have a zoo in the Chicago area, but it's nothing like this. Its "claim to fame" is that it is free of charge so that anyone can have access. I like that," Nancy added.

"Yes, although I can understand why most places have to charge admission, it's great when the truly magnificent museums and galleries are open to everyone," added Jonathan. "The National Gallery in London, for instance. It's genuinely a marvel, and anyone interested can walk right in. Perhaps I can show it to you someday."

This startled Nancy. The thought that he was considering seeing her again in the future made her shiver. Unheard of. "Yes, perhaps," she squeaked out hesitantly.

They began walking toward the park and quickly came to a stand of rental bikes.

"Have you seen these before?" asked Jonathan. "We'll each check the tires and pick out our favorite. Then all I need to do is swipe my credit card, and we're on our way. We can return them anywhere we see a rental area. It's great."

"We have something similar in Chicago; only they use scooters. They seem to be everywhere!" added Nancy.

"All aboard. We'll head this way," Jonathan pointed to a bike path. "We won't ride on the roads unless we have to. It's much safer and just as scenic on the path."

"That sounds great to me. I haven't been on a bike in years, and it's all I can do to ride it without being concerned about being run over by a bus!" replied Nancy.

Within a couple of minutes, Nancy was riding like a pro. "I guess what they say is true…it's like riding a bike. Once you learn, you never forget. What I did forget is how much fun this is!" And surprisingly, my boots are working very well." Even though she had to concentrate on her technique, she loved the wind and the sun on her face and the freedom she felt riding at a moderate pace.

They rode around the park, stopping to watch some kids feeding the ducks at one of the ponds. Before long, they had circumnavigated the park. "Please, can we do it again?" pleaded Nancy. "I love it!" So, they began again. This time around, Nancy could see the sights and appreciate the park. The trees were huge and green, the lakes crystal clear and smooth, and many families were having picnics on the grass. "What a serene and lovely way to spend a day," thought Nancy. "Why haven't I done this before?"

Eventually, they came to the entrance of the zoo. "Would you like to go in?" Jonathan asked.

"Oh, yes, please," replied Nancy enthusiastically.

Jonathan smiled at the glee on Nancy's face. "She's like a child experiencing this for the first time," he thought. "Has she been so deprived of these simple pleasures? If so, why?" He was even more intrigued by this lovely, complicated woman.

They found a return station for the bikes and made the short walk to the ticket counter. "May I buy the tickets for the Zoo?" asked Nancy. "I'd like to. You've been so kind, and it's just a small way I can say thank you," she explained.

"If it means that much to you, thank you," replied Jonathan. Even in 2022, he wasn't used to being treated by his date to anything. It was a nice gesture, and he appreciated it.

Nancy reached into her purse for her wallet, and feeling an unfamiliar object, drew out a flash drive. "Strange," she said. "Where did this come from?" Only after delving into her foggy brain did she vaguely remember the encounter. She slipped the drive back into her purse without giving it a further thought.

They spent the next two hours meandering from one enclave to the next. Jonathan's favorite exhibit was the polar bears. Nancy's was the otters and monkeys. "They just like to play so much," she explained. "They seem so free to have fun without worrying about anything."

That made Jonathan wonder what Nancy had to worry about.

"Are you hungry or thirsty?" he asked Nancy.

"As a matter of fact, yes, I am…to both," she replied, smiling.

They found a small beer garden by the side of a lake and enjoyed the last of the September day as the sun began to set.

"Today, you will enjoy real German food," he said as he ordered schnitzel and beer for both of them. "It might not be good for the figure, but it is great on the palate," Jonathan added.

They both relished the tasty food and the cold beer. Only when they were finishing did Nancy look into Jonathan's eyes and begin to communicate what she was truly feeling.

Nancy drew out the flash drive from her purse with a questioning look. Jonathan saw the expression on her face and asked what the problem was.

Nancy answered honestly, "I don't know. I need to tell you something. I have cherished our short time together. You have made me happier than I have been since I can remember. But I am not what you think I am," then hesitated.

"Go on," said Jonathan.

"Last night after you left, I hit one of the clubs. I didn't mean I just went, but I was there for hours. I drank and danced until someone put something into my drink. After that, things became fuzzy. Nothing bad happened to me…nobody tried to kidnap me, at least I don't think so, but something strange happened. While I was high on Ecstasy someone had slipped into my drink, a strange man approached me and gave me this to mail to someone in theU.S.once I got home. It didn't seem strange at the time, but now it doesn't seem right. As a matter of fact, it seems VERY wrong."

"You are right in feeling that way. What else?" asked Jonathan.

"Now that I think about it, why would he approach me? Was it my American accent? Or was I targeted for a specific reason?" she asked.

"That's a possibility. What else happened?" asked Jonathan.

"Nothing. I left the club and went back to the hotel alone. It doesn't sound that bad, but I feel terrible about this. Should I just throw the flash drive away?"

"No!" replied Jonathan. "That would be the worst thing you could do. Whoever gave you this knows who you are. He wouldn't have given it to just any stranger. It is important to find out what's on the drive without endangering you or anyone else."

"But how can I do that?" Nancy asked. "I may be naïve, but I know better than to stick an unknown flash drive in my computer."

"You are right about that," added Jonathan. "Do you have the address where it is supposed to go?"

"Yes, I believe so," as she rummaged through her purse and brought out a slip of paper.

"Good. Nancy, do you trust me?" he asked while searching deeply into her eyes.

"As much as anyone I know," she replied. "Why?"

"Because I have contacts here in Berlin who can help us," he replied. "Would you let them take a look at it? We could then decide what needs to be done."

"Yes," was Nancy's answer. She tried to explain the circumstances of the night before but was interrupted.

"Later, Nancy. You owe me no explanations. We just met, and there are no entanglements. I had a great time with you both last evening and today. Simple as that. Let's figure out what this is, and then we can discuss other things."

"Just one thing Jonathan," Nancy interjected. "My flight home leaves tomorrow morning at nine o'clock."

"Then we'd better get started," said Jonathan with determination.

Chapter 5

Jonathan immediately called his contact. Nancy only heard half of the conversation.

"It is a flash drive that was surreptitiously given to an acquaintance. I need it analyzed now if possible."

After a brief pause, Jonathan said into the phone, "Good, we will be right over." He turned to Nancy and said thoughtfully, "We have about ten hours before you have to be at the airport. Do you mind losing a night's sleep to find out what this is?"

"Of course not!" she exclaimed. "Should we be taking this to the police instead?"

"Nancy, I am the police," replied Jonathan. "Interpol."

Nancy's jaw dropped in surprise. She would have never suspected this kind and gentle man could be in law enforcement. She collected her things, and they headed for the closest taxi stand.

"Jonathan, you don't need to involve yourself in this. This is my fault, and I can get myself out of whatever mess this is," declared Nancy.

"Nonsense, this is what I do for a living. This may be nothing to worry about, or it could be something very serious. I want you to know which it is before you leave. It sounds extremely suspicious to me, and it is important we find out," explained Jonathan.

"Thank you for this. I'm sorry," she said sincerely.

"You're welcome," Jonathan said as he hailed a taxi and opened the door for Nancy to slide in.

They arrived at a nondescript stone building with no identifying markings within twenty minutes.

"We're here," stated Jonathan. "We will need to get you a visitor's pass. I think it is important for you to tell us everything you can remember about last night."

Jonathan greeted the guard, showed his ID, completed the necessary paperwork, and handed the visitor's badge to Nancy.

"Come on, I have people who want to meet you," he said as he pushed the elevator button.

As they stepped off the elevator, Nancy saw a large room with at least fifty cubicles. Since it was late Saturday afternoon, only a few people were at their stations. After introductions were made to two of the agents, they all got to work.

"How did you get this?" asked agent Schulz.

Nancy explained the encounter, including how she had been slipped the Ecstasy. There was no judgment on the agents' faces—just curiosity. Nancy had expected some condemnation for her actions and was pleasantly surprised it didn't come.

"Don't be embarrassed," interjected Agent Richter. "We have heard a lot worse. You are young and bound to make mistakes. You did nothing illegal. It's just a good thing Agent Harris was there. OK, let's see what is on the flash drive."

They proceeded to a particular computer with anti-viral programs for this purpose. When the information on the drive appeared, the agents' concentration became very focused.

"Miss Calloway, please turn away," ordered Agent Schulz. "I don't want you seeing this," he added protectively.

On the monitor was a very amateur video. It was homemade in someone's basement. The lighting was dark except for a spotlight on a young woman wearing only a torn black corset and skirt, similar to what Dolcé had worn the night before. She was bound to a metal armchair with zip ties on her wrists and ankles and a rope tied tightly around her waist and to the back of the chair. Her hair was blood-streaked, as was her face. Her expression of pure horror was masqueraded by thick black eye makeup and running mascara. She was screaming, but nobody could hear her to come to her rescue.

A man dressed all in black with a hood hiding his face approached the woman. He held a dagger high above his head menacingly. The woman tried to struggle, but it was hopeless. Her eyes were as big as saucers, with a look of terror as the knife drew closer. A piercing scream was heard as the knife bit her breast, and blood streamed. It was a superficial cut. The torturer wanted to savor the pain he inflicted.

The film continued until, eventually, the knife was slashed across her neck, the woman bled out, and all movement ceased. The unknown man cut off a lock of the woman's hair. "For my collection," he mumbled.

Agent Schulz had turned a pale green. Agent Richter had had to excuse himself, and he vomited into the nearest trash bin. They had seen horrible scenes of violence, but nothing like this. It took a few minutes after closing the program before anyone could say anything; the shock was so severe.

"Oh my God!" is all Agent Schulz could say, still in shock. "What have you gotten yourself into?" he questioned while he turned and looked at Nancy.

Jonathan had only seen a fleeting glance of the young woman's murderous attack and eventual death. One glance was enough. He stood between Nancy and the monitor, protecting her from the gruesome scenes.

Nancy had also gotten a few glances of the carnage. The similarity to what she had looked like last night had not escaped her consciousness. The realization that the poor girl in the film could have easily been her struck her as if she had been slapped across the face. She was so severely shocked that she began trembling violently and had to be helped to a chair. She began sobbing uncontrollably, not only for herself but for the wasted life of the poor innocent girl who couldn't have been more than twenty-two.

Getting down to business Agent Schulz said, "I've heard of snuff films before, but I never knew they actually existed. But knowing human nature and how sick it can be…it doesn't surprise me. The wanton brutality is neither forgivable nor forgettable. There are just too many sickos out there, and we need to find and stop as many of them as we can.

"What do we do with the flash drive," asked Nancy innocently.

"Let's think for a few minutes," added Agent Jonathan Harris. "The drive is evidence, but we must pretend that Nancy never found the contents. Whoever gave her this did it for a reason. We need to discover what that reason was. Was it a warning? Or just an easy way to circumventU.S.customs?"

"What do you think if we make a copy and give Nancy the original drive to mail as instructed when she gets home? We have an address, even though it is a post office box. We can have it staked out by the local police to see who picks it up," suggested Agent Richter, now that he had gotten over the initial shock.

"Won't that put Nancy in danger?" asked Jonathan.

"She will be in danger regardless. I believe the danger will be lessened if she follows instructions," answered Agent Schulz. "We will be able to do the forensics on the copy. It's important that Nancy send the original with her fingerprints on it and none of ours and quietly go on with her life as usual. We don't know how sophisticated these people are. Most are psychos who enjoy the pain of others. This is way above mere killing. This is an organization. Otherwise, how would they have picked Nancy from the crowd? Was it planned, or did they hear her speak American English and choose her randomly? How did they spike her drink so easily? There are many unanswered questions."

Whoever they are, we need to get to the bottom of this before some other innocent becomes the next victim," added Agent Richter.

"We need to go over exactly what happened last night," Agent Schulz said to Nancy. "We need every detail you can remember. Nothing is too inconsequential. We're not trying to grill you or be unkind, but this is our only chance since you will leave the country early tomorrow morning. It is important that you get on your scheduled flight. They may have people watching."

Nancy began at the beginning, recalling everything she could. Despite her remarkable date with Jonathan, she felt embarrassed to be telling her deepest thoughts and feelings about her adventure and why she needed to go out to the club. She did not see judgment on his face, just concern. That freed her to be specific, although she didn't feel like any of the details she remembered would help to find the stranger who gave her the flash drive. She knew he was tall, maybe 6 foot 2 or 3, with a black leather coat, scruffy beard, and spikes in his ears. But that described half of the males in the club!

One thing she did remember that made him stand out: the stranger had a tattoo on the left side of his neck. "It was an iron cross with black and red outlines. The center was a shaded black, with something that looked like a black spider web surrounding it," explained Nancy.

"Well, that's something at least," added Agent Richter.

It soon became apparent that Nancy had no more to add. It was suggested that Agent Harris take her back to the hotel and accompany her to her door, which he did.

"Don't open the door for anyone tonight," declared Jonathan when they arrived at her room. "Not even Room Service," he added. "I will be back at 6 a.m. to take you to the airport," he said in an all-business tone of voice.

"I'm so sorry, Jonathan. I had no idea," she exclaimed apologetically.

"I know. It's OK. As I said before, we had a good time together without judgment or commitment," Jonathan said quietly. "I'd still like to get to know you better the next time we run into each other," he added with a smile and squeezed her hand. "But tonight, you'd better pack and get whatever sleep you can. Six a.m. will come very quickly. "Good night," he said with a light kiss, which made Nancy smile.

"Good night, and thank you for everything," Nancy said sincerely and disappeared behind her closing door.

The following day Jonathan rang her room at precisely 6 a.m. Dolcé had no desire to go to the clubs, even though she knew it was Sunday morning and they would be going strong.

She had learned a valuable lesson and was happy to be alive and well. Nancy was packed and ready to go. They arrived at the airport with enough time to have a coffee before Nancy headed for the gate.

"Here is my card. It has all my official information. I will be in touch as we learn more," said Jonathan. "Be very careful when you go home. Mail the flash drive as instructed, and don't tell anyone about it. Nobody!"

"I won't; I promise," answered Nancy. "Besides, who would believe me."

"Report any unusual events, no matter how small. You may be in danger or not. I cannot know at this point. We will do much of the legwork here in Berlin and at my office in London. This is an international issue, not just a local crime."

"I will," said Nancy. "Jonathan, you are a wonderful man; I want you to know that," she added. "I am very fond of you!"

"And I am fond of you, too," he said sincerely. "Perhaps our paths will cross again. I would like that."

Nancy's heart sang even though she knew they would probably not meet again. A kind, decent, respectable, handsome, and sexy man liked her, truly liked her despite her quirks.

They said their farewells; Nancy went through security and immigration without a problem and boarded her plane without incident.

"Goodbye, Germany," she whispered. "It's been quite an adventure," as the plane lifted off the tarmac on its way home.

Chapter 6

After settling in and having a welcomed meal on the plane, Nancy stretched out as far as possible to get some much-needed sleep. Instead of searching for her next male conquest, she was thankful that the seat next to hers was unoccupied. "How things have changed in the last seventy-two hours," she muttered. Before drifting off, she took stock of the events since leaving Chicago three days previously. "What an adventure," she added and passed into a deep, dreamless sleep.

Nancy awoke when the announcement was made that they were descending into Chicago O'Hare airport. She had slept like the dead for over nine hours without stirring and felt refreshed after reacquainting herself with her environment. She was stiff and had to use the toilet, which she did quickly before the flight attendants demanded everyone to be in their seats with their tray tables and carry-on luggage stowed, window shades up, and seatbacks in the fully upright position. She hadn't even had time to figure out what her next steps would be. It was Sunday afternoon in Chicago. That would give her time to go home, freshen up a bit and then find a self-service post office. She needed to do all her errands that afternoon because she would be back at her nursing job at the regular time on Monday morning, the very next day.

Luckily, Nancy was able to clear immigration quickly. Since she did not have to wait for checked baggage, she zipped through customs without delay. Within twenty-five minutes, she was hailing a cab. Because it was Sunday, traffic was light, and it took only one hour to get home. She couldn't stay awake on the ride, so she again drifted off and was surprised when the cab pulled up in front of her apartment building. She paid the fare, obtained a receipt, and paused to look around her environment before entering the building, climbing the steps, and returning home.

"Strange," she thought as she looked around the apartment. "I was sure I had left the hall light on when I left." Nancy remembered what Jonathan had said to her: "Report anything unusual." She inspected the apartment thoroughly and saw nothing out of order. "Perhaps the bulb burned out while I was gone," she whispered to herself. She would report the abnormality just in case. But later. Now she was on a mission to get to a post office as soon as possible and rid herself of the tiny object that had become an incredibly heavy burden.

She found a padded envelope and quickly slipped the flash drive into it, sealed it tightly, carefully addressed it with a Sharpie marker, and slipped it into a pocket of her slacks. Dropping her suitcase on the bed, she splashed her face with water and brushed her hair quickly before grabbing a sweater and her purse and heading for her car parked in the lot behind the building. She smiled when the engine turned over without hesitation. "I don't know why that surprised me," she said to herself. "It was in fine condition when I left, and that was only three days ago. It's not as if it's been three years, although, in a way, it feels like it."

Nancy found the nearest post office and was glad to see it had a self-service machine. She followed the steps, filled out the tracking form, paid for the postage, and attached it to the envelope. With a little "good riddance," she placed it in the outgoing mail slot and turned to leave the building. "I hope this is the end of it," she said, but she doubted it. "This seems too easy to be finished. I can only hope and pray that it is."

Nancy caught up on some necessary errands before returning to the apartment, where she made herself some dinner and did two loads of laundry…her Sunday routine. She thought about calling Jonathan but realized it would be after midnight in Berlin. She would call him in the morning before leaving for work. She was determined to get to bed early. Although she had slept well on the plane, she was still fatigued to her core and needed a good night's rest before beginning her busy week.

The next morning, Nancy, as usual, picked out a crisp white uniform and dressed impeccably. She didn't run because she had to stop by the courier office on her way to work and drop off the reusable container and her reports. Travis came through the front door when she arrived at the office. "How did things go?" he asked.

"Fine," she said honestly. "No problems whatsoever! The University had the stem cells before noon on Friday and gave me a receipt. I can't wait for another assignment soon," she added.

"Well, it might be sooner than you think. I'll have more information for you tomorrow," replied Travis.

"Sounds great!" she said enthusiastically. "Ok, I'm out of here to go to my day job. Toodles!"

Travis waved to her as she left the room.

Nancy arrived at her nursing job precisely at 7:55, as she always did.

"How was your trip?" chimed Maria from the other room. "I want to hear all about Berlin."

Nancy knew better than to say anything about her extracurricular activities, so she answered noncommittedly, "The flight was good. I met a very nice man, and we had dinner together.

The assignment was easy, and the city was fascinating. I wouldn't call it beautiful because there are too many reminders of its malevolent past. Horrible things happened there during the middle of the last century, and you can still feel the evil. Otherwise, it was great. They have a huge park like Central Park there with an excellent zoo. I even went bike riding, and I haven't done that since I was a kid."

"Well, it sounds like it was a successful all-around trip," replied Maria. "I'm glad you had the opportunity to see it. When is your next assignment?"

"I don't know, but Travis said he will have information for me tomorrow," answered Nancy. "Now, who's on my list of patients to see today?"

After receiving her schedule, Nancy remembered she hadn't told Jonathan about the abnormality in the apartment. "Darn, I got distracted." Because her time was short, she texted Jonathan instead of calling. "Arrived safely without incident, except a light I had left on was off. I checked the bulb, and it is working. Should I be concerned?"

She received an immediate response. "Was anything else amiss?"

"No," she replied. "The door and windows were locked, and nothing seems to have been moved or taken."

"It may be nothing, but it is better to be safe. Be sure to get extra locks for the door. Look around for bugs," was Jonathan's reply.

"Bugs?" asked Nancy

"Electronic listening devices, not crawling insects."

"Oh, I'm such an idiot. I'm at work now, but I'll check when I get home," said Nancy.

"Do you have a weapon?" asked Jonathan.

"I have a taser but no gun," she replied.

"Make sure to keep it charged and with you at all times. Better safe than sorry," he responded. "Does anyone have an extra key?"

"Only the landlord and she has never come into my apartment without permission the entire five years I have lived here," said Nancy.

"I don't think anything can be done, but be careful. Be sure the corridors are empty before entering, especially on the stairs. Deadbolt the door and put extra security hardware on the windows," Jonathan advised.

"Yes, Sir," she responded. "I will get that done today. I've got to get to work. Thank you for everything," she wrote sincerely.

"My pleasure," he wrote back. "Talk to you soon."

Nancy ended the connection. Jonathan didn't seem overly concerned about the incident, so she didn't dwell on it. She needed to concentrate on her work, although she called a locksmith and arranged to have two more deadbolts installed on her door later that afternoon.

The day was uneventful. She moved from patient to patient, who were happy to see her again after her short absence. It wasn't until after work that her mind wandered back to the change in her apartment. "Was someone casing her home? Had they been looking for something? If so, what could it be?" A shiver coursed through her body just thinking about the possibilities.

Nancy's apartment had always been her sanctum, her sanctuary. Very few people had seen it, and fewer had been invited for a meal or a drink. Dolcé NEVER brought her conquests home. She also never used her real name when she went out. She did not want people to know where she lived. What was so disturbing was that someone had possibly invaded her safe place, her castle, which highly alarmed her. Nothing like that had ever happened before. Did it have something to do with the club in Berlin? But why? The questions kept bombarding her mind as she did her job, until she made them stop by focusing on the task at hand.

When Nancy got home, she locked the new deadbolts and added the new key to her keyring. "Better safe than sorry." She remembered Jonathan saying. She checked the windows to make sure they were securely shut. She checked the closets. She found her taser and plugged it in to fully charge overnight. Nothing looked out of the ordinary, but things felt different as if someone or something was watching her. She looked for hidden cameras or microphones and found none. "I'm being paranoid," she thought. Paranoid or not, she was determined to be cautious and carry her taser with her at all times.

The week passed uneventfully until Travis called. Nancy answered her phone with a little jolt of nervousness, knowing that he would be calling with another assignment. "Hi," she answered the phone happily.

"Hi to you too," said Travis. "I have another assignment for you."

Nancy's heart jumped, knowing she would be on her way out of Chicago again. "Sure, what is it?"

"It's to London this time. Are you up for it?" asked Travis teasingly. He knew that she would jump at the chance. "You'll leave a week from Thursday. This way, you will have the weekend to explore the city of Big Ben. I'm talking about the famous clock, not one of the guys who hang out in the neighborhood pub."

"As if," Nancy joined in on the fun. "Give me the details later when I stop by the office. And Travis, thank you."

"You're welcome," he added. "You did a great job on the last trip, and we want to use you as much as possible. All the arrangements have been made with your hospice people. They know how much you want to do the courier assignment and want you to be happy."

Nancy was thrilled; not only because she would be going to London, but because she knew Jonathan would be there and they might be able to see each other.

Nothing out of the ordinary occurred for the rest of the week. Patients to see, three-mile runs every morning, and no sign of any disturbance in or around the apartment.

On Friday, Nancy prepared to become Dolcé. "Two dates with a nice guy are not going to change me," she insisted as she shed her nurse's uniform before making dinner and having a Manhattan, which she preferred when drinking at home. She took the cocktail into the bath she had drawn and sipped it slowly as she melted into the fragrant bubbles she adored so much. Her bath lasted for over an hour. She was not in a hurry. The clubs didn't get started until ten at the earliest.

It was her habit to show up at a bar or club around then and not much later. If she arrived later than much later, she found her prospects diminishing, either because they were drunk or stoned and not attractive to her or they had found another partner for the night. Ten was the bewitching hour, at least here in Chicago. Berlin, she had learned, was completely different. It had been an education for her. She had thought she was the wildest person, but she was a pussy cat compared to the Berlin crowd. "It's all in a person's perspective," she thought philosophically.

Chapter 7

Nancy entered the bathroom, and Dolcé emerged one hour later. Her transformation had been complete. Dolcé had decided not to go as a Goth hipster tonight but chose a more blatantly sexy, sophisticated look instead. "And the look is magnificent if I do say so myself," she muttered as she inspected herself in the mirror.

Dolcé was in all her glory, dressed to the nines in a gorgeous sequined minidress that hugged her curves nicely, with a neckline that plunged well below her perfect breasts that seemed to defy gravity. The array of blue and turquoise sequins overlaid on the black background fabric cascaded vertically like raindrops, gently sliding down the contour of her body, inviting hands to follow them. "Like braille," thought Dolcé with an impish grin. Her underwear consisted only of a black lace thong she saved for special occasions.

She let her long black curls flow over her shoulders, partially veiling her exposed cleavage. It was like saying, "I dare you to brush me away to reveal the treasure underneath." Her make-up was as much a part of her disguise as anything else. She tweezed her eyebrows to a perfect arch, then applied a black pencil for definition. The luxurious false eyelashes were applied next, causing her already dramatic eyes to be downright powerful. The eyeshadow was smokey with a black undercoat covered by an iridescent silver top coat. The eyeliner was bold without the "wings" that many women thought enlarged their eyes. Her eyes were brilliant without them. Four coats of black mascara were applied, giving her the mysterious without being trashy appearance she had hoped for. The look was finished with light foundation and blush positioned carefully to highlight her cheekbones and bright red lipstick. "Perfect," Dolcé said out loud to her reflection.

She slipped on her four-inch strappy sandals and grabbed her small black sequined cross-body handbag containing lipstick, a credit card and ID, her phone and a taser, fully charged, and two doses of Molly. She also pinned a tiny GPS Travis had given her to the inside of her dress, just in case she found herself in an unfamiliar situation. Before leaving the apartment, she grabbed a black pashmina, knowing that September nights in Chicago could get very cool. Making sure the door was fully bolted shut, she descended the stairs just as her regular Uber driver arrived to take her to her destination.

"The Ritz Carlton Hotel, please," instructed Dolcé. She desired to start the night with some class. She wanted a beautiful lounge with beautiful people and many lonely horny businessmen. "How are you doing, Dwayne," she asked the driver.

"Very well, thank you, Miss Dolcé," he answered politely. "You look especially exotic and beautiful tonight!"

"Thank you. Are you working late tonight? If so, I will call you to take me home. From where I'm not sure at this point," Dolcé added frankly.

"That's all right, Miss Dolcé. Friday nights are hectic, and I'll be available until about 4 a.m. You text or call me, and I'll pick you up as usual," he said. "You are one of my best customers. You know I'll always take good care of you.

The ride took twenty-five minutes and gave Dolcé plenty of time to plan her attack. She would go to the Torali Lounge inside the Ritz Carlton and see if there were any prospects. If not, she would head to the Primary Night Club only two miles away. The dress code was more relaxed there than she liked, but she could always find someone who would want to take her home. She might need to compromise, but it was only for one night. "Think positively," she told herself.

The Torali Lounge was impressive with its high ceilings and beautiful modern chandeliers, plush furnishings, and numerous places to sit at the bar. The one downside is that it only stayed open until midnight. That did not give her much time to strike up a conversation and arrange for the night's entertainment. Entertainment was how she described her encounters. Nothing more, nothing less. She never paid for, nor was she paid for, that type of entertainment. Weekends were for fun in whatever way it came, as long as she felt protected. Businessmen were usually safe. The higher the status, the more they had to lose if things got out of hand. And it seldom did. Dolcé knew how to control the scene.

Dolcé strolled to the bar and settled in with confidence. Every male eye in the lounge followed her. Even the men with wives or dates. They couldn't help it. She was the most fascinating creature most men had ever seen. She ordered a Manhattan straight-up with Maker's Mark bourbon and a cherry with a stem. She couldn't help taking the stem into her mouth, tying it into a knot with her tongue, and depositing it gently on her cocktail napkin. She was sure at least eighty percent of the men in the lounge observed her little tradition.

She didn't have to pay for the drink. Within two minutes of its arrival, the first eager prospective suiter sat next to her, signaled to the bartender that he would pick up her tab, and began his pick-up line. Although she was polite, Dolcé quickly told him she was not interested. "There are many better ones to pick from tonight," she thought as she scoped out the room.

It was like a revolving door for the next half hour. Men would approach Dolcé, give their pitch, and leave after a few minutes. Finally, Dolcé was approached by a man that interested her. He wasn't terribly handsome but was very well dressed in his Armani sports jacket, turtleneck sweater, neatly pressed jeans, and well-polished classic Gucci lace-up shoes. He was also well-spoken and didn't succumb to the typical cliché lines. He sat next to her, offered to buy her a drink, which she accepted, and began talking to her like they had known each other for years.

Dolcé mentally went through her checklist. He made her laugh: check. He listened as well as talked: check. He didn't come on too strong but made his interest known: check. He was from out of town and didn't get to Chicago often: check. He wasn't wearing a wedding ring: check, although that wasn't a deal breaker. He was staying here at the Ritz, so transportation wasn't a problem: check. Was he a dangerous serial killer? Dolcé could not be sure, but she didn't see any micro expressions that might indicate he was overly stressed or psychotic. She always had to go with her gut feeling with that. And thank goodness, her gut had not steered her wrong.

Dolcé also clarified that she was not a professional and was just out for fun. He responded well to her candor. It became clear that there was a mutual understanding of intentions and desires, and it wasn't long before he began leading her out of the bar into the lobby and to the elevator.

"Before we go any further, do you have protection?" asked Dolcé seriously. She never risked getting HIV for a night of fun. She always asked the question, but she made sure she was always "carrying."

"Yes," he answered.

"OK then," she replied. "Lead on McDuff." She didn't know why she said that. It just seemed appropriate and made them both chuckle.

When they entered his room, there was no urgency to "get the deed done." Dolcé asked if he wanted a dose of Ecstasy to heighten the enjoyment. He agreed, as long as she also imbibed. He admitted he had never had it before. Dolcé patiently tutored him on what to expect before assuring him that it was of the best quality and that nothing extra was added to the formula.

He…she called him He because his name wasn't necessary…ordered room service drinks and a carafe of iced water. After ingesting the small pill, she knew it would take about forty-five minutes for the effects to be felt. They began casually kissing and caressing each other while listening to music from Pandora as they waited for the drinks to arrive. Neither wanted to be caught "with their pants down" when the room service waiter knocked on the door.

Dolcé was lucky tonight. "He" was a gentleman and enjoyed the Molly ride. After the drinks were consumed and the effects of the drug kicked in, all inhibitions dissolved. Clothes were shed and thrown wherever they landed. The skin was stroked with the other's skin. Sensations were heightened, although the drug lessened his sexual performance. It didn't matter to either of them. They were on a high and having fun.

Eventually, Dolcé suggested they go to a late-night club, but "He" wasn't up for going out, and she reluctantly acquiesced. Besides, she was having fun and felt safe. It was only Friday night. She always had tomorrow night to go completely wild.

They both fell asleep. Dolcé awoke at 3:30 a.m. and quietly called Dwayne to pick her up. She slipped from the room without disturbing "Him" and without leaving a note or any evidence that she had ever been there. She wanted and needed to stay anonymous. By 4:30 a.m., she was safely back at her apartment, temporarily satiated and ready to sleep until noon at least.

Chapter 8

Morning morphed into the afternoon before Nancy awoke. She checked the clock and slumped back into her luxurious sheets and duvet. "It's only twelve-thirty. I can sleep for another three hours," she whispered before falling back asleep. This was her weekend ritual. Friday night was Dolcé's serious party time; sleep late on Saturday that evening, head out to the clubs for a less energetic party and possible sleepover and then be home by noon to begin her sobering transformation back to Nancy. Nancy would then prepare for the work week ahead of her and be "wide-eyed and bushy-tailed" Monday morning.

The phone rang. "Hello," she answered sleepily.

"Oh, did I wake you?" asked Jonathan. Nancy sat straight up in bed with instant attentiveness after recognizing his voice from the first syllable.

"I was out late last night," explained Nancy. "I'm surprised to hear from you. What's up?"

"I have news about the little object you received in Berlin. I'd rather not discuss it while you are inside your flat. Would it be possible for us to talk for an hour? Can you be somewhere else at that time?" he asked.

"I guess so. You've got me curious now," said Nancy

"Don't say anything, but I believe you are being followed, and your place was bugged," said Jonathan.

"I checked and didn't see anything," added Nancy.

"These are professionals. You would need to be an expert to find the kind of bugs they planted," explained Jonathan. "Just call me when you are outside."

Nancy was wide awake now. She quickly slipped on her running outfit and left the building. When she was outside, she dialed Jonathan's number. "Hi again. So, what's going on?"

"I don't want you to be alarmed, but some bad shit (pardon my French) has been going down. There was a lot more on the flash drive than just the video. We broke the encryption and found that you stumbled upon an entire organization of really bad guys. The film was the least of it. They are involved with human trafficking on a huge scale—International, including most of North America and many places in Europe and the Middle East. We still don't know who gave you the flash drive or why.

We believe it was someone who was a traitor to the organization and wanted the information forwarded to the police or similar. There is no way anyone in the organization would want this information to be exposed," explained Jonathan.

"So, how do I fit into all of this?" asked Nancy with determined focus. "Why would my apartment be bugged, and who did it?"

"We don't know that yet, but it appears that you were purposely targeted at the club. Perhaps the man with the tattoo panicked and slipped you the flash drive because he heard your American accent. But perhaps someone knew that you were at the club and followed you there," said Jonathan.

"Very weird. I didn't know I would be there until I left my hotel room. I must have been followed. Do you think the bad guys drugged me? I thought it was the mysterious tattooed man, but that doesn't make sense now," said Nancy.

"Don't freak out, but perhaps you were drugged to kidnap you and either sell you to the highest bidder or to make you the star of their next film," Jonathan interjected.

"Oh, my god! Really?" exclaimed Nany.

"We don't know anything yet, but I'm calling to warn you to be extremely careful. Do you have your taser with you right now?" asked Jonathan.

Nancy was ashamed to have to say she didn't.

"Don't go anywhere without it. Nowhere. I will arrange to have your flat swept for bugs this afternoon if that is OK with you," added Jonathan.

"Of course," replied Nancy. "Thank you for warning me. I am terrified right now."

"The organization will do just about anything to get that flash drive back. Did you send it to your given address?" asked Jonathan.

"Yes. I mailed it the same day I got home. I have a tracking slip if that will help," she replied.

"Good. Please send me the tracking number, and we will follow up. We have had someone watching the PO Box you sent it to, but nobody has collected anything from that box. It has been less than a week, but the flash drive should have arrived yesterday or sooner," said Jonathan.

"Oh, Jonathan, I must tell you I have another assignment next week. It's in London! Are you going to be around next weekend?" she said eagerly.

"Yes, I should be. I got back three days ago and don't believe I will be assigned to go anywhere late next week, but things can change at a moment's notice.

We will have to try to get together for business and some pleasure," he added cheerfully.

Nancy's heart soared. This was the first man who had ever wanted to see her again after two dates. "I look forward to seeing you again," she added sincerely. "I'll send you the details."

"But for now, we need to focus on the issues. Someone is going to try to get that flash drive back. You don't have it to give. That puts you in a dangerous position. They will think you are lying if you say you don't have it. We need to find out something about these creeps. You may be able to help us if you are willing."

"Of course, I am willing. I need to feel safe in my own home once again. Just tell me what I can do," she said emphatically.

"For now, go about your normal routine and be very aware of your environment. Report anything that doesn't feel right, anything. Nothing is too small to report," said Jonathan.

"I haven't noticed anything unusual since the day I got home. I put new deadbolts on the door and live on the third story of my building without a fire escape near my windows. They are all locked and haven't been disturbed, to my knowledge. Nothing seems to be moved or taken, but I will check again. Just send your people over as soon as possible, and I will let them in to inspect the apartment," she said.

"Good. I'll be in touch this week, and please plan on having a thorough debriefing when you get to London," said Jonathan. "It's serendipitous that you will come to London when we need your assistance."

Dolcé couldn't help but chuckle. She had a thorough "debriefing" last night! She wisely chose not to share that humor with Agent Harris. She did say, "Yes, what a happy coincidence."

"OK, until later then, cheers," said Jonathan and disconnected.

Nancy let the conversation soak into her consciousness. Then she shivered, knowing she could have been the victim of a horrific crime while in Berlin. "I wonder how those clubs keep their patrons safe. Or how many innocent young people disappear and are never seen again? And do the club owners even care?" She doubted it!

Looking around and seeing her environment in a new way, Nancy no longer felt protected in her own home. That was the one place she always felt secure. That was now in question and shook her to her very core. "If I cannot feel safe in my own home, where can I," she asked herself. Was someone watching her now? Did someone know her every move? The insecurity she felt as a teenager eked into her consciousness, and she suddenly felt extremely vulnerable and alone.

She hurried into her building and quickly locked all the deadbolts upon entering her apartment. She was breathless, not from the exertion of taking the stairs three at a time but from the adrenaline caused by an increasing and overwhelming fear. She spent the next hour straightening the place because she didn't want "the bug men" to see her apartment as less than immaculate, not that they cared or even noticed. Her routine was shot to hell, and it upset her equilibrium. She suddenly felt herself shaking uncontrollably. She became nauseated and could feel her heart beating rapidly and irregularly. She also became short of breath and began breathing with shallow quick breaths. She also felt pressure high in her chest and simultaneously, broke out in a sweat. Her hands started tingling. She knew that pain down the left arm wasn't a good sign. "Am I having a heart attack?" she asked as she lowered herself into a chair so she wouldn't fall. "You are too young and healthy to have a MI," she told herself. "You are having a panic attack!"

"Calm down," she said. "You've been in a lot worse situations before. You don't even know if there is any imminent danger!" That was the trouble…she didn't know anything for sure.

It took fifteen minutes of slow deep breathing (in through the nose, out through the mouth) and purposeful concentration until she felt better. "Wow, that was a doozy," she said to herself. "I hope that doesn't become a habit." She checked her vitals to be sure she was doing OK. Blood pressure: 124/72, Pulse a little high at 102 beats per minute, and oxygen at 99%. Her vitals were good, which helped assure her she would be fine.

The "bug men" arrived an hour later and swept the apartment. They found no listening devices or cameras, which relieved Nancy. "Maybe all this is in your imagination," she told herself, trying to quell her fear. Eventually, she was able to calm down enough to text Jonathan. "Nothing was found here," it said simply. She almost instantly received a reply from Jonathan. "Good, see you soon," was all it said.

The day had slipped away quickly. It was time for Dolcé to prepare to go out as usual. "You know what?" she said to herself. "I'm going to stay in tonight." She had only stayed in on a Saturday night when she had a fever of 102 and a bad case of the flu. It was unheard of for her to be at home on a Saturday night. Her decision was made because she was afraid to go out, knowing people could be stalking her without her knowledge. Knowing that her apartment was bug-free was of some relief, but she knew she was being watched one way or another. But how? And by whom? Why?

Instead of spending the next few hours preparing to become Dolcé, Nancy found a book and read it. "This isn't so bad," she thought. She found a movie on Netflix she had wanted to see.

"I am surprised my TV works. It has been so long since I turned it on," she chuckled. She made popcorn she found hiding in the farthest corner of a cabinet, changed into her most comfortable pajamas, rechecked the locks on all the windows and doors, and made herself comfortable on the sofa. "So, this is what normal people do on a Saturday night," she commented to herself. Halfway through the movie, she fell asleep and didn't wake up until 2 a.m..

The night was young, and the clubs were still open, but Nancy chose not to go out even though she felt refreshed and recharged after her evening nap. "No, it's just not safe. I'm wild, but I'm not crazy. I would have to be crazy to take any unnecessary chances tonight," she said to herself as she headed to the bedroom. She climbed into bed and quickly fell into a deep, dreamless sleep.

Chapter 9

Nancy's week began like most of her weeks. She jogged her three miles every morning, dressed carefully, and arrived at her hospice job precisely at seven fifty-five, visited her list of patients, talked with the families as needed, and returned to the hospice office each afternoon when her shift was completed. What kept Nancy motivated this week was the knowledge that her routine would be broken and shattered by Friday...but in a good way. She would be in London for the first time and was very excited.

On Monday, during her lunch break, Nancy stopped by the local bookstore and bought a copy of Rick Steve's Guide to London. She spent any free time she had in the evenings studying it to help her make the most of her concise amount of time in the city that had always been at the top of her "bucket list." So many sights, so little time," she said to herself.

She made a list of the "must-dos" while she was there. Shopping at Harrod's was at the very top of the list. She had dreamed about going there since she was a little girl. She had arranged to stay until Sunday, so she had a total of fifty-two hours to pack everything in she wanted to do. She knew that she would have to plan carefully, but she could get several sights seen if she grabbed meals on the run and didn't sleep until she got home to Chicago.

"Maybe I'm trying to do too much," she advised herself wisely. "Nah! I can be like the Energizer Bunny and not run out of steam until I pour myself back on the plane on Sunday!" she added, not so wisely.

By late Wednesday, Nancy was packing for her early evening flight to London the next day. Since her plane did not leave O'Hare until seven thirty, she had planned on working until 3 p.m. That would give her time to check in at the hospice office and pick up her stem cell container before heading to the airport. She would stash her suitcase and carry-on items in the car when she left for work in the morning. She had decided it would be more convenient for her to drive herself to the airport and park in long-term parking for the three days she would be gone than take a taxi. That way, she could hop in her car when she arrived back at 6 p.m. on Sunday. "What a whirlwind," Nancy said to herself.

She checked the weather forecast for London and noted that it would be cool and rainy while she was there. "It isn't London without rain," she thought and put a travel-size umbrella in her suitcase. Nancy thought of taking some "clubbing" outfits with her but decided against it.

She knew that any free time she had would be spent with Jonathan, whether it was business or pleasure. She would do everything in her power to assist him and his fellow agents in catching and prosecuting the slime that was trafficking innocent adolescents. Nothing was more important to her, not even Harrod's.

So, into the suitcase went sensible working clothes and a couple of casual outfits in case they had time to rent bicycles again. She had had so much fun on the bike in Berlin that she would love to tour London the same way. A pair of semi water-proof shoes went into the suitcase. "Am I getting old?" she asked herself when she saw all the practical instead of pretty or sexy items in her bag. She did pack one set of frilly undies to make her feel alluring, even if nobody would see them.

Her pre-departure mantra had become: "Passport, ticket, money." She was obsessive about ensuring everything was ready and available when the time came. "Oh, one thing I forgot," she said as she made sure the GPS Travis had given her was in her handbag. "Now I'm ready to go."

She found it challenging to keep focused during work on Thursday, knowing that she would be on a plane to LONDON this evening. It was so exciting. She had always wanted to go to London and see the sights. She looked forward to viewing Big Ben and Buckingham Palace as well as Trafalgar Square and The Tower of London. She also wanted to go to the British Museum and the National Art Gallery. She knew she wouldn't have enough time to see a play or a musical, but she could go by the theaters and imagine how wonderful it would be. She wanted an authentic pub lunch, a pint of Guinness, and maybe a game of darts. She wanted to ride upstairs in the front row of one of the red double-decker buses. She didn't care where it was going; she just wanted the experience. And she wanted to ride the Tube, or what would be called the subway in the United States. She wanted to see it all, but knew she couldn't. "Oh well, at least I'll see some of it, and who knows, maybe I'll be going back again soon and can start where I left off."

And, of course, she was excited about seeing Jonathan. She hated admitting it, but he had changed her more than a little bit. Partying didn't quite have the luster it had before. There was something comfortable about being with a good person. One who seemed to like her for her, not for her incredible body or a quick lay. She would also be spending time with "Agent Harris." They had serious business to attend to. She might spend most of her precious hours in London in an office at Interpol. But that was OK. It was necessary. The sooner the police broke up the human trafficking ring, the sooner she would feel safe again. Safety was now her top priority.

After work, she stopped by the courier's office and picked up the package with the stem cells and her detailed instructions. Travis reminded her to keep the GPS with her at all times. Nancy thought that was a little strange but didn't question it. She had so many other things to think about and keep organized.

She was to take a taxi from Heathrow airport directly to The London City Cancer Center and deliver the stem cells to the lab. Once that was accomplished, she would be free for the weekend. "Simple enough," she thought.

The drive to O'Hare was uneventful, and she quickly found a convenient parking place. A co-worker had suggested she take a picture of the parking spot so she wouldn't have to remember where her car was at the end of her trip. "What a great idea," she had said to her acquaintance. Now all I have to do is remember to take the picture." Nancy took out her phone and got a usable, if not beautiful, picture of her car and the space number before taking her luggage out of the car and heading for the terminal.

Nancy was becoming an old pro at maneuvering through O'Hare. "I'll have to apply for a TSA pre-pass," she muttered when she saw a long security line. "Or maybe even a Global Entry membership. That would make things much easier both coming back into theU.S.and going out since it also included the TSA pre-pass. I'll apply for it when I get home next week," she told herself.

It wasn't long before she was boarding the flight. In contrast to her last journey, she wasn't scoping out possible hook-ups for her free time in London. She was preoccupied with thinking about seeing Jonathan again and wondering what she would learn about the investigation. She was fatigued from the long and busy day, so after dinner, she immediately made herself as comfortable as possible and closed her eyes. "Thank goodness I can sleep most anywhere," she thought as she slipped into a restless slumber.

Just like her last flight, she awoke when the plane began its descent into Heathrow airport. She had just enough time to quickly run to the loo (British speak for toilet) and splash some water on her face. As expected, Heathrow was a zoo. Thousands of people were everywhere. Signs were saying "Way out" instead of exit. "Was John Denver a part of designing this airport?" she mused. "No, that was Far Out."

She followed the herd of humanity down seemingly unending corridors. It reminded her of rats in a maze and was just about as humane. Finally, she came to the immigration hall. Hundreds of people, including families with small children speaking many languages, were ahead of her. "This is going to take hours," she said, frustrated. And it did. One-and-one-half hours later, she presented her passport, got it stamped, and was unceremoniously welcomed to the United Kingdom. Her feet hurt from standing so long, and she was stiff from the flight, but that did not dissuade her. She was in London!

Nancy then headed outside to find a taxi. Luckily, the line was short, and she was in a cab within minutes. It was an old-fashioned black boxy taxi with the driver on the right-hand side. "This is going to take some getting used to," she noted. She instructed the driver to take her to the London Clinic Cancer Centre, and they were off. The ride took a little over 30 minutes, and unfortunately, it did not take her past any sights. "That's OK," said Nancy to herself. "I'll get to see plenty later today." She was curious about how people get accustomed to driving on the left in such heavy unforgiving traffic. "I guess they are just used to it."

They arrived at the Cancer Centre a few minutes after eleven. As before, the taxi driver agreed to wait while she delivered her precious cargo to the head of the lab. They were back on the road within 20 minutes. "I love this job!" she whispered. "Where else can you travel like this with the only responsibility to hand deliver a package? How was I so lucky?"

It was only three miles to the Royal Garden Hotel in Kensington. The hotel was chosen not only because it was comfortable and beautiful but because of the location near Kensington Gardens and Harrod's Department Store. "If I get a chance, I will do some major shopping! I don't know how I can finish everything in just two days. It's nearly impossible." The taxi drew up to the hotel entrance, and the driver removed her bags from the boot (English for trunk) after she paid for the trip and remembered to get a receipt.

The hotel was gorgeous and was across the road from some beautiful gardens. She stepped through the doors and was blown away by the incredible lobby and the well-dressed and pleasant front desk personnel. Luckily, she was able to check into her room without delay. She called Jonathan as soon as she entered the room, not wanting to waste even a minute. "Jonathan, I'm here and ready to go," she said excitedly.

"OK," he replied. "I'll be there in forty-five minutes. We can catch a quick lunch and then come straight to the office. I'm afraid the sightseeing will have to wait until later. This can't wait. I hope you understand."

"Of course I do!" Nancy proclaimed. "I'll meet you outside the front of the hotel in forty-five minutes, so you don't have to worry about parking. You will recognize me, won't you? It's been so long since we last saw each other," she said teasingly.

"I think I can remember what you look like unless you're in one of your disguises," he teased.

"Now, that's a great way to begin. A little laughter goes a long way to break the ice," she thought to herself.

She spent the next half hour showering quickly and changing into fresh, practical clothes. "This is business. The fun will come later If we have the chance," she said, wondering what the day would bring.

Chapter 10

"Welcome to England!" exclaimed Jonathan as he drove up to the curb, and Nancy opened the passenger side door.

"Thank you; I'm so excited. Gray skies and all," replied Nancy surveying the ominous-looking clouds.

It was evident by the smiles on their faces that they were mutually happy to see each other again. "So, I thought we'd catch a quick lunch at one of my favorite pubs on the way to the office. Is that good with you?"

"You must have read my mind. I was hoping for a pub lunch, and now you are making my dream come true," she replied cheerily.

Jonathan miraculously found a parking place directly outside the pub, The Three Feathers, and the two entered the crowded and noisy bar. "Can you find a table? I'll get us drinks. Would half a lager be OK with you?" asked Jonathan.

Nancy didn't understand. She didn't speak "British English" yet. "Half of what?" she asked innocently.

"I'm sorry. I should interpret it for you. Half a pint of beer in your language," Jonathan said teasingly and headed for the bar.

Nancy enjoyed the gentle kidding. It was new to her, and it demonstrated affection when Jonathan pulled her leg. She joined in by saying, "Jolly good, old Pip" in a very horrible English accent. He cringed a bit and then laughed. "Good try," he said. Their time together had started well.

Nancy found a small round table near a window and waited patiently for Jonathan to arrive with the drinks. She enjoyed people-watching. The pub was packed chiefly with men standing around, chatting with their friends and downing massive amounts of beer. The pub was thankfully free of cigarette smoke, unlike the sidewalk outdoors, and Nancy remembered that Brits were no longer permitted to smoke inside public establishments, including their local pub. She appreciated breathing without the smell of stale tobacco in her nostrils. And she was thankful that Jonathan didn't smoke.

"Is it strange that the Brits drink so much at lunch? Does anything get done in the afternoons?" They were rhetorical questions that weren't meant to be answered. She just wondered because she knew she wouldn't be able to function with a pint or two of ale in her gut.

She would probably have to take a nap. She knew England did not have a traditional siesta like the Southern European countries such as Spain, Italy, and Greece. "You would think they would need a siesta too!"

Jonathan appeared with two small frosty mugs. The beer was cold, which pleasantly surprised Nancy. She had heard that the beer here was served warm.

"The lager is served cold. It's bitter that is served at room temperature. People think the flavor is better when it is warm. You'll have to be the judge of that yourself," explained Jonathan. "And, I took the liberty of ordering lunch for both of us. Otherwise, we might not have had time. You can have whichever you prefer, Shepherd's pie or Steak and Kidney pie. It's pie whichever you choose," said Jonathan loudly over the din.

"I haven't had either one before, so you choose for me," said Nancy, a little overwhelmed by the new sights and sounds. The noise was nearly deafening. "At least everyone is having a good time," she said, rationalizing the din.

When the lunches were delivered to the table, the plates had the pies on them and a vast portion of chips (British for French fries) and soggy-looking peas. "How many armies are they trying to feed?" asked Nancy, tasting the Shepherd's pie.

"Yum," she said enthusiastically. "That's good." Inspecting the pie to see what it was made of, she saw no typical pastry crust and wondered why it was a pie, not a casserole. She saw ground meat that she assumed was beef, a variety of veggies in a brown gravy with a cheesy mashed potato "crust." Whether it was a pie or a casserole, all Nancy knew was that it was delicious!

The conversation was a challenge over the noise of the rowdy lunch crowd, so it was put on hold until after they finished eating. "I couldn't eat another bite," said Nancy, pushing her plate away. She had eaten less than half of the meal.

"I know; the portions are humongous," added Jonathan. "Sometimes it's quantity over quality. Luckily, they have both here. Did you like your first pub lunch? Can you now check that off your "to-do" list?"

"Yes, and it was everything I had hoped for," Nancy replied. "Thank you. You have made this Chicago girl very happy."

"Now we have to hurry to the office," Jonathan said, changing into his "Agent Harris" mode. "People are waiting for us."

"Yes, sir," Nancy said as she saluted him whimsically.

Interpol headquarters in London was only two and a half miles away from the pub, but it took them almost half an hour to get there due to horrible traffic and congestion.

"Yikes," said Nancy. "It would be faster for us to walk. I guess that's why most Londoners don't own cars and take the bus or the tube."

"Good observation. If everyone here were as smart as you are, we would be there by now," Jonathan chuckled.

They finally arrived at the Interpol building, parked, and entered. As in Berlin, they had to go through a security check, obtain a guest pass for Nancy, and then were allowed to go to Agent Harris' office, where he gathered five agents for their meeting. After introductions were exchanged, they all got down to business.

"Ms. Calloway, thank you for being here. Your input may be instrumental in finding and stopping this criminal syndicate," Agent Morris said.

"You are so very welcome. Anything I can do to help will be my pleasure," said Nancy.

"You understand that we cannot share most of the case information with you. Things need to be kept confidential at the least and Top Secret mostly," added Agent Barnhardt.

"I understand that anything that is said in this room is not to be repeated," said Nancy emphatically.

"Good, then let's get started," said Agent Robinson, who was leading the meeting. "First of all, thank you, Ms. Calloway, for freely giving the flash drive to Agent Harris. It has provided us with a wealth of information. It had the video of that heinous crime and lists of contacts in over ten countries, including the US, Germany, the UK, Saudi Arabia, and others. You accidentally came upon one of the largest organized networks of human trafficking we have ever known."

"All I did was find the flash drive in my purse and give it to Agent Harris," said Nancy humbly.

"Yes, but that was the key to beginning this investigation. We are trying to locate the man who gave you the flash drive and need any information you can give us on him," continued Agent Robinson. "He could provide invaluable details and tell us why he gave you the flash drive in the first place. Did he say anything to you?"

Nancy thought carefully and knew that Dolcé was stoned out of her mind at the time and wasn't in any condition to recognize anyone then, much less now, rationally. She tried, however. "He didn't say much, and I couldn't hear because the music was so loud. Everyone had to shout to be heard at all," she continued. "I believe he had a deep raspy voice and spoke to me in English with a German accent."

"That's good. Please continue," encouraged Agent Robinson.

"He was very tall. Maybe six foot two or three. He may have been wearing boots that made him look taller than he was. He had on a black leather coat that went down to his knees. I remember because I thought he must be hot in that heavy coat. It was almost like a cloak. He had longish black hair…to his chin, not his shoulders. He had a scruffy short beard…more like he hadn't shaved in a week than a real beard. I believe his eyes were brown, but I cannot remember. He was slim but muscular, and he tasted like peppermint. We kissed a few times while dancing," she said in explanation, not looking at Jonathan. "He smelled of tobacco. But the most remarkable thing about him was the tattoo on the left side of his neck."

"That's very good. Please describe the tattoo," interjected Agent Peterson, who was taking careful notes.

"I looked it up when I got home. It was a stylized Iron Cross with a black outline shadowed with red. It was about three inches across," she stated.

"Did it look like this?" interjected Agent O'Reilly, showing Nancy a picture of a traditional Iron Cross.

"It was similar but with black and red outlines. It had black shading in the center. But the most interesting thing I remember was the black spider web surrounding the cross. It was creepy in so many ways," she said and shivered. "Wasn't the Iron Cross a symbol of the Nazis?"

"Yes, but originally it was a military medal given by the King of Prussia," Jonathan explained. "How do you think it was used in his case?"

Nancy pondered the question for a minute. "I have no idea, but it could be something that has to do with the gang he is in. Or just that he likes creepy insignia tattooed on his neck."

That made sense and no sense. Just then, their conversation was interrupted. "Like this?" asked Agent O'Reilly, who had sketched what she had described.

"Yes!" cried Nancy.

"Great. Now, can you remember anything else?" asked Agent Robinson.

"Not really," she added. "Someone had slipped some ecstasy in my drink, and I was feeling no pain. Do you know why the person who spiked my drink chose me? And, do you think it was him or somebody else?"

"We don't know that right now, but we will try to get the answers to your questions," replied Agent Robinson. "Perhaps they were planning on kidnapping you because of your youth and beauty," which made Nancy blush.

"Or maybe the mystery man wanted to approach you because of your obvious American accent. He might have thought you'd be more susceptible to accepting the flash drive if you were high. We are not here to judge," he reminded Nancy and everyone else in the room. "We are here to gather facts so, you can tell us anything." Nancy remembered Jonathan said the same thing.

"There's not much more that I can remember, I'm afraid," said Nancy sadly.

"What about at home? Has anything unusual happened since returning from Berlin?" asked Agent Robinson. Nancy glanced at Jonathan, who nodded. That gave Nancy the courage to continue.

"Well, yes, although it's more of a feeling than something tangible," she said quietly. "When I got home, the hall light was turned off, and I am sure I left it on. Agent Harris had a team sweep for bugs, but didn't find anything. Nothing was conspicuously moved or out of place, but I knew someone had been there. And I feel like someone is stalking me. I have never seen anything suspicious or anyone in particular, but I can feel someone watching me. I know that sounds strange or paranoid, but it's real to me."

"Not at all," said Agent Peterson. "Thank you for your candor. Now, let's talk about the flash drive. Agent Harris has explained to us how you obtained it and the address you sent it. Do you have anything to add?"

"No, not really," she said. I sent the flash drive to the PO Box address I was given the same day I returned from Germany. I used the self-service machine near my apartment and got a tracking number. It was delivered to the box the next Saturday. I'm sorry, but that's all I know." After a moment's hesitation, she asked if anyone had picked the flash drive from the box.

"We can't say," said Agent O'Reilly sympathetically. "It is part of the investigation and needs to be kept confidential, even from you. It's for your own good."

"I understand," said Nancy. "Is there anything else you need?"

"Yes, if you could go through the pictures of possible men that fit the description you gave us," added Agent O'Reilly.

"Of course," Nancy said. She realized that she would be kept away from being an active team member as a witness. She wanted to be more involved, and decided to express her desires to Jonathan when they were alone. In the meantime, she was led to a computer and began flipping through what seemed like thousands of portraits of men with scruffy beards.

After forty-five minutes of mind-numbing searching, Nancy stopped. "Here, this is him!" she howled involuntarily to nobody and everybody. The agents within hearing distance reacted to her exclamation by running to see what she had found. "If it is not him, it looks a lot like him," Nancy explained.

"Wolfgang Zimmerman," agent O'Reilly read from the monitor. The unusual tattoo was clearly visible on his mug shot. "German citizen with a long rap sheet of petty crimes over the last ten years. His last known address was in Berlin. I believe you have found our man, Ms. Calloway," he said adamantly and smiled broadly at Nancy. "Well done! Not many people would have stuck with the job at hand as you did. This will be invaluable to our investigation."

Nancy couldn't help but beam with pride and happiness. She had contributed something unique that nobody else could. Those deep seeded insecurities she had felt from a very early age were beginning to crumble. She started to believe in her self-worth. It had taken twenty-five years, but it was a milestone, and Nancy knew it.

It was time for Nancy to leave. Jonathan walked her out. "Do you need me to drive you back to the hotel?" he asked.

"No, you stay here and help to shut the operation down," Nancy replied. "It will give me a chance to explore on my own. Can I take the tube from here?"

"Are you sure?" he asked again. Nancy nodded. "OK then, it's a short walk to Chancery Lane tube station. There are machines to buy your ticket," he said while digging into his pocket, drawing out some coins, and offering them to her. "There should be an ATM where you can exchange money. Until then, take this. It's enough to get you started. Be sure to keep your ticket, because you will need it at your destination. Take the Central Line west to Queensway station. It should be about seven stops from beginning to end. It's easy. There are maps in each car, so you shouldn't get lost. Once you get to Queensway, you can walk to the hotel or grab a taxi. It's a nice stroll. I think you'll like it. Use Google maps to find your way. I'm sure you won't have any trouble. If you do, just call me."

"Thanks," she said, waiting for Jonathan to mention plans for later.

"I need to stay here now, but I could meet you later if you'd like," he suggested. It was as if he had read her mind.

"Of course, I'd like," she said. "Friday night is usually my time to "howl at the moon," as you know.

"I'll meet you at eight this evening. We'll figure out where to go then. Right now, I need to go back to work," he said, kissing her on the cheek. "Cheers for now. Oh, and Nancy, it's good seeing you again," he added sincerely.

Chapter 11

Nancy was excited and a little nervous about being on her own so quickly in such a big city. "Nothing ventured, nothing gained," she thought. "You've wanted to see London all your life, and now you are here. Make the most of it!"

With that in mind, she decided to try hitting the sights instead of heading to the hotel. She bought a map from a kiosk on the way to the tube station to get her bearings. When she arrived at the station, she suddenly remembered that Travis had given her an Oyster Card to use during her trip. It had fifty pounds sterling credit on it. She would tap the card on the turnstile and then could go anywhere in London she wished without having to deal with coins. "That was nice of Travis to include this," she commented to herself. "Now, where do I want to go first."

The Hop-On Hop-Off bus tour in Berlin had been so good that Nancy decided to explore the city first with a tour. It was still gray outside but didn't look like rain, so she decided to risk the open-air double-decker bus tour. The closest location to catch the tour was Covent Garden, only one mile away. She added Covent Garden to her Google maps and was on her way in no time. "No need to take the tube now," she said. "That will have to wait until later."

Nancy enjoyed the twenty-minute walk to Covent Garden, observing the older and varied architecture of the buildings along the way. She also learned the hard way that someone crossing the road must look right, not left. "Wow, that was a close one," she exclaimed after nearly being run over by a double-decker bus.

Covent Garden was incredible. No longer the early morning bustling fruit and vegetable market of the past, it had been transformed into the West End's hub of shopping, dining, and entertainment. Thousands of people milled around the square, window shopping, sitting "al fresco" at one of the many restaurants, or just enjoying some spontaneous entertainment from one of the buskers (English for street entertainers) who littered the area. She found the correct bus stop and only had to wait for a few minutes before paying for a two-day ticket, climbed up the stairs, and made herself comfortable while enjoying the beginning of many amazing sights. "This is only one of three different tour routes," Nancy told herself. "I'll have to continue my ride tomorrow. There should be just enough time!"

Then Nancy got a brilliant idea. She had Paid Time Off coming to her. Why not stay a whole week? She would be able to get to know the city and would have the time needed to discover the insides of the monuments and museums instead of quickly passing them on a moving vehicle. She called Maria, her boss at the hospice office, where her idea was approved.

"When I heard you were going to London, I figured you would want to stay longer. You have earned your time off, so enjoy it," said Maria. She also called the courier office and received a similar statement of approval. Travis explained that there would be no additional pay, and any expenses would be hers.

"Of course," chimed Nancy, excited to know she would be staying longer. "It's amazing what you can accomplish from the top of an open-air bus!" she said, smiling from ear to ear. Nancy was always frugal at home and had a good nest egg of savings, unlike many of her colleagues who live paycheck to paycheck, so she was financially able to take this spontaneous detour. She decided that she would have to change hotels, however. The Royal Garden Hotel, at $280 per night, was a little too rich for her blood. She quickly brought up the app for hotels.com and found a safe, modern, and comfortable room in the same neighborhood for half the price. She figured she would just be sleeping there, so luxury was nice but unnecessary. She booked the room for seven nights and then changed her airline reservation via the app on her phone. "What did we do before Smart Phones?" she asked herself. She was once again able to relax and enjoy the tour.

In her excitement, Nancy hadn't thought to tell Jonathan of her plans. She would love it if he could see her often on her week-long stay but realized he had a job to go to and wouldn't be able to be with her during the day. That was perfectly fine with her. She had always found her way in life, and this week would be no different! But hopefully, this week would be much more fun than her everyday life.

Awed by the city's sights, sounds, and smells, Nancy tried to absorb as much as possible in one sitting. "I'm like a dry sponge, soaking everything in," she thought. As the end of the 1-hour Green Route tour approached, Nancy began to feel weary and decided to return to the hotel. She knew better than to nap to avoid jet lag but wanted to clean up and unwind before going out this evening. Looking at the time, which was already five o'clock, she realized it wouldn't be long until Jonathan, hopefully not Agent Harris, arrived to take her out.

As promised, Jonathan arrived promptly at eight, and Nancy met him in the lobby. They greeted each other warmly with a hug and a European-type kiss before Jonathan suggested they have a quiet drink in the hotel bar before going out. "We have a lot to talk about without distractions," he said. Nancy agreed, and they headed for the piano bar off the lobby.

Their conversation began with small talk and then got serious. Agent Harris wanted to brief Nancy on the day's activities at work. He felt she deserved to know since she had been instrumental in getting the investigation out of neutral into full steam ahead. "Everyone at the agency was very impressed by you," he began. Nancy smiled. "Your statements have made all the difference in the case. We now have a solid lead and will begin interviewing Mr. Zimmerman as soon as we can locate him." He continued to tell her of their progress, at least as much as he could share. "How was your day?" he asked, reverting to Jonathan from being Agent Harris.

"It was great," Nancy said enthusiastically. "You have an amazing city that I have just begun to explore. One that I want to learn more about," she added as she told Jonathan about her change of plans. Her smile faded slightly when she saw the frown on Jonathan's face.

"I am glad that you can stay longer," Jonathan replied. "I just hope you are not staying just for me." Nancy began to get nervous when he continued, "because I've been dispatched back to Berlin tomorrow for a few days. I think I'll be back by Thursday, which would still give us some time together before you go home."

Nancy was relieved knowing Jonathan wanted to see her but would be working. Her insecurities popped into her psyche for a moment, and it bothered her. "That's just fine," she exclaimed. "I have so much I want to see and do. You don't have to show me around. I understand that natives don't even consider attending touristy events in their communities. How often do New Yorkers go to the observation deck of the Empire State Building? Only when friends or relatives come in from out of town! I don't want to drag you from your important work," she added. "And besides, we have no commitments to each other. You don't have to feel obligated in any way. I'm a big girl who can take care of herself!" she told Jonathan. Privately, she was thinking, "at least I hope so."

With the air cleared, they headed out. Nancy was glad she remembered to bring her lined trench coat because the night was wet and chilly. "I thought we'd head to Covent Garden. There are many places to eat, and it's pretty exciting, especially at night."

"Yes, I know. I was there this afternoon," Nancy said. "I was hoping to go back, so this is a perfect plan."

"Afterwards, we'll head over to the theater district. Piccadilly Circus is similar to New York's Times Square and is quite dazzling," he explained. "I don't know if Chicago has something similar."

"Not really, at least not on such a grand scale," she replied.

"We'll take the tube. I didn't bring the car because parking is a hassle.

It's much easier to get around by public transport. I hope you don't mind," he said somewhat apologetically.

"Mind, of course not! I love the idea!" she added enthusiastically. "Besides, it will allow me to try my Oyster Card."

The evening was spent pleasantly with Nancy in awe most of the time. She had never seen anything like it before. The lights, the people, and the music were all so extraordinary! It was all she could do to curb her eagerness to experience everything all at once. "It's a little like trying to drink out of a fire hose," she said to Jonathan, who was enjoying seeing his "old stomping ground" through new eyes. Nancy's joy was contagious, and Jonathan realized he hadn't had such a good time in months or even years.

The evening ended where it began, back at the hotel lobby, where they chatted over a glass of wine. Nancy told Jonathan about moving to a more affordable hotel, and he approved. "There are a lot of sleazy hotels in London. I'm glad you chose a nice but affordable one," he added and noted it on his phone. "We'll keep in touch over the next few days, and please let me know if you need anything."

"Jonathan, there is one thing," she said, hesitating slightly. "I still feel like I am being watched. Is that possible?"

"It's doubtful but not impossible," he replied. "To be safe, you might want to open the tracker app on your phone. That way, I can know where you are in an emergency." Nancy hesitated a moment. "Don't worry. I won't be keeping track of your movements. Remember...no commitments and no judgment!"

"Thank you. That makes me feel better," she said quietly. "You'll be like a guardian angel during my visit here."

"Not an angel, but for now, a friend who cares and wants you to be safe and well," he said sincerely while taking her hands and looking deeply into her eyes. "I think we understand each other. I look forward to getting to know you slowly over time. You do fascinate me, Nurse Nancy! You are one complicated and special person!"

They said good night with an affectionate hug and a chaste but sincere kiss before Jonathan went out the door.

Nancy went straight to her room without any thought of going out clubbing. "What is he doing to me?" she wondered as she prepared for bed, slipped between the incredibly luxurious sheets, and immediately fell into a deep and restorative slumber.

Chapter 12

Nancy couldn't wait to get her day started. The priority was to pack and switch hotels. Then to get acquainted with the city. Since she would be staying for a few days, she didn't need to rush to see everything in one day. She had always heard about the great variety of stores on Oxford Street and wanted to begin there, knowing that Harrod's would be a fun excursion but would be out of her league and budget. She would need at least one, if not more, party outfits. Dolcé would never agree to go to a club in jeans and a sweater, and she was anxious to hit the clubs tonight. Nancy's blossoming relationship with Jonathan was all well and good, but it wouldn't keep Dolcé from sampling whatever nightlife she could. And whatever British men she could. She desired to experience all that London had to offer!

Nancy decided to walk to her new hotel, which was only a mile from the Royal Garden Hotel. She needed the exercise, and luckily, the sky had cleared up, and the day looked promising. Again, she was fortunate to be able to check in early. After quickly dropping her bags in her room, she headed for Oxford Street and Selfridges Department store. She had heard so much about it, including that it had been open for over a hundred years. First things first. She needed a sexy and fun ensemble for tonight. After all, Saturday is the second most important day of the week to party.

Nancy decided to try public transportation on her own this morning. She found the directions, walked the very short distance to West Cromwell Road Tesco stop, took the bus Route 74 towards Baker Street station, and got off successfully at Portman Street before walking to Selfridges less than half a mile away. "That was fun," Nancy admitted.

She spent the next two hours exploring the shops and boutiques on Oxford Street before ending up at Selfridges, where she knew they would have the widest choice of evening attire. She also liked buying something from such a famous department store. She experienced a small episode of sticker shock. The dresses she liked were all about $350 when the exchange rate was considered. "The same dress in theU.S.would be about one-third of the cost." For that reason, she chose to buy only one outfit and use it for all her nights out on the town. She usually didn't like wearing the same ensemble twice, but she would make an exception. Besides, there were plenty of different haunts in London, so she could go to another place every night without worrying that someone would notice she was wearing the same dress.

It was still early when Nancy finished shopping, and she decided to have lunch before setting out on her sightseeing excursion. She was gobsmacked to learn that there were twenty restaurants and bars in Selfridges, each with its own theme. She chose Alto by San Carlo cafe because it was on the roof, had spectacular views, and she loved Italian food. The menu was extensive, serving cicchetti, which are smaller dishes similar to tapas in Spain. Nancy wanted to try something she had never had and ordered the Spiedino di Pollo (chicken skewer wrapped in pancetta) and the Truffle and Pecorino Ravioli (pecorino is a type of sheep's cheese similar to Parmesan). Both dishes were delicious, along with a glass of chilled white wine recommended by the waiter. "I always heard that British food was horrible," Nancy commented. She had been pleasantly surprised.

After lunch, she joined the Red Hop-On Hop-Off bus tour, which lasted over two hours and drove by most of the more prominent attractions in central London. The weather was good, so Nancy again climbed up the stairs to get a bird's eye view of the sights without worrying about her view being blocked by other vehicles. She couldn't get over how amazing the city was! When the tour stopped at Buckingham Palace, she decided to exit and spend some time admiring the gates, the Royal Guards, and the throngs of people taking pictures while trying to make one of the guards crack a smile. None were successful, of course.

While she was gawking at the sights, a young man approached her and said hello. She was surprised but acknowledged him with a pleasant greeting. She was eager to meet new people, and this seemed like serendipity. He was friendly, around 30 years old, well dressed, and had what Nancy thought was speaking poshly, but Nancy had to admit she couldn't tell a posh from a cockney accent. They all seemed exotic to her. "What the heck," Nancy said. "Why not get to know him better? He might be someone to go out with tonight." They chatted for a while, and he offered to buy a drink for Nancy at a nearby pub.

"No thanks," Nancy said politely. "I need to get back to the hotel to take a nap before getting ready for tonight."

"Oh, where are you going? Will you be alone?" he asked.

"Not if you want to meet me," Nancy added. "My name is Dolcé. What's yours?"

"Peter. OK then, how about if I meet you at your hotel," he suggested.

Dolcé wanted to keep things as anonymous as possible. "No thanks. How about if I meet you at the Carwash Nightclub at eleven o'clock? I will be wearing a red mini-dress and will be around the main floor bar." Nancy didn't think much of the encounter, finished sightseeing around the palace and then decided to take the tube back to the hotel.

She found Hyde Park station without a problem, scanned her Oyster Card at the turnstile, followed the signs to the southbound platform of the Northern Line, and waited for the train to arrive. The underground was a blast from the past in several stations, the walls covered with white tiles that reminded her of a public toilet, and smelled like one too! Nancy remembered reading that the London Underground was the first in the world, first started in the 1860s, was used extensively as a bomb shelter in War II, and carried up to five million people a day! "Very impressive, I must say," Nancy commented to herself. She did that a lot, commenting to herself. That's because she spent so much time alone as a child, she gradually learned that she was her own best listener. It became a deeply ingrained habit that she continued into adulthood. If people looked at her funny when they caught her talking to herself, she just shrugged and ignored them.

The train arrived, and Nancy quickly found a seat after the previous riders had departed the car. She could read the map above her head in each car to know how many stops she had to count before getting to her destination. She enjoyed hearing the soothing British female voice announcing the next stop's location. She also enjoyed reading all the advertisements and public service announcements on the walls of the car. It kept her busy until it was time to disembark.

She kept hearing, "Mind the gap," warning the patrons to safely step over the space from the train onto the platform. "Minding the gap," she mimicked as a bit of a joke to herself. She loved riding the tube. She saw people of all different nationalities speaking incomprehensible languages and wearing all varieties of clothing. For example, on one ten-minute ride, Nancy heard English, French, possibly German or Dutch, some Arabic language…perhaps Farsi, Chinese, and some African language she couldn't decipher.

Nancy had heard that the elementary school system in London had 160 languages spoken by its students. "Just try being an ESL teacher here," she quipped. "Amazing!"

Before she knew it, the train had stopped at the Gloucester Road station, and she quickly gathered up her belongings and stepped onto the platform. "Now, I need to figure out which way is out," she said, looking around her. The crowd was all moving in one direction, so she decided to follow. She had to go down corridors, up escalators, down more corridors, through the turnstile, and up one final flight of steps to get to the street. And wouldn't you know it, she chose the wrong exit and ended up on the opposite side of Cromwell Road. Instead of trying to fight the steady and fast-moving street traffic, Nancy soon found it was safer, wiser, and more legal to head back down the stairs to the station and choose the correct exit.

She had missed the signs directing her to the right side of the street earlier. "Live and learn," commented Nancy and headed back up the long flight of concrete steps that took her outside. "Maybe that should be my mantra from now on," she added thoughtfully. "No, just my mantra for today. I like too many mantras to limit myself to just one," she said. And then added, "a lot like men," with a wry smile.

Finding the hotel from the tube station was easy. "I'm getting the hang of the city. And it's only been two days," she thought with a satisfied feeling.

The late afternoon and evening were spent writing in a casual journal. Nancy had never bothered to put her feelings on paper, but this seemed unique. Little orphan Nancy had found her way around one of the busiest cities in the world with aplomb and loved it.

She called Jonathan from the room where she could have the privacy they needed. Instead of waiting for Jonathan to ask her how her day had been, she asked about his. He had his "Agent Harris" voice. "Thanks to your help, we have made some headway on the investigation. We have people in Berlin looking for Zimmerman and should be locating him soon. Once we do, we will be able to determine his connection with all of this. We are hoping he will be an informer. Why else would he have passed the flash drive onto a stranger? It could blow the case wide open if we can recruit Zimmermann."

"Wow, it sounds like you're not letting any moss grow under your feet with this," said Nancy a little tritely. She didn't know what else to say. "Have you got any ideas of where the organization is operating?"

"Not yet," he added. "We have some leads we're following, but it may take some time."

"So, how was the sightseeing today," Jonathan asked and reverted to his friendly voice.

"It was so good!" exclaimed Nancy. "The shops are amazing but very expensive! How can people afford it?"

"Many times, they can't," Jonathan explained. "People will save up for months to buy one great dress; that's what they do. London has always been expensive, but it's worth it. Even if four or more friends have to live together and share the costs, they will if it means staying in a great part of town. People in their twenties and sometimes into their thirties even continue living with their parents if it makes financial sense."

"Yikes, no thanks," exclaimed Nancy a little too emphatically. Jonathan noticed.

"Anyway," he said. "I'm sorry I won't be available to see you much in the next few days. Maybe around Thursday, I should be back in town."

"That's OK," Nancy blurted. She wanted to be on her own tonight. "You've been so kind to me already. I'll be fine on my own and enjoy the challenges the city provides. I'll probably go out to one of the clubs tonight. You know me…I have to have my weekend clubbing fix."

"Please be careful," was all Jonathan said, sounding more like a parent than a potential lover. "And text or call if you need anything."

"I will. You go get the bad guys, Tiger," she said and hung up the phone.

The phone call brought Nancy's thoughts back to the reality of the case. She had been lucky in Berlin, and she knew it. She took Jonathan's words somewhat to heart and tonight was determined to limit her alcohol to one drink per hour and to abstain from drugs of any kind completely.

Chapter 13

"I'm in London!" Nancy had to repeat herself to believe it. "How did I get so lucky!" as she prepared to go out. "Tonight, I am going to be siren red and light up the town," chimed in Dolcé. And that's precisely what she had planned. The mini-dress she had purchased at Selfridges was made of a luxurious bright red satin with a corseted bodice, concealed hook and eye fasteners in the front, a sweetheart neckline, frilled shoulder straps, and a gathered hem that came to four inches above her knees. The dress fit Dolcé perfectly, both in dimensions and in character. It would be ideal for what she had planned for tonight. She had checked out many possible clubs in the weekly entertainment newspaper called "Time Out." The Carwash Club caught her eye today. It was known for its colorful dress code, reminiscent of the 1970s, featured long-running pop and disco music, and a shining disco ball. It sounded like pure fun. "It's a far cry from the Goth clubs in Berlin," she noted. "A new club, a new city, a new disguise. It's all good."

Dolcé's hair and makeup had to be different tonight, too. She had luckily remembered to buy a curling iron with an option of either 110 or 220 current. She had heard horror stories of girls who had burnt their hair by using a curling iron without the converter. Even worse, she had heard that a friend of hers blacked out an entire building by simply plugging in her hair dryer and turning it on medium speed. Dolcé certainly did not want to do either thing! She carefully curled her long hair into gentle ringlets to brush out later. She picked a bedazzled headband to help pull her hair back. The look was perfect.

The make-up was next. The disco era was all about blue eyeshadow and sparkles. Dolcé found just the right shade in her "emergency travel kit," which she always had packed and ready to go. She made "cat eyes" from the shadow and eyeliner, flowing far beyond the end of her eyes, almost into her temples. The blue in the shadow gave her already icy turquoise eyes a somewhat ethereal quality. Very bold but mysterious. She then applied tiny rhinestones onto the inner upper eyelids that sparked every time she blinked. To compliment her dress, she used the same shade of lipstick. The result was dazzling; she had to admit. What a contrast to the black Goth look she wore in Germany! She slipped on her black strappy sandals, and the look was complete.

She was nearly ready. Stopping for a minute before leaving the room, she located the tracking device Travis had given her and carefully pinned it to the inside hem of her dress. She also left a quick note addressed to Jonathan, telling him where she was heading and when she expected to be back. She didn't have a buddy to ensure her safety, so this had to be the next best thing. It would have to do. She didn't want to bother him and didn't want any interference. A note is as good as anything else…just in case.

She grabbed her coat, knowing it could be cold and rainy by the time she returned, and headed out the door. With her newfound confidence in figuring out her way around town, Dolcé headed to the Gloucester Road tube station, took the Piccadilly Line east for four stops, then changed to the Jubilee Line north and got off at Bond Street one stop up. "Easy peasy," she said out loud to herself. She was riding the tube on a Saturday night which was very different than during rush hour. The cars were only half full. The riders were younger, often in groups, and dressed up to go to their favorite pub or dance club. Seeing them gave Dolcé some ideas for dressing later in the week if she decided to go out (which, of course, she would…are you daft?!).

Dolcé quickly found the nightclub and was greeted at the door with a flourish. "I've still got it," she said a little smugly. She paid the ten-pound admission fee, including her first drink, checked her coat, and then explored. Like so many nightclubs, Carwash had three levels with different themes and styles of music on each floor. Dolcé enjoyed the happy exuberance she was witnessing everywhere. Couples of mixed genders were dancing freely, as were groups of women. It didn't seem to matter whom you danced with as long as you were dancing. Dolcé joined in and was engulfed quickly into the happy scene as everyone danced to the Bee Gee's famous song, "Staying Alive," "Who says Disco is dead?" squealed Dolcé to anyone who would listen. Her enthusiasm and practiced dance moves caught the eyes of some of the men around her. She happily accepted invitations to dance but did not attach herself to any one guy. She was thoroughly enjoying the feeling of just letting herself feel the music. And obviously, the people around Dolcé were enjoying watching her! She was experiencing a little bit of Dolcé heaven…she was the center of attention and admiration from many angles.

Eventually, Dolcé had to stop and take a breath. Only then did she realize it was after eleven and Peter would be looking for her. She quickly made her way to the ground story bar, watching for Peter in the throngs of people. She suddenly stopped, not believing her eyes. Not ten feet away from her was a very tall, thin, but not gaunt man dressed in low-riding bell-bottom trousers and a loose-fitting hippie-style retro shirt. She recognized him from the very distinctive Iron Cross tattoo on left side of his neck.

He looked straight at her and then began moving towards her, quickly but not menacingly. Through her shock at seeing the German stranger, she reacted immediately under the upstretched arms of her fellow revelers and running in the opposite direction of the man she recognized as Wolfgang Zimmerman.

Thankfully, Dolcé saw Peter at the bar having a casual drink. She approached him swiftly and silently and was next to him before he could react. "Oh, thank goodness you're here," she began breathlessly. "I'm sorry to involve you in this so quickly, but I believe I am being stalked and am quite frightened." Peter reacted instantly, placing himself between Dolcé and the alleged threat, even though he could not see anyone. "Where?" he asked, inspecting the dance floor.

"He was right over there," Dolcé exclaimed while pointing to the center of the room. "Oh, perhaps I was mistaken," she added when her stalker was no longer in sight. "I'm sorry. Can we start over?"

"Are you sure?" asked Peter. "You seemed pretty upset for a minute."

"It must have been my imagination," she said to Peter and then to herself, "Honestly, Dolcé, your mind is playing tricks on you." It wasn't long before she and Peter were chatting despite the deafening music. Soon they joined in dancing with the others. Dolcé noticed that Peter was a good dancer. Uninhibited and rhythmic…just how she liked her men. She was enjoying herself again and snuggled into Peter's chest during the next slow dance. "Nice," she thought.

Peter was also enjoying the slow dancing with Dolcé. She was gorgeous, a great dancer, and affectionate.

Suddenly Dolcé tensed. "What is it," Peter whispered.

"He's right over there," she pointed to the tall stalker she recognized from Berlin.

Peter then did something unexpected. He pulled out his phone and spoke briefly before shielding Dolcé from possible danger. Suddenly five young men in street clothes surrounded the man with the neck tattoo, grabbed him by the elbows, and escorted him out from the dance floor. Peter took Dolcé's elbow to also guide her out of the room.

"What's going on," she questioned with total amazement showing on her face.

"I'll explain once you are safe," he said concisely.

They entered the corridor where the five other men had handcuffed the stalker and seated him in a chair away from the crowd.

"Who are you?" asked Dolcé incredulously.

"I am Detective Peter Mathews of the London police force. Your friend, Agent Jonathan Harris, asked that I keep an eye on you tonight," he explained. "No, not to keep track of you personally, but because we had received word that Wolfgang Zimmerman was in London looking for you," he added quickly.

"How can that be?" asked Dolcé, not believing what she was hearing. "I only knew I was coming here earlier today."

"I'm not sure how, but they have been able to track your every movement," Peter added. "Do you have any idea?"

"Perhaps!" she exclaimed. "Jonathan can track my phone, but I haven't told anyone else. However, I have a GPS tracking device that belongs to the courier service I work for. I pinned it to my dress just in case I had trouble. Could it have been hacked? I can't imagine any other way anyone would know where I've been and where I'm going. I didn't think I was that predictable. I should be furious with Jonathan for intruding on my privacy, but to tell you the truth, I'm very relieved," she said with a sigh.

"We hoped you would feel that way. Now, we have a witness to interview. Do you wish to be a part of it? You are, after all, involved up to your eyeballs," Peter noted the obvious.

"Well, I guess our dancing shoes have turned into gumshoes, so why not!" said Dolcé, now quickly morphing into Nancy teasingly. "Too bad. You cut quite a rug," she added while looking Peter straight in the eyes.

Chapter 14

"We have got to stop meeting this way," said Nancy glibly after recognizing a number of the Interpol agents sitting around the conference room table. She didn't feel glib at all. Last night's sighting of Zimmerman had rocked Dolcé/Nancy to the core of her being. She was glad to be safe with so much police protection, even though she felt she was being treated a bit like a naughty child.

After Zimmerman was apprehended at the Carwash Club, Officer Peter Mathews escorted Dolcé back to her hotel for a good night's sleep. He arranged to pick her up and take her to the Interpol office at 9 a.m. sharp.

"We are glad you are safe, too," Agent Robinson said. "Things could have gone in a much different direction. Why don't you tell us what happened last night."

"Nothing much. Peter, Officer Mathews, had seen me at Buckingham Palace earlier in the day. He chatted me up, and we had arranged to meet later that night. I was not aware at the time that he was a police officer," began Nancy. "It is my understanding that he was on assignment from Agent Harris to watch over me and assist if I got into any trouble."

"Does trouble usually follow you?" asked Agent Robinson sarcastically.

"Not normally, but since I began traveling to Europe, I guess so," she said thoughtfully. "I like to go out on weekends and have never had any real trouble I couldn't handle myself. That is until a couple of weeks ago."

"Are you in the habit of making dates with total strangers on the street?" asked Agent Barnhardt in a fatherly tone.

"Not normally, but I am always anxious to meet new people," Nancy said innocently but knew Dolcé was there laughing at the mild deception. "I often will meet someone in a club."

"To answer your original question, after arriving at the club, I got a drink and walked around for a while before joining a group, and we all danced together. It was simple as that. The group came and went, changing the mood of the music. I was enjoying myself and lost all sense of time," Nancy added.

"Were there any drugs involved?" asked Agent Robinson.

"Not that I was aware of," Nancy replied honestly, glad that she had decided not to imbibe, for once. "I didn't take any drugs voluntarily, and I felt no effects of anything but the couple of Manhattans I had."

"Then what happened?" asked agent Barnhardt.

"Nothing much. I was dancing, and suddenly looked up to see the man I had encountered in Berlin. He was dressed for the evening, in disguise, or a costume, as you would say. Even with the different clothes, he was easily recognizable because of the tattoo on his neck. I will never forget that!" she explained and shivered involuntarily. "Our eyes connected, and I knew he was looking for me. I panicked and ran away from him as quickly as possible. Then, I remembered my date with Agent Mathews and found him. Thank goodness he was there!"

"Zimmerman didn't find us right away, but when he did, it seemed like he was intent on speaking with Dolcé," added Officer Mathews. "He didn't approach her because I was present. Nancy identified him, and he was quietly arrested and taken away. There was no violence, and I doubt that any other clubgoers knew anything had happened.

"Why do you think he was looking for you?" chimed in Agent Peterson.

"I honestly have no idea," sighed Nancy.

"Did he seem menacing as he approached you last night?" continued Agent Peterson.

"I don't know. He wasn't scowling, and I didn't see a weapon, but my gut reaction was to run away when I recognized him. That's all. I wish I could give you more," Nancy said apologetically.

"That's OK. We have him here to interrogate. We would like you to stay close by if we need to ask more questions. Will you do that?" asked Agent Robinson.

"Of course!" she said emphatically. "I'd like to be a part of all of this. It does involve me, after all."

"We don't normally allow witnesses to become an active part of the case, but we will make an exception. We believe you will be able to extract information from Mr. Zimmerman more effectively than we can. He is asking to speak to you. Are you willing?" asked Agent Robinson.

"Again, of course I am willing!" emphasized Nancy.

After a short briefing and wiring her to a communication system, Nancy was led to an interrogation room with a simple table, two chairs, and a large two-way mirror. "This looks just like the rooms I see on TV," mentioned Nancy to herself. "All I need are two huge guards."

As she entered the room, she saw the guards standing in two of the four corners, with Mr. Zimmerman handcuffed and shackled to an iron bar permanently attached to the table. "Yup, just like on TV."

She sat across from the prisoner. "Is there anything you'd like to say to me?" was all Nancy could think to ask, leaving an open-ended question as she had learned to do in the Army. When he didn't immediately respond, she asked again with a slightly different approach.

"You sought me out in Berlin," she began. "Why?"

"Because you reminded me of the young woman in the film," Zimmerman said quietly. "So young. Maybe not so innocent, but certainly neither you nor she deserved to die that way. They had chosen you to be next, and I couldn't let that happen."

Nancy trembled with shock. The reality of her close call struck her like a slap in the face. It took a moment for her to compose herself, then she said, "Thank you."

"Gerne geschehen," he replied.

Nancy rose and left the room, visibly shaken. She conferred with Agents Robinson and O'Reilly for a few minutes before returning and sitting at the table across from Zimmerman.

"Are you willing to work with Interpol to stop these people?" she asked. "If the answer is yes, they are willing to work with you, but you will need to tell us everything you know."

"That is why I am here. I had to be arrested in a public place against my will. Otherwise, they would have stopped me," Zimmerman added.

This changed everything. Suddenly Interpol had a precious asset. One who was willing to cooperate and more. Everyone, including Zimmerman, the Agents, and Nancy, was aware of his importance. It was time to make a deal and begin in earnest.

Agent Robinson called his superior officer with the update. Permission was given to ease restrictions on Zimmerman, and the meeting was moved to a conference room where all team members could be present and participate. No longer was Zimmerman a hostile witness but a willing collaborator.

"What do you want?" asked Robinson to Zimmerman.

"I want them stopped!" Zimmerman replied. "I want immunity and whatever protection you can give me. I am willing to return and pretend to be on their side while reporting to you. You see, I hate these people and what they are doing. I have made some mistakes, but now I need to atone."

"Why now?" asked Robinson.

"They went too far. They don't know it, but they took a cousin of mine. I want to get her back and make them pay," replied Zimmerman.

That made sense to all involved. "We will grant you immunity if you can assist us in shutting down this operation. How will you live afterward?" asked Robinson.

"I don't care about myself; I want them stopped. I will take immunity, but that is all. I ask Ms. Calloway to continue with the investigation if she is willing."

"Yes, I am willing. I want to get those bastards, and if I can help, it would be my honor," said Nancy emphatically.

"It's highly unusual, but if all parties are willing, an exception will be made," instructed Robinson. "Now, let's begin.".

The proceedings began with everyone being notified that their conversation was being recorded and careful notes were being taken. Agent Robinson led the interrogation.

"Please state your full name and address," Robinson stated.

"Wolfgang Zimmerman, Berlin, Germany. I am a German citizen with a valid passport," Zimmerman began.

"Have you ever been arrested?"

"Yes, for minor crimes. Mostly in the last three years. Petty theft. I went to prison for four months, and that is where I met the organization's members," Zimmerman added.

"Who or what is the organization?"

"It is a very organized cartel involving people from Mexico, the US, the UK, Germany, Albania, and Saudi Arabia. Although they dabble in weapons and drugs, their primary business is human trafficking. Illegal immigrants from Central America are smuggled into the US, where they are sold or traded to work as slaves in factories worldwide. Children of both genders are sold into the sex slavery business. Young beautiful Eastern European women are lured into the UK and Germany by people promising them careers in the modeling business. Once they arrive, their money and passports are taken away, they are drugged and imprisoned without hope of release. In extreme cases, the troublemakers are made examples of. You saw the film. That young woman was deemed a troublemaker, and she was disposed of."

"Were you able to decipher the information from the flash drive I passed to Ms. Calloway? Most of the information you need is there. Names, places, transportation networks. Everything I could find" asked Zimmerman.

"How did you get the information?" asked Agent Peterson.

"Germany has become the hub of its operations over the last year. The man behind it all, Maximillian Gerhardt, is in Germany running the process. I have seen him only once, but that was enough. Like any other megalomaniac, he surrounds himself with his henchmen. Nobody can get close without reason. I am a tiny cog in the big wheel of his institution. But I have kept my ears and eyes open. I have kept every little bit of relevant information over the last year until I could pass that information to the right people.

"Tell us about the destination of the flash drive. To whom did you send it and why?" asked Agent Peterson. "Nobody has shown up to claim it at the address Ms. Calloway sent it to."

"That was what I believe you call a Hail Mary in your language?" said Zimmerman. "I could not keep the flash drive any longer, and I didn't want Ms. Calloway to be stuck with it, so I had her send it to a dummy address. This way, it could be retrieved, but M.s Calloway would not possess it in case someone went looking. It was lucky that Ms. Calloway gave Agent Harris the flash drive to copy. Sheer coincidence."

The meeting continued for hours. Questions were asked and answered to the best of Zimmerman's ability. New questions were then asked until everyone involved seemed to have a good sense of the organization and its workings.

"This is massive," said Robinson.

"That is the understatement of the century," added Agent Peterson and all the others in attendance nodded their heads in agreement.

"Now what?" asked Agent Harris.

"Now we get the information to the agencies equipped to deal with this and begin a coordinated campaign to bring Gerhardt and his cronies down once and for all," said Robinson.

"What do we do with Zimmerman and Calloway?" added Agent Harris. "We need to keep them safe."

"Zimmerman needs to stay with us for the time being. Of course, Ms. Calloway may return to her vacation plans with an escort at all times. We will call on her again once we have a better idea of how to proceed."

"Yes, sir," said Agent Harris. "That will be my honor and privilege."

Chapter 15

"Well, that was quite a morning!" exclaimed Nancy to Jonathan as they arrived back at her hotel. "This has certainly turned out to be quite a trip! And I've only been here slightly over forty-eight hours. I sure do know how to pack in a lot of excitement in a short amount of time… most of which I'm sure we could all do without!"

"To put things mildly, my dear," said Jonathan with a hint of fondness. "You sure have made my mundane life anything but boring. Now, let's try to keep you safe for the next few days. I'm afraid you will have to put up with either myself or other officers assigned to your security."

"I'll be glad of the attention. Both because I enjoy your company and because you make me feel safe. So, I won't have to work very hard to put up with any of you!" she said as she batted her eyelashes in a mockingly flirty way.

"That's good because you're stuck with us for the duration," Jonathan added. I suppose we should have something for lunch. It's already well past midday. There's a chippy around the corner if you're interested."

Nancy had to think for a minute to figure out what a chippy might be. "Could you translate that into American, please," she laughed.

"There's a fish and chips shop around the corner," Jonathan explained.

"Oh, I'd love it! I've heard so much about the famous English fish 'n chips wrapped in newspaper," she replied.

After arriving at the chippie and receiving their order, Nancy was surprised when Jonathan began pouring malt vinegar over his lunch. "Try it," he said. "It's delicious."

She did and decided he was right. "I'd weigh three hundred pounds if I lived here with all these heavy lunches. Would it be possible to get some exercise this afternoon? I haven't been for a run in days, and I feel like I'm stiffening up."

"I don't have any running clothes with me, and I have to stay with you at all times now. How about a bike ride instead? There are some to rent just a block away."

"That sounds great. Let me change, and I'll be back in ten minutes," suggested Nancy. Jonathan nodded his agreement.

The two easily found rental bikes nearby and happily rode through Kensington Gardens and Hyde Park in just a few minutes. The leaves had just started turning their autumn colors while the garden flowers were still blooming. It was a lovely Sunday afternoon, and many Londoners were outside to enjoy what could be their last warm Sunday for months. Families were picnicking, groups of students were reading or debating, and some brave souls were catching the last of the summer rays in bikinis. "Quite idyllic," thought Nancy.

As they approached Hyde Park Corner, Nancy heard some yelling. "Oh, that's just Speaker's Corner. It's been there forever," commented Jonathan. "People stand on their soapboxes and lecture to anyone who will listen. At any time, you may hear someone expounding on the virtues of composting, the dangers of climate change, or that we are all damned to hell for our wonton ways. It can be very entertaining if not educational."

They continued their bike ride for another half hour, crisscrossing the parks and gardens and crossing over the Serpentine, stopping to watch the swans gliding across the calm water. "Did you know the Queen owns all the swans in England?" asked Jonathan in his most posh scholarly voice.

"No, I didn't," replied Nancy. "How does she manage?"

"Quite well, I imagine," added Jonathan.

They stopped in front of Kensington Palace to allow Nancy to take a picture. "It must be very strange to live in a home that is also a palace. I would hate to live in such a fishbowl, where people are peering into your windows to get a glimpse of you at any time of the day or night," Nancy stated matter-of-factly. "And where people are traipsing through your home all day long."

"I understand what you mean," said Jonathan. "Although their private quarters are not open to the public."

"I just value my privacy so much that I cannot imagine the pressures of being on display all the time," added Nancy. This gave Jonathan a little insight into Nancy's life, and he made a mental note of it.

They parked the bikes and decided to have a cuppa (cup of tea) since it was late afternoon. They found a café on the water and had a pleasant time chatting about life and the day's events before stopping by a grocery store for some provisions and then heading back to the hotel.

"I've been meaning to give you this," said Jonathan as he drew a small device out of a pocket. "It's a GPS similar to the one your courier service gave you. I want you to keep this with you at all times. Day and night. On your person, not just in your purse. It needs to be somewhere not easily found, so hanging it around your neck is not a good idea.

We will be able to keep track of you on our vigil to keep you safe."

"Thank you," she said. "I will swap this with the one Travis gave me since my assignment with them is complete. I'll just put it in my suitcase for the duration. I don't want to get them mixed up."

As they arrived back at the hotel, Nancy said to Jonathan, "It's been a big day. I think I'll stay in tonight."

"I think that is wise. Although we cannot require you to stay with your protection, we recommend it. Just until we know more about what is going on. You stumbled onto an extremely dangerous group of people, and I would hate to see you get hurt," said Jonathan. "I am quite fond of you, Nancy Calloway," he said, "and want you around for a long time to come. For now, we need to keep things professional. Once this is over with, who knows? I'll be in touch in the morning," he added and turned to leave.

"Thanks for everything, Jonathan," Nancy called sincerely. "You're exceptional," she heard herself say as she saw him wave farewell to her.

The Dolcé-in-her urged her to change into evening clothes and hit the town, but the Nancy-in-her prevailed for once. It was still early, and she had a lot of pent-up energy, so Nancy changed and went to the hotel's gym for a thorough workout. An hour later, she emerged sweaty and feeling invigorated. She showered and had a light dinner before finally relaxing and allowing herself to begin processing the events of the last two days. Had it only been two days since arriving at Heathrow? That didn't seem easy to comprehend.

First, she replaced the GPS given to her by Travis with the one given to her by Interpol. This gave her a feeling of well-being…not that she was being tracked, but that she was being tracked by "the Good Guys." Not that Travis was a "bad guy." It's just that he didn't have anything to do with what had been going on and didn't need to know her movements while she was on vacation. Once again, it was a privacy issue for her. She wanted to keep her private life private.

Nancy then began mentally recreating the events of the last sixty hours. She had arrived at Heathrow on time and had no difficulty getting through immigration or customs. She delivered the stem cells as contracted and checked into her hotel without any deviation from the plans. Nothing stood out to her as unusual. It was only after her assignment was complete that extraordinary things began happening. Was everything a set-up? She now knew that the "chance" meeting with Peter in front of Buckingham Palace was anything but chance. Had she been followed the entire day? Why hadn't she felt it? What would have happened at the nightclub if Peter hadn't been there? Would Zimmerman have drawn her into a dangerous situation? Was he as beneficent as he professed to be?

How did he know she would be at the nightclub? Was she being followed/ tracked by more than one entity? If so, why?

There were so many unanswered questions that her brain started spinning. Should she call the airline and get on the next flight home or stick it out in London to see if she could help with the investigation (which is what she wanted to do)? Life had become predictable at home. Work during the week, conquests and encounters during the weekends. Week after week. Without adrenaline, danger, or challenges. It made her miss her Army days in Afghanistan. She had never felt more alive than she did during a battle and its aftermath. A melancholy came over her, thinking of how she missed being in the middle of the fight. At that moment, she decided to be instrumental in bringing those trafficking bastards to justice, whether or not Interpol wanted her. She would stay in London and do whatever it took.

With that decision made, Nancy opened the bottle of wine she had bought earlier in the day, drank deeply, and let the warmth of the dry red liquid envelope her until she sank into a deep sleep.

Chapter 16

Nancy awoke with a determination of spirit she hadn't experienced for a very long time. She knew what she wanted...no, needed...to do and that was to be an instrumental part of shutting down the cartel. She had never considered herself a heroine but certainly wanted to feel like one now. It wasn't courage or even stupidity she was feeling; it was rage. How dare those men enslave other human beings? How dare they separate children from their families and trade them for the perverse pleasures of a few wealthy deviants. How dare they crush the futures and dreams of beautiful young women who are only trying to improve the lot they were born into? How dare they, indeed!

Nancy's determination came to a boil as the phone rang, and she heard Jonathan's voice at the other end of the line. "Good morning," he said cheerily. "What would you like to do today?"

"I'd like you to take me back to your office," she said with conviction.

"But I don't believe they need you today," he answered.

"Oh yes, they do! They have no idea just how much they need me right now. And if they don't know, I will teach them! Look, Jonathan, I will not sit quietly and let those vile creatures continue devastating lives. I not only want to, but insist on being a part of this. I believe I can play a vital role in bringing them to justice if Interpol only gives me a chance."

"But we don't recruit civilians," began Jonathan.

"Well, you'd better make an exception and quickly. Either take me to your office, or I will find my way," she insisted.

Jonathan could tell she wasn't joking with him. He quickly got on the phone, talked for about a minute, and then signaled Nancy to follow him to the car parked outside the front door. "Come on, get in. I've been instructed to do as you ask."

They arrived at Jonathan's office twenty-five minutes later. The conversation in the car had been minimal. Both Jonathan and Nancy were caught up in their thoughts. Nancy was trying to figure out a way to convince Interpol to use her as an asset, and Jonathan was trying to figure out a way to change Nancy's mind.

The formalities at the entrance were quickly completed, and Nancy led the way to Jonathan's office, where the other agents were waiting for their arrival. Before they could say anything to contradict her,

Nancy began by saying, "I stumbled upon this by accident, but I don't believe there is a better person to assist you with this investigation than I am. Let me tell you why."

"First, I am already personally involved. I know as much, if not more, than any of you. I was the first contact, the one that Zimmerman approached. There must have been a reason for that. Yes, I looked completely different than I do now. I am a master of disguises and use them most weekends. Do not judge. They can be very effective. I was the one who identified Zimmerman. Something none of you could do."

"Second, you may not know it, but I have a solid martial arts and warfare background. I served in Afghanistan in a combat zone until I was injured and honorably discharged from the U.S. Army. I am a trained nurse and combat medic so that I can help with any injuries. I am thoroughly trained with handguns and am not afraid to use them if necessary.

"Third, I have a vested interest in bringing Maximillian Gerhardt and associates down. Perhaps you forgot, but I was to be next on their list of unwilling film stars. That's personal!"

"And fourth, I am freely and willingly volunteering; no strings attached. I believe that I can be an invaluable addition to your team. I understand and respect the chain of command and am willing to do what is needed day or night."

"This is highly irregular," interjected Agent Robinson, "but I wish half of my Agents had your dedication and determination. If you are willing to take orders and be an active part of the team, I will agree, with gratitude, to have you come aboard."

Nancy was surprised that the decision was made so quickly and showed her pleasure at being accepted into the fold.

"I need you to go with Agent O'Reilly, who will test your skills," Agent Robinson continued. "We will then give you a crash course on the basics. You will be in plain clothes, so there is no need for formal initiations or uniforms. You will not have a badge. This is a very temporary assignment, you understand. Once we complete this case, you will be going home again with our gratitude."

"Understood, sir," said Nancy respectfully as she was led out of the room into her future.

The day flew by. Nancy was taken first to the infirmary for basic testing, including vitals and a physical exam, which she passed with flying colors. Next, she scored highly in the firearms range. "It's like riding a bike," she kept saying when the active-duty agents couldn't compete with the high level of skill she demonstrated. Then she was taken to the gym for some self-defense testing. On her way out, she overheard a seasoned agent say,

"I wouldn't want to go against her in a blind alley any time soon. She looks like an angel but has the devil in her when she's riled up." That was the nicest thing anybody had said about her in years! It made her smile and humbly swell with pride. She was back! As if that wasn't enough, as she entered the conference room, every one of the Agents stood up and applauded her. "I've never had a standing ovation. Thank you, kind sirs," she said to all of them.

"Kindness has nothing to do with this! Where have you been hiding all this time? You have missed your calling!" exclaimed Agent Robinson.

Nancy glanced around the room and saw Jonathan's look of wonder on his face as if he was asking who she was. "Oh, if you only knew," she said silently to him.

Things got down to business once again, this time with Nancy as an entirely accepted team member.

The highest priority was to figure out what to do with Wolfgang Zimmerman. Should they let him go? Should they keep him in protective custody? Should they use him as bait and as an undercover informer? How much can they trust him? Does it matter? Nancy took the lead and suggested she spend a few hours with him the next day. She would be able to find out where he was coming from and to get as much information about his part in the organization as possible. Her motivation in getting to know him better was to work with him to infiltrate the organization. She could pose as his new girlfriend. She wasn't sure whether or not she would be recognized but doubted it because of her heavy Goth appearance in Berlin. But she needed to be sure. Only he could tell her that. She was willing to serve as bait to get close to the organization, but didn't want to go in blindly.

Before anyone realized it, it was quitting time. Nancy had made an indelible impression on everyone, and it was difficult for her to get out of the office because everyone had something they wanted to say to her. Jonathan took over and excused himself and Nancy, and left the building.

"Do you want to get some dinner," Nancy asked Jonathan. "I'm starving—my treat. I insist. You've done enough for me already."

"Sure. That would be great," Jonathan answered. And then added, "by the way, who are you?"

"Go to dinner with me, and I'll tell you," replied Nancy.

They found a small Italian bistro that allowed them to have a private chat and a glass of wine. Once they ordered, the conversation began in earnest. "Do you want to know all about me," Nancy asked seriously. "I'm very complicated, and you may not want to hear everything I have to say."

"Yes, I do want to learn all about you. The good, the bad, and the ugly. And it sounds like there are lots of each in your life," replied Jonathan. "Remember, no judgment."

"And what about you?" asked Nancy. I know practically nothing about you, except you are charming, friendly, not bad to look at, and cop."

"Gosh, you described me to a tee in just one sentence. I am quite boring compared to you, I am sure."

By the time the post-meal coffee arrived at their table, Jonathan's jaw was practically hanging on its hinges. He had never known anyone like her. Nancy had held nothing back. It felt good to tell all. She had never seen a therapist but knew she should have. This was the next best thing. Jonathan would either accept her for who she was or not. It was as simple as that. Even though they were attracted to each other, Nancy did not have an overwhelming need to please Jonathan. She felt she could be totally candid with him, and she didn't need to pretend or hide. She had never felt that way before. She didn't know whether to be relieved by or afraid of those emotions.

Jonathan was gobsmacked by Nancy's story. He didn't know how to react to the things she described. Her early childhood, her never feeling like she belonged, her wild days (former and present), her Army days (the best she had ever known), all of it. He was more fascinated than anything. How Nancy had survived was beyond his comprehension. And how she had become the woman he had come to know was now known to him. He wasn't repelled; he was transported by her ability to adjust and persevere. "I don't know what to say," was all he could muster.

"You don't need to say anything. I don't need your opinions. You asked, and I told you," she said. "It's as simple as that. If you still want to be my friend, so be it. If not, it's been nice getting to know you a bit."

"Of course, I still want to be your friend!" he exclaimed. "You're the most remarkable person I have ever met. And the most unusual," he added with a smile.

Nancy laughed too. "That goes without saying!" she giggled. "Now, take me home, please."

"With pleasure," he replied.

Chapter 17

Nancy woke up feeling like a new life had begun. A life with purpose and excitement. A life where her skills were valued and unique. Screw the danger. This is what she was meant to do; help free an untold number of people from being captive in a living hell. She couldn't wait to begin her day and arose early to get a four-mile run in before she was scheduled to be at the Interpol office.

She had declined a ride with Jonathan beginning this morning. She would take public transport to "work" and be treated just like everyone else. It thrilled her to see the facial expressions of her new (though temporary) colleagues brighten as she entered the conference room. She also enjoyed the friendly acknowledgments of her presence and greetings of welcome. It was now time to get down to work.

Agent Robinson began by summarizing the case to the entire group, including the information extracted from the flash drive. Afterward, he made assignments. "With your agreement Nancy, I would like to assign you along with Agents Harris and O'Reilly to Mr. Zimmerman."

"I was hoping you would say that," replied Nancy. "If he turns out to be the asset we believe he is, I would like to work with him to infiltrate the organization."

"Are you sure?" asked Robinson. "It could be extremely dangerous."

"That is the only reason why I agreed to all of this. I not only want but need to see this through. It's personal to me. Very personal."

"All right then, let's get Zimmerman in here," ordered Agent Robinson.

Robinson broke the Agents into groups with specific assignments.

Nancy, Zimmerman, Agents Harris, and O'Reilly's assignments related to Zimmerman's involvement with the organization. Names, places, details only he could know and divulge. Nancy asked to have a private conversation with him. She wanted to go with him to infiltrate the group and needed his input on the best way to achieve it. Zimmerman did not believe anyone would recognize Nancy since they had only briefly glanced at Dolcé, and she was Goth at the time. As long as she changed her major appearance, different clothes, makeup, and perhaps a long blonde wig, nobody would suspect her of being the same person.

It would be preferable to stay in London, but if traveling back to Berlin was necessary, Nancy was willing to do it. She was aware that it was going to take more than the four more days she had officially applied for and called her bosses to tell them she would be away longer. Her boss at the Hospice encouraged her to stay as long as she needed. She had earned it. Travis, however, questioned her about her prolonged stay. Noncommittedly, Nancy explained that she wanted to explore the city and country more extensively while she was there. He couldn't very well say no. She was a casual employee at best, so he assented begrudgingly. "That was a little strange," Nancy commented to herself and then forgot about the interaction.

An Inter-Agency wide offensive was quickly mounted, including the U.S. FBI, U.S. legal attaché offices in Berlin, London, Riyadh, and Mexico City working in close contact with their country's equivalent to theU.S.FBI, all coordinated by London's Interpol office. Sting operations began being planned, information gathered was shared, and plans were made to shut down the large and dangerous international organization.

Nancy was not one to let others do the job she could do so well. When her idea of going undercover to expose the British and/or German gang was shot down, she protested loudly.

"There is nobody more qualified to go undercover than I am. Zimmerman and I have discussed the idea in detail. I can access information nobody else can gather by posing as his girlfriend. Although I do not speak German, I can do an adequate British accent for my back story. Zimmerman met me here in London, and we became close. I would accompany him to gatherings and meet the organization's other wives and girlfriends. He believes I would be accepted into the group without much trouble. It could be dangerous, but I would take the risk, and Zimmerman would do his best to protect me. I freely and willingly accept whatever risk there would be.

Discussion continued between the Administration and the agents. Objections were made and answered. Nancy's safety was debated extensively. Everyone eventually agreed that she was in a position to assist like nobody else and that she was well-trained and experienced in self-defense and combat. If anyone was qualified, she was. By the end of the afternoon, Nancy was a full-fledged team member. Financial arrangements were finalized. All her expenses would be paid/reimbursed, and she would be paid a stipend. Nancy was not as interested in the money as in accomplishing the goal. She would do anything to bring the organization down. Anything!"

Once the decision to include Dolcé was finalized, shopping for an appropriate wardrobe began. Vintage shops were scoured. Dolcé wouldn't be dressed in all new clothes. Zimmerman liked his women casual and a bit hippie. And sexy. He described in detail what his ideal girlfriend would look and act like. The clothes and make-up were easy to find and incorporate. The behavior would take some practice, especially the accent. She needed to NOT be an American. That would have been too obvious. Dolcé spent the entire evening with an elocution coach to help her develop a specific accent she could sustain. She also needed coaching on British mannerisms. Things like eating with the fork in her left hand and using a knife, how to make and drink tea correctly, counting with her fingers the British way, and rude hand signals she would be using were just the beginning. All these were foreign to Dolcé and needed practice before she could present herself properly as Zimmerman's girlfriend.

Zimmerman signed a formal agreement with the agency to serve as an informer while actively working on behalf of the agency; while posing as a contributing member of the organization. He was issued a GPS so he could be tracked by Interpol and agreed to have it surgically implanted, so it was undetectable during a general search. By four o'clock, he was given his freedom after being beaten up slightly to make his story of being arrested and interrogated against his will more believable. He stayed in London under Gerhardt's orders, who wanted him close by.

Zimmerman was welcomed back into the criminal fold once his superiors interviewed him. They didn't like the idea that he had been in police custody for two days and wanted to know precisely what had been asked and answered. He was strip-searched, which was expected after a group member had been arrested. The search came up clean, which Zimmerman knew it would. Zimmerman very convincingly conveyed his hatred and contempt for the cops, especially since he had been roughed up during interrogation…which the police were known to do if they could get away with it. The bruises and abrasions Zimmerman had helped to perpetuate his lies. Within a couple of hours, he was again "one of the boys."

The ruse had begun and was working. The code name for the operation is Save the Children, or STC for short. The organization became known as TBG (the bad guys…simple and to the point.)

Chapter 18

Nancy was now Dolcé full-time. Zimmerman was her boyfriend and protector. Or was she his protector? Only time will tell.

She was in her element, disguised and dressed up. She loved being incognito but also attracting attention simultaneously, which she was doing at the moment. Today, instead of her conservative jeans and practical sweater and boots, Nancy, now Dolcé, was the center of attention as she walked down the street. The morph was complete, and she was stunning.

Her flowing black hair was now medium golden blonde with streaks of highlights, thanks to a three-hour session at a nearby salon. Dolcé had not wanted to have her cover blown by wearing a wig that could slip or not look natural. The result was spectacular. Soft, flowing, seductive. Exactly hippie enough with just a bit of sophistication.

Dolcé's makeup was much softer too. She applied a natural foundation with a hint of blue/turquoise shadow on the eyelids to accent her incredible eyes. An understated brown eyeliner pencil was added before a thin layer of brown/black mascara. Minimal blush added color to her cheeks, and to top it off, she dabbed a soft pink gloss on her perfect lips.

Dolcé's disguise also extended to her wardrobe, one of many costumes she had purchased. Today's outfit consisted of a mod printed turquoise relaxed V-neck blouse with a flowing silhouette that hugged her waist, then flared to her hips, and long flaring sleeves that gave a comfortable feel. Partnered with a denim mini skirt and "fuck me" thigh-high stiletto boots gave her look the perfect combination of intentionally sexy but casual.

She knew she had nailed it as she walked down the street to the tube station. Both men and women turned to watch her as she passed by. She couldn't ignore the admiring looks of both genders and smiled. But it was only when she arrived at the office that her time and efforts were truly rewarded. She entered the conference room for an early morning report, and although every pair of eyes in the room was glued to her, none of the men greeted her by name. They did not recognize her, even though she was expected at the meeting. It took over a minute for the first agent to realize that it was Nancy in disguise.

"Oh my god, is that you?" Agent O'Reilly shouted. Even Jonathan had not recognized her, especially since Nancy had donned a pair of lightly tinted sunglasses that partially camouflaged her eyes.

The rest of the Agents recognized her at about the same time. Chaos took over for a couple of minutes as each Agent exclaimed their surprise and admiration.

"That Zimmerman is one lucky bloke," someone was heard exclaiming.

"Well, I guess that was successful," Nancy announced to the throng. "Is there anyone now who doubts my capabilities?"

The consensus was No; nobody doubted her incredible chameleon-like talents, or any other skills for that matter.

Once the commotion over Nancy calmed down, each group leader gave a short synopsis of the previous day's progress, details learned that were considered essential to disseminate, and plans and goals for the next few days. Assignments were given, and everyone went to their desks/stations and began their work earnestly.

Dolcé would meet with Zimmerman today to compare notes and begin the charade of being a couple. They needed to agree on their back story and become familiar enough with each other to make that story believable, both academically and physically. They also needed to find an efficient way of communicating outside of standard texts and cell phone calls, especially in an emergency. Agents O'Reilly and Harris listened carefully to Nancy's concerns and gave her valuable advice on achieving their goals. She was very appreciative of each pearl they shared with her, knowing that one of them might save her life. She was also grateful for the oversight they would give every minute of the day. Two undercover police officers were assigned to act officers to act as covert bodyguards and keep her safe.

Agents Harris and O'Reilly spent the day working on locating Gerhardt and his headquarters. Local police were put on stakeouts at the most probable locations and reported directly to them with any possible leads.

At noon it was time for Dolcé to meet Zimmerman for lunch. It would have been out of character for Zimmerman to be seen lunching in the Kensington area, so they decided to meet in Camden Town. Dolcé looked at the Tube map carefully and chose her route. She would leave Gloucester Road station on the Piccadilly line going east, change to the Northern Line at Leicester Square going north for five stops, and be there in approximately one half an hour. She used her Oyster Card and found the journey crowded and exhilarating, especially since three eligible-looking men approached her at a short distance. She politely but firmly declined their salacious offers with a shrug and a wave of her hand. "You don't get if you don't try," she said philosophically.

Ascending from the Camden Town tube station onto the street was a bit of a shock to Dolcé. It was like she was entering an entirely new universe.

Gone were the stately buildings and well-dressed, upwardly mobile pedestrians scurrying to their shopping trip or to take their children to the park. She saw brightly painted building facades with elaborate street art, and hundreds of punksters perusing the dozens of market stands selling everything from fresh vegetables to studded dog collars. The atmosphere was one of controlled heavy metal madness. She could only imagine how wild and crazy the place would be on a Saturday night, and she liked it.

She was to meet Zimmerman at the Buck's Head Pub on Camden High Street near the tube station. After spending a few moments getting her bearings and asking a passerby which direction she should go, getting into the spirit of the area, she meandered through the market, stopping at a stall when something caught her eye. She even bought a pair of dangly earrings she liked before running into Zimmerman outside the pub. They smiled brightly and gave each other a warm hug and kiss as they came together, knowing someone may be watching and the charade had to be 24/7. Besides, Dolcé enjoyed his stubbly kiss. "This assignment could be nicer than I anticipated," she commented to herself. With his arm around Dolcé, Zimmerman gently directed her inside the pub, where they found a table and ordered lunch and drinks.

"This is like being in another dimension," said Dolcé to Zimmerman.

"Yeah," he said in his German accent. "Isn't it great?"

"Totally," answered Dolcé. "Even the menu was out of my realm. I have never heard of fried chicken, waffle pieces, and maple syrup on a pizza. I guess it's no worse than ham and pineapple."

They sat close to each other for two reasons. First, anyone watching would see their intimacy, and second, they could chat without outside external ears overhearing them. They exchanged pleasantries and a kiss or two between bites, especially when they felt they were being watched, which they did. But that wasn't unusual for Dolcé. She was watched everywhere she went because of the pure sex appeal that oozed out of every one of her pores.

They were able to get some business talk in too. "What should I call you?" asked Dolcé.

"Zimmerman is fine. Everybody calls me that. Nobody uses my Christian name except my mother," he chuckled. "And that is only when she is angry with me. So, she uses it a lot! She always seems to be angry with me. And what is your name?"

"Dolcé Minetti, if anyone asks. Minetti is a made-up name, so don't try to find me in any Chicago phonebook," Dolcé smiled. "So, how did we meet?"

"I met you in the market a week ago Saturday in the afternoon, after I returned to London from Berlin. The market is generic enough of a place that we won't have to describe it in detail. Let's say we met at the stand that sells spiked dog collars. That's as good as anything. We'll be sure to go by there when we finish here."

"That sounds good. What do I do for a living?" asked Dolcé.

"What are you good at?" asked Zimmerman. "We don't want you to work in a shop because someone may go looking for you."

"No, I'm not a shop-girl. I work as an assistant with a CPA nearby. That should answer the question but keep people from asking more."

"Yeah, good thinking," said Zimmerman smiling. "None of my acquaintances will be interested in you for your brain. Not with a body like yours. And besides, my co-workers are just a bunch of drunk losers trying to get along. They are not going to want to learn about you as a person; they're only going to care about how much sex we have and how good you are in bed."

Dolcé was repulsed just at the thought of his acquaintances but stayed silently listening.

"I live nearby in a flat with two other guys. They are lower down on the ladder than I am, so they answer to me. They are complete animals, so don't be surprised when you meet them," said Zimmerman, somewhat apologetically. "I'm sorry if you have to be exposed to their lifestyle. It is not mine. But I am only here temporarily, so I don't make waves. At least I have my own bedroom."

"Oh, since we're here, please tell me more about how you met and became involved with the cartel," said Dolcé.

"It's not difficult to get in at the ground level. You have to be desperate and be able to follow instructions from the bosses. I met one of the members when I was in prison for a few months, and they recruited me. My friends and my family had given up on me. I don't blame them; I was a drunken mess, high all the time—a real loser. I had nowhere to go and no future after prison until I met them. They gave me a job and a place to live. In the beginning, it was enough. I looked away and refused to see what was happening. I did what I was told and have risen in the ranks. But my eyes were opened, and now I hate everything they do and are. It wasn't one thing that made me hate them so much; it is everything," Zimmerman hesitated before saying ..."Now I want them all dead."

Dolcé had listened carefully, studying his facial expressions as he spoke. He seemed completely sincere and dedicated to destroying the same people who had, in a way, given him his life back. But at what cost? His monologue had convinced her that he was frank in his convictions.

He wanted the cartel dead, figuratively and literally.

"Wow, how do you really feel about them?" she asked sarcastically with a big smile.

Zimmerman picked up on the joke and smiled too. "Now you know how and why I feel the way I do. We need help to bring them down."

"It's so strange how everything happened. You picked me to receive the flash drive; I accidentally met an Interpol agent simultaneously. Even me being in Berlin and now in London. It's almost as if someone or something is pulling my strings, like a puppet," she said, realizing there were many coincidences in the works. "Or maybe they are not coincidences, but someone was pulling those invisible strings," which made her cringe. She did not want to think about that.

"We now have each other's basic information. We will have to improvise when interacting with our co-workers. I will try to say as little as possible when I'm around them. My British accent isn't very convincing, and I don't want to give us away," said Dolcé.

"Agent Harris needs to speak with you as soon as possible. Give him a call from a pay phone if you can find one, or use the burner phone I have for you, but not from your personal or work phone," she added. "He will expect to hear from you sometime this afternoon and will give you more information and any instructions he may have."

"OK, I will contact him as soon as I am able. I have to be very careful," said Zimmerman. "And you also have to be very careful. These people are ruthless. They have no respect for human life and will kill anyone who gets in their way without mercy."

Dolcé shuddered, knowing what he said was the entire truth. These people were more than dangerous. They were treacherous and amoral.

"Oh, I have something for you before I forget." Zimmerman passed a new flash drive to Dolcé, which she stowed in her bra quickly and inconspicuously. He said further information needed to be passed on as soon as possible. Dolcé handed him a burner phone he was to communicate with the Interpol agents.

"Thank you," was all Zimmerman said.

They were almost done with their lunch and were drinking the last of the pint, this time a Guinness instead of the lager that always accompanied a pub lunch, when they heard a voice calling to him.

"Hey, Zimmerman!" it called. He looked up and saw one of his cronies in the organization. "Mind if I join you?"

"Sure, pull up a chair," he answered. "What's going on?"

"Nothing," the stranger answered. "Well, well, well," he said, leering at Dolcé. "Someone had told me you have a new girlfriend, but I didn't believe it," looking Dolcé up and down again. "And, how did you get so lucky, you old sod!"

"Just my turn, I guess," Zimmerman replied. "Jack, this is Dolcé. Dolcé, Jack," he said succinctly, introducing them. Although he appeared uncomfortable by the meeting, he knew this was a good coincidence. Jack would go back and tell everyone about his new squeeze, which would give the relationship legitimacy when he brought her into the group later in the day or week.

Dolcé waved to Jack and tried out her new accent. "Nice to meet you, Jack," she said in her slightly Cockney twang. Introductions complete, Jack dominated the rest of the conversation with Zimmerman, pretty much ignoring Dolcé. "Definitely a male thing," thought Dolcé with mild disgust. "But this is good. Jack considers women as accessories without ears or brains. I imagine most of the guys in the group are like that. The women can come and go, mostly forgotten as long as they don't make waves. This is a powerful asset."

Jack told a few crude jokes that neither Zimmerman nor Dolcé wanted to hear, but they laughed anyway. They wanted Jack to like Dolcé and return with good reports, which he did. After twenty minutes and emptying his pint, Jack stood up and left without as much as a farewell. "No social skills," thought Dolcé. Every tiny observation she made now could be important later.

"Well, that was interesting," Dolcé said after Jack's disappearance. "And very timely. We couldn't have asked for a better encounter." Zimmerman agreed and gave her shoulder a light hug. She liked it. "Where does he fit in?"

"He's one of the lowest flunkies. He is an errand boy. He does whatever he is told to do by the higher-ups. If someone needs beating up, he'll do it. If they need him to deliver a drug shipment, he does it. They say jump, and he asks, "how high?" I was there not too long ago. I climbed in the hierarchy because I can follow instructions, am sober on the job, listen without talking back, am organized enough to keep things straight, haven't skimmed any money off the top of earnings, and have gained their trust," he said almost proudly. "That loser will never get anywhere except maybe into an early grave. I know he's stealing a little bit here and a little bit there. It will catch up to him eventually. Probably sooner than later, and I hope I'm not around when it happens. Or even worse, they ask me to "correct" the situation. Not that I care about him, but the thought of beating someone so badly it puts them in the hospital, or killing them outright, doesn't sit right with me anymore."

"I can understand that, and I'll keep those things in mind," said Dolcé. "Are you almost done?"

After leaving the pub, the two roamed the market, happily trying on hats and sampling many pastries the vendors had on display, like a real couple spending a quiet afternoon together. As they strolled, they kept constant communication, sharing observations and instructions while they knew there was no possibility of being overheard. The investigation was still in the early stages. Interpol did not want to tip their hand too quickly and possibly blow the case, but they also understood that the longer things took, the more suffering the victims experienced.

Zimmerman shared that something big would be going down in a few days, but he needed to learn precisely what or when. He would keep his eyes and ears open and report anything he thought was important. Dolcé had no reason to doubt his claims. They spent another hour together before going their ways and after arranging to meet the following evening at a club. Zimmerman could no longer risk going to the Interpol office. If spotted anywhere near there, his cover would be exposed.

Dolcé had time to review the lunch date while taking the tube back to the Interpol office. Her report to Agents Harris and O'Reilly was detailed and complete, including the encounter with Jack. She also handed over the new flash drive to have it analyzed and the information distributed later that day. The three worked for the remaining afternoon, trying to anticipate and mitigate danger to devise possible scenarios that Dolcé may find herself in. Dolcé knew she needed to be prepared to defend herself in all situations. She could not carry a gun but needed to use whatever other weapon may be available to her if necessary. After finishing at the office, she went to the Interpol gym and worked out with a Martial Arts instructor. She wanted to make sure she was as ready as possible for whatever came her way.

When Dolcé finally arrived at her hotel, it was well after 8 p.m.. She picked up a salad to eat in her room, along with a bottle of crisp cold white wine. She had earned it. Things had gone well at lunch. Too well, in a way. Dolcé was attracted to Zimmerman's rough and commanding but gentle demeanor. She liked the way he smelled. And kissed. "That is going to make this assignment VERY fun or far more dangerous," she said as she opened the wine. "I wonder which…or both."

Chapter 19

It was Thursday morning. Nancy woke up bright-eyed and bushy-tailed, ready to meet the day head-on. Then she looked in the mirror and saw Dolcé staring back at her. It was a shock at first, but then she welcomed Dolcé into her day, knowing how important she would be over the next few days or weeks. Besides, Nancy secretly liked Dolcé's bold outlook on life. She was always willing to try new things with new people at any time or at any place. Nancy knew that she did not have a dissociative identity disorder. Still, sometimes the contrast between herself and Dolcé was so polar opposite that she believed other people might think she did.

"No matter," she said to her reflection. "I/we are going to kick butt today. First, at the office and later tonight when I meet Zimmerman." She knew that she had to prepare carefully for her evening date. She had to be completely believable and yet ready for anything that could happen, including going home with Zimmerman if the opportunity was ripe. Zimmerman wasn't the kind of man with platonic relationships with his women. His dates were usually fueled by booze or drugs and nearly always ended at either his or her place. Tonight should be no different, especially if his "friends" would be watching. Nancy hesitated a bit, but Dolcé was all in. "In for a penny, in for a pound," she said to the mirror.

Nancy wasn't expected at the office until early afternoon, so she spent the morning working out and preparing her wardrobe for that evening. She ducked into The House of Henna for a couple of temporary tattoos. She had noticed that both Zimmerman and Jack had multiple tattoos and felt it was an almost expected accessory. She wanted to blend in, especially up close but didn't want to get a real tattoo.

Choosing the designs and the best locations for the tattoos was a challenge. There were so many exquisite patterns that she needed help from the tech who convinced her that a sun was a very "hippie" tattoo. She wanted the designs to be visible but not apparent. The first, a sun, went on her left shoulder blade. It was the perfect location to show the tattoo when wearing a halter top or something backless.

The design was intricate, with sixteen rays, four straight beams jetting from the quarter-hour points, and 12 curved rays interspersed throughout. Between each ray, there was a dainty teardrop. In the middle of the sun was the face of a beautiful and exotic goddess, with her eyes closed, rosy cheeks, and plump, pouty lips. "Gee, it looks a little like me," Dolcé observed. She loved it. It was feminine and serene but powerful.

The second tattoo was a simple rose placed on her right breast. She wanted something uncomplicated and pretty that would be visible with most of the tops she had picked out.

It was difficult for Dolcé to sit still for the two and a half hours it took to apply the tattoos, but she knew her patience was worthwhile when she saw the final product. "Gorgeous," she said admiringly to the tech. "Thank you very much."

Nancy felt tension in the air when she arrived at the office. "What's going on?" she asked the first agent she saw.

"Things are going down soon," he said as they entered the conference room.

Agent Robinson was standing at the head of the table, ready to begin. The Agents settled into their chairs, and the chatter subsided into silence. "Gentlemen and ladies," he began. "We have come across information that will enable us to hopefully bring "The Bad Guys-AKA TBG" down for good.

"Eastern European women, especially Romanians, are being sex trafficked to Britain on an industrial scale," he began. "Vulnerable women are lured to the UK with the promise of modeling careers or other attractive employment, only to find their 'hosts' take away their passports and money once they arrive. They are then forced to have sex with clients to pay off their debts. Organized crime groups advertise their victims to buyers on sex marketplace websites and host them in pop-up brothels, often in rental homes or hotels. These women are particularly vulnerable because they are moved around, isolated and controlled. They are rarely able to work off their debts, and become involuntary slaves to their handlers (pimps). Some of the victims are drugged regularly…and worse. As you witnessed in the video, the perversity has no boundaries. That poor woman who was 'snuffed' isn't an isolated case."

A wave of conversation broke out among the agents. Robinson allowed the spontaneous pandemonium to continue for a minute before once again taking control of the presentation. "Up until now, we have not been able to pinpoint the ring leaders. We have had successful sting operations where undercover detectives have placed ads on websites commonly sought out by suspects seeking illegal sex acts, and arresting the perpetrators when they show up for the appointment. But that focuses on the johns, not the organized crime group itself. Thanks to our German informer, Wolfgang Zimmerman, we now have enough evidence to go after the syndicate in the London area."

Another outburst of spontaneous conversation broke out among the agents and Nancy. It sounded like a pep talk in the locker room before a big football game. Everyone was wound up and pumped. Enthusiastic cheers were heard down the halls. This was truly exciting news!

"Ok, settle down," called Agent Robinson, holding his hands in the air, encouraging everyone to take their seats. "We have been able to get the location of TBG's headquarters here in London and are now working on warrants. Gerhardt is not the man in charge in the UK. A man named Samuel Bingham is. We know where he lives. He uses his home as the syndicate's headquarters. He conducts business with his employees there, but he has other locations where the dirty business occurs. There are warehouses around town used as storage facilities and who knows what else. Just use your imagination. The warehouses will not be our primary targets; the brothels are. Hopefully, by bringing down these houses in one big sweep, we will ultimately be able to confiscate their prized real estate."

"We are working with Scotland Yard and the local police to establish coordinated sting operations throughout Southern England. All this will take place within the next week, so I will need everyone to give us 100% over the next few days, the weekend included." There was no dissension in the ranks, no disguised grumbling. On the contrary, the enthusiasm was palpable. Robinson had motivated each agent to have a single purpose of accomplishing that goal. Once and for all, getting the head criminals off the streets and rescuing the innocents. A roar of agreement went up as Agent Robinson smiled upon his "flock." He was very proud of his people.

Specific assignments were made, and once again, everyone either returned to their desks or gathered together as a team to get started.

Agents Harris and O'Reilly huddled along with Nancy. The shit was about to hit the fan, so to speak, and all were aware of the danger the next few days would bring, especially to Nancy/Dolcé. The plan was for Dolcé to hook up with Zimmerman this evening and return to his chosen place. Depending on the situation, this might be to his apartment or Bingham's hideout. Once inside and accepted, she was to gather any specific information she may encounter, especially the location of where the women were kept, and, if possible, to make contact with them. Zimmerman would serve as boyfriend and protector while performing his criminal duties to avoid suspicion. He was aware of the locations of most of the houses since he inspected them regularly, but not all of them. Everyone knew it would be a very delicate balance. If either Dolcé or Zimmerman were discovered, it could mean torture and possible death. Nancy/Dolcé assured all involved that she was willing to take the risk.

Nancy also asked to have the Interpol GPS tracker surgically implanted under her skin. She felt the minimally invasive procedure could save her life if she and her possessions were thoroughly searched. Or if she was taken to a location against her will and without Zimmerman's knowledge.

Interpol officers could pinpoint her exact location and get to her within minutes, unlike the hours or days without the GPS. Usually, it would be considered an illegal invasion of a person's privacy. Still, Dolcé was not only permitting them but also demanding they do the procedure for her state of mind. She would only feel safe with it embedded into her and transmitting at all times. "Screw privacy right now. Give me safety and time," Dolcé exclaimed.

Over Jonathan's protests, she was sent to the infirmary, where the procedure was completed in less than fifteen minutes. She had a tiny incision at the back of her hairline that was nearly invisible, even if someone looked for it. The GPS was only temporary and could be removed as quickly as it was implanted.

Jonathan's (as well as Agent Harris's) admiration for Nancy grew as he became more familiar with her. She was the most competent and complicated woman he had ever known. "No shit Sherlock," he mumbled to himself. She fascinated him with her chameleon abilities. This included her personality as well as her appearance. She was like the wind. Blowing in one direction one moment and from a completely other direction the next. "She probably isn't marrying material, but what a wild ride a relationship would be with her." Jonathan realized how sexist that statement was and regretted saying it. "Sorry," he said to anyone who may have heard.

All he knew was that he wanted to protect her in any way he could, whether a romantic relationship developed or not.

"Do you have some time we could spend together later this afternoon?" he asked Nancy. "We have become so involved in the investigation that we haven't had a chance to be together."

"I'd like that," she replied. "I don't need to be at the club until midnight this evening. Can you come by my hotel around seven?"

Then Nancy and Agent Harris went back to focusing on the upcoming challenges and the case details. It was surprising how they both could slip easily from a personal to a professional relationship.

Nancy went for a short three-mile run before getting ready for her date with Jonathan. She looked forward to seeing him and changed into her Autumnal casual outfit of jeans and a sweater. It was warm and comfortable. "Kind of like Jonathan," Nancy observed.

Nancy had not had a chance to do much sightseeing once she had been introduced to Interpol, so Jonathan suggested they go to the South Bank of the Thames, close to the London Eye. "The Eye is closed at night, but the views of Parliament and Saint Paul's Cathedral from the South Bank are spectacular. We can also walk by the Globe Theater, and if you want, we can get 'yard' tickets for only five pounds and watch a few minutes of whatever production is being performed. We can leave at any time without anyone looking at us accusingly. It might be a nice introduction for you, in case you ever come back to London. There are also lots of places to eat and drink there, so we can stroll until we find something we both like."

"That sounds like an excellent plan," agreed Nancy. "Jonathan, you always make our time together so special…and so normal. Normal to me is not boring; it is welcomed sometimes. And one of those times is right now."

They walked to the South Kensington Tube Station, took the Circle Line east for six stops, and arrived at Blackfriars station by seven-thirty. They then walked across the Millennium Pedestrian Bridge, and only then did Jonathan allow Nancy to look back. When she looked back to where they had just been, she saw the magnificent dome of Saint Paul's Cathedral lit up. Nancy's breath was taken away by its splendor. "Oh, Jonathan, it's incredible!" she exclaimed breathlessly.

"I thought you'd like it," replied Jonathan. "We locals take the sights for granted. Seeing things through a tourist's eyes is fun for a change. Now, on to the brink…" as he pointed toward the east. "Shakespeare awaits," he explained.

They strolled less than two blocks before arriving at the Globe Theater. Tonight's performance, "Much Ado About Nothing," had just begun. Nancy couldn't believe what she saw. The theater looked like something straight out of Tudor times with the whitewash on the walls, the exposed wooden beams, and the thatched roof.

"This new theater was built to duplicate Shakespeare's original theater as closely as possible. It opened to the public in 1997 and has been performing in the summer every year since. They don't do plays in the winter because the only theater parts covered against the elements are the stage and the seating areas. If it's raining and you are one of the 'groundlings', you better with a yard ticket, you better have a raincoat or umbrella. You can get very wet," said Jonathan in his best Tour Director voice.

"Well, I guess it's a good thing it is not raining tonight," Nancy said unnecessarily.

"Do you want to go in?" asked Jonathan.

"Won't we be interrupting?" asked Nancy timidly.

"No, the yard tickets are for the peasants, which we are tonight. You stand and watch the production and can walk around to your heart's content. Let's go in. We can leave after you have seen enough for tonight."

They bought their tickets and walked into the theater. Nancy was once again awestruck seeing it in all its glory. The seated and standing audience was utterly engrossed in the play, laughing at all the right places. "You're right," whispered Nancy. "There's no roof above us." Jonathan just chuckled affectionately.

They stayed for nearly 45 minutes and wanted to stay longer but knew their time was limited. "Wow!" was all Nancy could say. Jonathan shared her feelings.

They once again strolled on the walkway, but this time turned west towards the London Eye. The night was cool and clear, and their conversation was light and easy. They did not talk shop this evening. They wanted their time together without stress or anxiety about the upcoming operation.

As they rounded the bend of the river, the Houses of Parliament with Big Ben came into view. Again, Nancy was awestruck. "Oh my gosh, it's magnificent! I have seen pictures of Big Ben hundreds of times but never imagined it was so beautiful!" Just then, Big Ben clanged out the half-hour in its deep tones. Nancy squealed with delight, which made Jonathan laugh.

"How can someone so complicated also enjoy such simple pleasures?" he asked himself. Of course, it was a rhetorical question. "Let's find somewhere to have a drink and something to eat," he said to Nancy.

"Great," was her answer. She was having a marvelous time, and it showed on her smiling face.

They chose to get a quick casual takeaway called Great British Fish and Chips. They sat at the picnic-type tables munching on their greasy and delicious dinner while drinking in the atmosphere around them as well as an obligatory pint. For Nancy, this was a dream come true. A month earlier, she would have never imagined she would be here, absorbing this magical city's sights, sounds, smells, and tastes.

"Thank you, Jonathan," she said gratefully.

"For what?" he asked, genuinely puzzled by her gratitude.

"For just being you," she replied. "And for the way you make me feel so special."

"First of all, you are exceptional. Second, it is my honor and privilege to introduce my home to you," Jonathan said sincerely.

All too quickly, the evening had to end. Dolcé needed time to regroup and prepare for the possible arduous and dangerous few days to come. After a quick tube ride home, Jonathan dropped Nancy off at her hotel lobby.

"Be safe, Nancy," he said emphatically and disappeared.

Chapter 20

Dolcé was more excited than nervous as she prepared for the evening, knowing that it may extend overnight or for the entire weekend. She found packing difficult. If she had been home, she would have thrown a duffle bag into the trunk of her car. However, she had no personal means of transport here in London and nowhere to stash anything but an overcoat and a medium-sized handbag. She was also hesitant to carry anything that would be considered a weapon in case she was searched. She was able to find a metal nail file that had a sharp tip. "This will have to do for now," she said to herself. Besides a weapon, she was hoping to take essentials like a toothbrush, a change of underwear, and a shirt with her. And, of course, condoms. They were always a part of her overnight kit. Thankfully, those small items fit into the pockets of her jacket or in her purse. She chose the most versatile and practical of her new hippie outfits. She also wanted to look particularly attractive, not only to Zimmerman but to any of his "friends" they may encounter. It never hurt to be able to distract them if necessary.

Zimmerman had suggested they meet again in Camden since it was close to where he was staying in temporary digs with two of his co-workers. A place called The Worlds End was chosen. It was across the street from the Camden Town tube station and stayed open late since the heavy metal nightclub in the basement had a special license to remain open until 4 a.m.. It was convenient and offered a choice of dance club or pub in one; perfect for their needs.

Dolcé arrived shortly before midnight and had no trouble finding the pub. After checking her coat, she entered the main bar. She saw that several men and two women surrounded Zimmerman as she arrived. Zimmerman saw her and welcomed her with a hug and a deep kiss. Dolcé knew it was for show, but she liked it. He tasted of beer and cigarettes, although there was no smoking inside the pub. With his arm possessively wrapped around Dolcé, he introduced her to the group and then went to the bar to get her a drink. The guys looked her up and down more than once and grunted a hello before returning to their male-dominated bluster about football, bikes, and booze. They didn't think twice about her being accepted into the group. It was clear to Dolcé once again that the women were considered accessories and not active members of the discussion.

The rough English accents with so much swearing were difficult for Dolcé to understand, but she concentrated on listening and keeping quiet. She was there to observe, not to make friends. She also watched the two girlfriends to see how they related to their dates and each other.

The men were mostly in their late twenties to early thirties, big with beer bellies, and uneducated. Nancy would have called them crude. Dolcé just thought they were slobs and cruel. The friends were covered with tattoos, many of them with skulls and snakes. Dolcé noticed that each of the men, including Zimmerman, had an identical crown tattooed on their left forearm. She concluded it was a membership sign of their brotherhood in crime. Like Lord Voldemort's Dark Mark with his followers, the Death Eaters in the Harry Potter series of books and movies. She also noticed that one of the two women had a similar tattoo. "Is she being sex trafficked? And is that why she has the same tattoo?" Dolcé wondered but didn't dare ask out loud. She looked for the telltale signs of the woman with the tattoo being trafficked: being overly submissive, having bruises or burn marks, being significantly younger than her boyfriend, and avoiding eye contact. The signs were there but subtle. Anyone unaware of the situation would probably not notice. Dolcé was very aware of her surroundings. Even more so now that she knew she was among the enemy.

She wanted to be able to speak privately with Zimmerman but couldn't find the opportunity for nearly an hour. The loud Heavy Metal music blasting from the overhead speakers didn't help. It was frustrating, but Dolcé was patient, which paid off. She eventually excused herself and asked where the lady's toilet was. Zimmerman said he also had to go and followed her after pointing the way. They were able to exchange a few words. They arranged to leave together at 2 a.m. and go to his place. There they would be able to communicate more effectively. "Yea, right…communicate," said Dolcé sarcastically, which made Zimmerman smile. After returning to the table, Zimmerman and Dolcé relaxed into each other and were very believable as a couple. Nobody questioned Zimmerman about her, either with words or actions. When they left together, it seemed like the most natural thing in the world. That was exactly what everyone had been hoping for. Dolcé was in.

Zimmerman's shared flat was less than a ten-minute walk from the pub. It gave them time to plan the rest of the evening/night. It was decided Dolcé would stay over and hang out at the flat for a while after he left for work in the morning. Zimmerman assured Dolcé that she would be safe for the night and that their conversations if kept at a low volume, would not be overheard. Of course, any moaning would be heard and expected by his flatmates. The idea of putting on a show for them tickled and excited Dolcé a bit. She knew they would be drooling with envy by morning!

They arrived at the flat, which was precisely what Dolcé expected to find. Grubby furniture, beer bottles, and dirty dishes on every flat surface in the kitchen and living room. "Typical bachelor pad. Gross!" murmured Dolcé. At least Zimmerman's room was relatively clean, and it seemed like he had made an effort to make her comfortable. The sheets were clean, and the bed was newly made. There were no clothes on the floor, and to Dolcé's great relief, there were no signs of bugs or other small critters in the room. There was even a small chair where she perched herself as they settled in.

"This is the first opportunity we've had just to talk privately," began Dolcé. "Tell me more about yourself," she encouraged.

"I'm thirty-three. As you probably figured, I grew up in Berlin in a not-very-happy family. I wouldn't say I liked school, so I dropped out when I was sixteen. I worked odd jobs and got into the typical trouble kids get into. Smoking, drinking, and drugs. I've done most drugs but was never addicted to anything. My drug of choice is cocaine because it gives me energy. And, of course, beer. I drifted for several years, and then I met some guys who promised me the kind of cash I needed. I began selling drugs to anyone who would buy them. I got caught and went to prison here in the UK for a few years. My "friends" disappeared when I was arrested. I met my new "friends" while I was in prison. I've been with the Organization for three years now. At first, it was OK. They had me dealing mostly with the intermediaries. I never really had to see the women or children we use. Then about a year ago, they "promoted" me to be one of the managers, one step above the handlers, otherwise known as a pimp. I'm in charge of six houses of women, including collecting the earnings and making sure their pimps are keeping everyone in line and that production stays high. If there is a problem, and there are lots of them, they call me."

"Just the other day, I had to find and retrieve a runaway. We don't have many of them since most of the girls are emotionally or physically beaten into submission. Even if they wanted to escape, there was no place for them to go. They have no papers or money; they don't speak the language, and ironically their only support system is the other enslaved girls. Many of them are brainwashed into believing that as horrible as things are, they would be a lot worse elsewhere."

"When I do have to get involved, things are not nice. She was punished and is in pretty bad shape right now. I wouldn't say I like it. In fact, I hate it. Dealing drugs was OK, but this is just depraved. I am not a cruel person, and my job makes me one. If I were a nice guy, the system wouldn't work. Gerhardt keeps people in line, including the trafficked and the traffickers, by intimidation and threats of violence. Sometimes the violence is real.

If they had any idea of what I was doing, I'd be tortured and killed within a day. My life would be worth nothing. Right now, I feel like my life is worth nothing."

"I got myself in so deep I could not figure a way out. I had to do things that were highly illegal and immoral. I'm no saint, but now I can't sleep. I'm a mess from what I've had to do and see. I think your people call it PTSD, but we have no therapy. It got to the point that my lack of sleep was making me sick. I was in Berlin trying to distance myself from the people here in London when I ran into you. The killing of that poor girl was, as you say in the US, the straw that broke the camel's back. I was not there when it happened, but I heard about the film and the senseless torture and death, and I couldn't do anything to save her. I knew I needed to stop these people one way or another. The only way I knew how was to document as much as possible and then pass it on. I saw you at the club that night, so free, so happy and so uninhibited, and also in such danger without knowing it. You are exactly the kind of woman they like to use. Someone drugged you to divert you and bring you into the fold. It wasn't me. I saw it coming and had to help you even though you had no idea of the danger you were in. At the same time, I saw an opportunity to pass the flash drive on. I knew it was dangerous, but I had no choice. It was then or never. I couldn't keep it on me. Thank goodness you passed it on to the right people. It was touch and go there for a while. And now, I've dragged you into this. I'm sorry."

"Don't be sorry. I volunteered for this. I haven't felt so appreciated and alive in my whole life! I thank you for it," replied Dolcé sincerely. "Whatever happens, you did the right thing. Speaking of which…what should I know right now. Whom should I stay away from, and how can I help?"

They ended up talking for another hour. Details came pouring out of Zimmerman. Locations of the houses where they kept the women, how they were transported, where they saw their johns, and how they were kept subservient. Whom to avoid and whom to be friendly to. Most important, he disclosed the names and addresses of the people in charge—the head mobsters or; more accurately monsters- and how to get to them. Of course, they lived in well-secured compounds with numerous bodyguards surrounding them at all times. They would be challenging to get to without SWAT-type teams and warrants. Dolcé listened very carefully and put the most crucial information on her phone. She didn't want to forget, but she didn't want to have any incriminating evidence if she was caught. Her phone had a password, not a thumbprint lock, so she felt somewhat safe adding the most vital information that was worth the risk.

The sun rose as they ended their talk; each of them was so exhausted that their brains didn't work anymore.

Dolcé surprised Zimmerman when she looked him straight in the eyes and said, "wanna fuck?" And they did. Over and over. The roommates complained about being woken up by the noise. Dolcé just smiled. Her mission was going well.

Chapter 21

"It's 1 p.m.," stated Dolcé to Zimmerman after slowly regaining consciousness and checking her phone. Not that it was unusual for her to sleep until the afternoon of the "day after the night before." It was unique, however, because it wasn't a Saturday. That was usually the only day of the week she allowed to indulge herself. She excused herself, though, knowing that the last week had been anything but ordinary for her. Here she was in London, England, in the middle of a vast and dangerous sting operation that could have ramifications in many parts of the world. And in bed with a felon who was an OK guy.

No, this was not her regular Friday. If she were home, she would have been at work in her starched white uniform, caring for mostly elderly folks who depended on her or someone like her. She felt a pang of guilt, knowing that her patients would be missing her. The regret was tempered by the knowledge that she was working on something truly remarkable and that her efforts would improve many people's lives.

She didn't feel guilty about the fun she had with Zimmerman in the wee hours of the morning. Dolcé never felt guilty about having sex. She considered it a natural part of her personality and her life. Other people may disapprove, but that was their problem, not hers. She chuckled when she heard Zimmerman's flatmates loudly complaining that they hadn't gotten enough sleep because of the noise.

"Bloody hell," she heard one complain through the closed door. "It sounded like gorillas going at it in the zoo."

"You should be so lucky," replied Zimmerman. "You're just jealous. Bugger off," he added gruffly but with a secret smile, which tickled Dolcé.

Both Dolcé and Zimmerman knew it was time to face the day and get moving, although they didn't want to interrupt their comfortable warmth. Dolcé was the first to stir, rising out of bed and putting on Zimmerman's robe while heading for the bathroom down the hall. Zimmerman took that opportunity to straighten up the bed and slip on a pair of jeans. His phone rang as Dolcé was returning to the bedroom. She was able to overhear what sounded like him receiving today's instructions. He did not try to conceal his conversation. After hanging up, he explained that he would have to leave in the next few minutes because a problem had come up.

"Could I go with you?" asked Dolcé.

"I guess it would be OK, as long as you stay in the vehicle," he replied. That was all right with Dolcé. She wanted to see first-hand what Zimmerman had described to her. It would give her a better idea of the operation and, if lucky, give her a view of one of the locations used to house the women. And it would allow them to talk more without the possibility of ears listening in.

They left the apartment a few minutes later without saying goodbye to the flatmates or their dates and departed in the company's white panel van. The van looked like thousands of others on the streets of London on any given day. That was on purpose. Anonymity was important in their line of work.

They stopped by a takeaway for coffee and a quick lunch before heading to their destination. The choice was between Chinese, Indian, or Fish and Chips. Dolcé had never had much Indian food and was afraid it might be too spicy for her, and as much as she enjoyed Fish and Chips, she had had it only the night before, so Chinese was chosen. Besides, Chinese was easy to eat on the run. And, to her amazement, it was perfect. Just another aspect of London that came as a pleasant surprise to her.

It took about half an hour to get to their destination. During that time, Dolcé and Zimmerman talked about his job and his assignment today, which was to meet with one of the pimps, collect the week's earnings, see if there were any problems, make sure nobody was skimming money off the top, and ensuring that the women were ready to work. This part of the job he didn't mind so much, as long as he could keep from thinking about how the money was being earned. To keep his sanity, he had to keep it impersonal and professional.

Dolcé was shocked when they pulled up in front of the pimp's house. It was in a nice middle-class neighborhood with well-kept two-story brick houses, including gardens in the front and back yards with kid's toys strewn everywhere. "I would never imagine there is the equivalent to slaves being kept in that house," she said with wonder to Zimmerman. "I imagined it would be some old abandoned warehouse with no running water or electricity on the waterfront. Maybe I've been watching too many old movies!"

"You'd be surprised at the different neighborhoods we have living quarters," explained Zimmerman. "We even have a house in the Kensington area. People would be shocked if they discovered what was happening under their noses. The people in the highest echelons of the organization are often executives of large corporations and sometimes very influential politicians. These are the same people who go to church, send their kids to fancy public schools and Cambridge University, and are on the Boards of prestigious charities. They are extremely powerful, and their wealth is immeasurable.

"We have fifteen houses just around urban London alone and too many to count across the UK. Each girl averages 150,000 Pounds Sterling a year in earnings. Multiply that by an average of 10 girls/house. After expenses, that's over twenty-four million tax-free pounds per year in income in London alone. That money is then laundered and used for other illegal and highly lucrative enterprises, like drug trafficking and firearms dealing."

Dolcé's jaw dropped. "I had no idea," was all she could say.

"That is a very true statement. No, you don't know how high up the chain goes," he added. "That is why it is nearly impossible to irradicate this problem. The police can attack one layer, but there are about ten others that need to be weakened at the same time. And, more often than not, someone in the police department is in the pocket of the organization. The corruption is very invasive. We are putting our lives on the line to stop this, and the chances of us making a lasting difference are very small. I just need to try."

Dolcé looked over at Zimmerman with shock and admiration. "You go get 'em, tiger," she said with enthusiasm. "Or should I say, Magilla Gorilla," she added with a twinkle in her eyes. Zimmerman did not understand the reference but got the main idea anyway. He puffed up his chest and beat it with his fists several times. The levity helped to cut the very thick tension in the van, and both laughed for a moment before facing today's challenges.

"You stay here while I go meet with Axel, the guy who oversees this, and a couple of other houses. It shouldn't take long if all goes well," he said as he opened the door and began to depart the van.

"OK. Good luck," said Dolcé. Zimmerman looked back at her with a mildly stunned face. He never considered he would need luck for this and had never been offered it so sincerely. It touched him and helped him believe just a little bit that there were good people in this world.

Dolcé watched him saunter up to the house, knock on the door and enter the house after a bedraggled twenty-something girl answered the door. She did not make eye contact with Zimmerman but just let him enter and quietly shut the door behind him. Dolcé observed carefully. The drapes were closed, so she could not see movement in the house. She lowered the window to hear anything unusual, which she did not.

After twenty-five minutes, Zimmerman left the house and nearly marched to the parked van. He was now carrying a medium-sized duffle bag Dolcé assumed was filled with currency. She was correct. "OK, onto the next stop," stated Zimmerman as he threw the bag behind the driver's seat, bucked his safety belt, turned on the ignition, and put the van in gear. Zimmerman saw the question on Dolcé's face and explained simply without being asked, "All went well here. The issue is at the next place."

He was able to explain in more detail as they drove the forty minutes to the next house. "Every house has its hierarchy. There are the new girls, then the more seasoned girls that have been with us for a year or more. Then there is always one house mother who acts as the manager. She is in charge and answers to her manager or pimp," he began. "She is a sex worker just like the others but is promised and sometimes given special privileges and some extra freedoms for her extra services. She knows not to bend the rules or try to escape. She understands the consequences because she has seen them first hand with others who tried to bypass the system."

Dolcé expressed her understanding and concern, not with words but with her facial expressions.

"The madam of the next house has reported trouble with one of the girls that her pimp has been unable to stop. He called me to get her in line. This is the part of the job I hate so much!" said Zimmerman emphatically. "I not only have to rough her up, but I also need to make an example of her for the other girls. It won't be pretty. I think it would be better to drop you off at a nearby coffee shop while I do this job. I don't want anyone to see you, and even if you're sitting in the van, someone may be watching and catching a glimpse. That would not be good."

Dolcé nodded quietly. She instinctively knew to keep quiet and not ask questions. It was like Zimmerman was going to war. He had to continue acting as the tough guy until the sting was complete. Otherwise, he would be found out, and that could be fatal to many more people than himself.

He slipped on a pair of leather gloves as they drove by the new location toward the coffee shop nearby. "Just act normally," he instructed. "Have a cup of coffee and maybe something to eat. It might be better if you don't chat anyone up. If someone approaches you (and the men always did), say that you're waiting for your fiancé. That should discourage them. Do what you do best, be nice but firm. I'll text you when I'm a couple of minutes out. I'd appreciate it if you would get me a coffee to go."

"Of course," she said quietly as she got out of the van before entering the coffee shop, not looking back. She ordered a large coffee and a scone topped with clotted cream and strawberry jam. She would have never ordered this at home, but she wanted to know what all the fuss was about when her coworkers raved about how delicious they were. "When in Rome" was now her new mantra. She had what she later recalled as a "culinary orgasm" after her first bite. She couldn't believe that something so exquisite could be served at such an ordinary establishment. "No wonder people love these," was all she could say, as she had to actively control herself from ordering another serving.

"Enjoying the scone?" she heard behind her. Typically, it was a young chap hoping to get lucky. "Yes, thanks," she replied in what she hoped was a passable English accent. "I'm just finishing up before my very large, very jealous fiancé comes to pick me up." This did the trick. She was alone once again. It made her smile.

As she was finishing the last crumbs, her phone buzzed. She quickly ordered a coffee to go, paid the bill, and stepped onto the sidewalk when the white van came into view. She hastily climbed into the van, and they took off quickly but carefully. Zimmerman didn't want to draw any more attention than absolutely necessary and wanted to avoid being pulled over by a policeman at all costs.

Dolcé noticed that Zimmerman was actively shaken up and knew better than to ask. She understood that if he wanted to talk, he would. And he didn't, not yet.

"We have one more stop," was all he said as they drove to one more unfamiliar neighborhood, "You can come in. I want you to see what goes on first-hand, just in case you end up in one of the houses during the sting operation. I will introduce you as my "girl" which means you are also a worker and more than likely a house madam. Do not smile or make eye contact, but you are free to wander around to get a good look. Try not to say too much, although most of the women don't speak any English and would not recognize your pathetic accent," he added with a smirk, which made Dolcé smile. "The visit should only take about ten minutes, so take advantage of your time. I will be barking orders to you, so please do not take offense."

Dolcé understood completely and was glad and a little honored to be trusted enough to be invited in. She knew it could be dangerous and would act her part with precision.

They soon arrived, and Dolcé followed him into the house with a bowed head and a subservient posture. Nobody seemed to notice her, not the pimp nor the girls. Women were just chattel, objects to buy and sell, nothing more. Especially here. Zimmerman introduced Dolcé as Coco, knowing the pimp or the house madam would not remember that name. He explained that he wanted her to inspect the quarters and report back to him. Nobody questioned his orders. Nobody would have dared. He was definitely in charge.

Dolcé quickly did a tour of the house. It didn't look too bad. The kitchen and living room were clean and seemed to have the essentials for living, including all appliances and a large flat-screen TV. Three of the four bedrooms housed four people on twin-sized bunkbeds, each filled with a sleeping girl. They didn't stir, even though no effort had been made by Zimmerman or the pimp to "keep it down." It was unnatural. Dolcé looked closer and noted that everyone was breathing regularly.

"The girls must be exhausted and sleeping now so they can work all night," Dolcé surmised. "Or perhaps they were drugged," she added to herself, not knowing how true her statement was.

The fourth bedroom was the house madam's, with a nicely made bed, a small desk, dressers, and a closet. "Not too bad," thought Dolcé. "Rank has its privileges if you call slavery in any way, shape, or form a privilege."

Dolcé was surprised at the seemingly civilized conditions of the house. Then she severely chastised herself for even thinking that any of this could have an ounce of civility. It was all abhorrent in every aspect, no matter how clean the kitchen appeared.

Suddenly, Zimmerman bellowed to her and summoned her to get back into the van. The visit was over. It had been eye-opening, to say the least. She quietly followed Zimmerman out of the house without acknowledging any of the habitants and slipped compliantly into the van.

"Would you please take me back to my hotel now?" was all Dolcé could say for the first few minutes. Today had been extremely disturbing, even without knowing the details of what happened at house number two. She needed time to absorb and digest everything she had heard and seen over the last eighteen hours.

"Sure," he said amicably. "You were great today in all ways. You are an amazing woman, and I am glad you are with us. We can talk later. I am sure you have lots of questions and would appreciate answers. I have the burner phone you gave me. I'll call you this evening."

Changing the subject, Dolcé asked, "Is it weird that you wouldn't be with your new girlfriend on a Friday night?" she asked. "I can be available if you need me."

"No, Friday night is usually stag night, a time to spend with the boys," he said. "So, you won't be missed by anyone but me!"

Dolcé was relieved. She had no desire to go out tonight. She wanted to go back to the hotel and take about five showers to wash the filth she had seen today; not literal filth, but the degradation of human life filth. If only it was that easy. It would take more than soap and water to wash the memory of those poor girls from her conscience.

She needed to call Jonathan and clue him in on everything (well, almost everything) that happened over the last day. And Dolcé knew that Nancy needed rest and recuperation after the emotional roller coaster they had experienced.

She kissed Zimmerman lightly on the cheek as the van drove up to the hotel entrance. "Thanks. It's been surreal, to say the least," she said as she exited the van. "I'll talk to you tonight. Be safe."

Chapter 22

Dolcé was exhausted and needed a nap, but she wanted to call Jonathon first. He answered after the second ring and asked how she was.

"Fine, but emotionally very upset by what I saw, and just physically tired. Can we meet later this evening so we can talk?" she asked.

"Sure. It's six now. How about nine?" he inquired.

"That's great. Can you come here? I'm just knackered, as you Brits say, and I can't even think about going out. You know how exhausted I must be if I pass up an opportunity to go out on a Friday night," she added.

"That's the truth," he agreed teasingly. He understood how upset she was when she didn't respond to his teasing.

"We'll have a drink at the bar, or you can come up to my room. Your choice."

"OK, I'll see you then," said Jonathan and hung up. It concerned him that she was negatively affected by her involvement with the case. He made a mental note to be sensitive to her mood this evening.

Nancy was back after showering for over half an hour, getting the smoke and sweat off her. However, it did little to rid her of the visions of those "sleeping" captives."

"Shake it off!" she told herself. "It won't do you any good to get too emotionally involved. You need to keep a level head." That was easier said than done!

"At least Dolcé had fun last night…or should I say this morning," she thought with a tired smile. "Now it's time to sleep for a couple of hours." She threw herself onto the bed and was asleep in less than two minutes.

Nancy was startled awake by her phone ringing wildly. "Hello," she said sleepily.

"It's Jonathan. Did I wake you up? I'm in the lobby. It's nine o'clock," he said.

"Oh my gosh, I forgot to set the alarm. Give me ten minutes, then come on up. Bring a bottle of wine with you if you want," she said, now more awake.

"Already done," said Jonathan confidently.

Nancy nearly panicked, thinking she couldn't get ready in ten minutes. Thank goodness she had showered and washed her hair earlier. She scrambled out of bed, straightening the sheets and duvet into some semblance of order. Then she threw on her comfortable jeans and a soft long-sleeved shirt. She didn't have time to apply any makeup, and for the first time in her adult life, it didn't matter to her. She knew that Jonathan wouldn't mind and probably wouldn't even notice.

Ten minutes later, there was a knock on her door. She answered it in her bare feet and bare face. Jonathan's face lit up when he saw her. "You look wonderful!" he said appreciatively.

That honestly shocked Nancy. How could someone think she looked great without make-up and fancy clothes? It made her catch her breath for a moment.

"Come on in, my Prince," she said graciously. "It's no palace, but it will have to do," and she even curtsied to him, which made Jonathan bow. Both giggled like children at the silliness. They didn't hug or kiss but knew their affection for each other was there.

They settled into the chairs supplied by the hotel. Jonathan then opened and poured the Cabernet he had thoughtfully brought with him. He put on his "Agent Harris" persona and began asking Nancy probing questions, which she answered readily.

Nancy described the other male members of the organization she had met, the exact locations of the three houses they had visited that day, her overall feelings about Zimmerman's sincerity in helping bring down the gang, the address of his apartment, and the names of his flatmates. She went into great detail about the structure of the organization. Most of the information Nancy shared was already known to Interpol and the local police agencies, but it was good to hear it first-hand. It helped to confirm what they already suspected.

Nancy didn't share her severe reaction to seeing the drugged women. She didn't want to alarm Jonathan and didn't want Agent Harris to keep her from continuing her mission because she was considered weak or too emotional.

"Did you feel that you were in any danger?" Agent Harris and Jonathan asked. Both wanted to know.

"No, I was accepted easily and completely. The guys liked my looks but didn't touch. They knew better. Zimmerman was the alpha male of the ones I met."

Jonathan appeared visibly relieved.

"Zimmerman seems very sincere in his desire to destroy the organization. He has made some terrible choices in his life, but I believe he's basically a decent man." Nancy spared no details while she relayed Zimmerman's recollection of his earlier life, his recruitment and initiation into the organization, his rising through the ranks, and his utter disdain for the violence he had witnessed and even perpetrated as part of his job.

Dolcé's wild and crazy time with Zimmerman was the only thing she left out. Nancy felt that that didn't need to be disclosed because it had no direct relationship to the investigation.

Agent Harris listened carefully and even took some notes. Once Nancy was done talking about her experience and began sipping her wine earnestly, Jonathan was again present.

"I'm putting away my Agent Harris hat," he explained. "This is just Jonathan now."

"And this is Nancy," she assured him. "But you know Dolcé is always an important part of me. I need you to remember that."

"I wouldn't have you any other way," he added sincerely. "She makes you mysterious and exotic, not to mention drop-dead sexy!"

Nancy smiled. Jonathan was the first person who understood both parts of her and accepted her unconditionally.

They spent the next two hours chatting and laughing about everything and nothing. Nancy thanked Jonathan again for sharing the Shakespeare experience with her. She wasn't sure she'd have the time to take in a complete performance, so she appreciated the introduction. She also thanked him for his friendship and so much more.

"There's nothing to thank me for," said Jonathan sincerely. "We have a great time together, and hopefully, we will be friends for years to come. Remember, no conditions and no expectations. Just honest and open friendship when we're not mired in some deadly police campaign."

That made Nancy laugh. He had switched gears in one sentence. She ended up choking on a sip of wine, and Jonathan assisted by pounding her on the back. That made her laugh so hard that she began wheezing, which made her laugh even harder. It took a couple of minutes for both of them to recover.

"Oh, that felt good," sighed Jonathan, and Nancy nodded. "I haven't laughed that hard in years, and although it hurts, it feels so good."

"Kind of like athletic sex," Dolcé chimed in. Jonathan found her statement true but also very amusing and began laughing again.

Just then, Nancy's phone rang. It was Zimmerman checking in. "Perfect timing," said Nancy. "Agent Harris is here and would love to talk with you," as she handed Jonathan the phone.

Nancy listened to the one-sided conversation for a few minutes until her mind began to wander. There didn't seem to be new information, so she stopped listening and zoned out. Then, about twenty minutes into the conversation, she heard something that made her cringe. Zimmerman had found out that a new shipment of women from Romania would be coming into Stanstead airport next Wednesday. This was the perfect time to commence Interpol's sting operation if they could organize everything in time. It would give them five days to get all the different departments and agencies ready for a coordinated strike. That wasn't much time for such a vast and multi-faceted campaign to be formulated. They knew, however, that this was their best chance of attacking the enemy at many different levels. It needed to be done immediately.

Jonathan handed the phone back to Nancy. She arranged for Zimmerman to call her again in the morning when they could make plans for later that day as things on both sides developed. She would be his go-between and forward orders from headquarters to Zimmerman. They hung up without salutations.

Jonathan was now back in his Agent Harris mode. "I cannot believe how much progress you have made in such a short time. The information you have given us will be invaluable. And the trust you have instilled in Zimmerman is amazing. You are truly an asset to anyone who knows you! I need to go now and report everything to Agent Robinson. I imagine he would like to see you in the office tomorrow. Can you be there?"

"Of course!" she said decisively. "Just call me in the morning with where and when, and I'll be there."

The friendship mood was broken, and both Nancy and Jonathan were all business. He stood up quickly, said his goodbyes to Nancy, hugged her affectionately, and kissed her on the cheek before abruptly turning and leaving the room. He was already on a mission, which made Nancy smile.

Nancy finished the bottle of wine, changed into her comfy pajamas, and turned on the TV for an hour of mindless entertainment. Sleep came to her easily after she switched off the screen and settled into a much-needed slumber.

Chapter 23

The Interpol office was buzzing when Nancy arrived the following day. Every agent was immersed in their work, either on the phone, in a serious conference, or diligently working on their computer. The focus was complete, and the nervous energy was tangible.

Agent Robinson waved to Nancy as she entered, summoning her into his office. "I hear you did some amazing work over the last couple of days."

"Glad to help in any way I can, sir," said Nancy proudly.

"You're going to be a huge help, especially on Wednesday, if you are willing to take the risk and continue with your mission," he continued. "We want you to stay with Zimmerman. We hear he will be actively managing/overseeing the pick-up and intervention of the Romanian women arriving on Wednesday. Your mission will be to act as Zimmerman's assistant and the women's handler as they are transported to the house. Of course, in reality, you and Zimmerman will act as their guardians and saviors. The plan is to have you transport the women to the house as is normally done. We would then close in and arrest anyone involved, including you and Zimmerman, to help keep your cover. This will only be one tiny part of the entire operation that we are planning for Wednesday, but a crucial one. Are you in?"

"Of course I am!" she answered emphatically.

"Good," Agent Robinson quipped back, already thinking of something else.

"Agents Harris and O'Reilly will work closely with you and Zimmerman to make the operation go as smoothly as possible. You will get the details from them. If you have any concerns or questions they cannot answer, please come to me. We will also have daily afternoon strategic planning sessions with all the Agents. I expect you to be there too."

"Of course," she replied.

"You're dismissed. Go find your agents…and Nancy, thank you, and good luck!" he said almost kindly.

Nancy found Agents Harris and O'Reilly huddled together over a map of London. Red circles were drawn on the map that Nancy correctly assumed were the locations of the houses. What surprised her was that there were so many.

A coordinated attack on each of them, plus rounding up the pimps and managers, would be a huge and extremely complicated undertaking.

Nancy imagined the operation was like the old poem written by John Godfrey Saxe called The Blind Man and the Elephant. Six blind men observed an elephant from different perspectives. The first concluded that an elephant was like a wall. The second concluded it was a spear. The third a snake, the fourth a tree, the fifth a fan, and the sixth a rope. Each man only observed a small portion of the animal and couldn't imagine the entire beast.

Robinson and his staff's responsibility was to take all the separate parts and observations from each individual agent or department and communicate them well enough so everyone would understand the big picture and work as one giant elephant. At the same time, they needed to keep the elephant confidential. It would take only one person to leak the information to undermine the entire operation. Understandably, it was an astronomically brutal feat. So far, Agent Robinson seemed to be doing an incredible job.

Nancy joined Agents Harris and O'Reilly. It was Saturday. They had four days to plan before the sting began. It was decided that it was more critical that Nancy get with Zimmerman and learn the ropes of the business than hang around the office. "We need you to pass on anything that might help; times, places, numbers of people at each location, and what kind of security they have. We need to know if the escorts carry weapons. If so, we need to know what kind. If they carry firearms, we need to know it. Whatever information you can get us may save a life."

Serendipitously, Nancy's phone rang, and it was Zimmerman. Agent Harris grabbed the phone and shared his hopes and concerns for the next few days. He wanted Zimmerman to know how dangerous things were going to get and how he expected him to protect Nancy/Dolcé as much as possible. They agreed that Dolcé would spend the next few days with him to perpetuate the ruse and understand the organization's workings at the sex worker's level. She had one mission, and she needed to concentrate on that one assignment. She didn't need to know about the upper echelons of the cartel. That would only make things more dangerous for her.

Dolcé's mission was to meet the plane at Stansted Airport, serve as Zimmerman's assistant and do whatever she could to guide the women to safety.

It was still unknown if Zimmerman would be alone to meet the plane, which would have been beneficial for the operation but highly unusual. Standard operating procedure stated that at least three of the gang members needed to be present. There were usually at least three of the gang members present.

Zimmerman would be in charge, and the other two would be there to be bodyguards for him and the new shipment of women. If anyone got out of line, they were instructed to do whatever was needed to remedy the situation. Anything.

Having the two bodyguards along would complicate things. They needed to plan for every contingency, and time together was the only way to accomplish that.

Harris handed the phone back to Nancy, who arranged to meet Zimmerman that afternoon at a neutral location. She asked him to drive the van to their rendezvous, if possible, because she wanted to take along some provisions she would not otherwise be able to carry on a casual date, including some basic medical supplies and a taser Harris had slipped to her this morning. She couldn't be caught with a weapon but felt she could hide it and have the taser available later in an emergency. It gave her a little sense of security.

Nancy knew that the shit was about to hit the fan, and once it did, all hell would break loose. She and Zimmerman had to focus on their mission and anticipate every possible problem. No detail could be overlooked. The ramifications of missing anything could be devastating.

Gone was the thought that Nancy would have time to do a little more sightseeing during her "vacation." She left the office and returned to her hotel after being supplied with medical supplies, a Kevlar vest, handcuffs, a police radio, and a Glock 17 pistol with two clips of seventeen rounds each. She hadn't expected to be issued a handgun, and before she left the building, she went to the rifle range in the basement to be sure she could handle it efficiently and effectively. She had never used this particular model before and wanted to be sure she was comfortable with the weapon. After spending an hour on the range, it was evident that Nancy could handle any handgun without a problem. The officer in charge of the range was so impressed that as she left the area, he called out, "See you soon, Miss Annie Oakley."

Upon returning to her hotel room, Nancy carefully locked the handcuffs and Glock into the tourist safe available to every guest. She was aware it wasn't particularly secure, but it was better than nothing.

Nancy knew the next few days would be hectic, so she took a short power nap before getting ready to meet Zimmerman. She packed a duffle bag, knowing she would be gone from the hotel for at least two days and nights. And, since she was known now to Zimmerman's flatmates, it wouldn't be out of character for her to bring a few necessities for a weekend at his place. She hoped it wasn't a false sense of security fueling her excitement as she packed. She knew Zimmerman would take care of her if he could, but also knew she wouldn't be able to depend on it. She understood as well that what she was about to do was the best thing she had ever done.

That included saving the soldier's life on the battlefield that fateful afternoon in Afghanistan.

At seven o'clock, Dolcé saw Zimmerman's van make a sudden turn into the hotel's parking lot. She was on the curb waiting for him as she had been instructed. Zimmerman wanted as little exposure to prying eyes and cameras. He knew that it was impossible to completely avoid CCTV cameras in London. The average commuter to a London office building from the suburbs was filmed an average of three hundred times a day. CCTV cameras were everywhere. Big Brother is definitely watching! Usually, he would be very wary of the cameras, but with the sting in progress, being on the cameras made him feel better about things. This was the first time in his life that the police would be surveying him for his benefit instead of his demise. It felt very strange to Zimmerman, but he embraced it for once. Tonight, he was more concerned about being observed by his own men. He didn't belong in Kensington, and everyone knew it.

They quickly left the posher area of town and drove to the Earl's Court area that wasn't far distance-wise but quite different culturally. The area was affectionately called "Kangaroo Court" because of the many Australians, including students, who settled there over the decades. There were hundreds of restaurants where Zimmerman was sure not to run into any of his cronies. He wanted some alone time with Dolcé…when they could converse without fear of being overheard by the wrong people and where they could relax a bit and just be themselves.

They drove by Addie's Thai Restaurant, and instantly, Dolcé had a Jones for some Shrimp Pad Thai. Addie's was famous for its street food served in the bar in the basement or upstairs in the more traditional restaurant. They agreed to have dinner in the basement bar, where they were less likely to be seen. The bar was also better because they were very casually dressed and didn't want to stand out negatively. Zimmerman quickly parked the van, and they walked the short distance back to the restaurant.

Dinner was delicious. They ordered several starters and two entrees and ate them Family Style, sharing all the plates with gusto. It was almost like an actual date. They each had a glass of wine, laughed, and shared some anecdotes from their lives before getting to business.

Zimmerman told Dolcé that two bodyguards would accompany them on their airport run on Wednesday. This made things more complicated, and their strategy needed to be altered. No longer was it a simple meet and greet at the airport and then a diversion of the van to a safe house. It was still the meet and greet, but the van needed to go to the house as was routinely done.

They would have to play the parts of the Bad Guys until they could safely extract the newly enslaved women from the house. Hopefully, with the help of the police, they would be able to devise a plan to do it on their own if backup did not arrive in time.

Dolcé wanted to make a dry-run to the airport, and then from the airport to the house they would be going to. She also wanted to tour the house itself so she would be very familiar with the floor plan and any possible places to hide a weapon or herself if needed. The house was vacant until the women arrived, so that was possible. Zimmerman was also responsible for ensuring the house was correctly furnished, so access was not an issue.

They decided to do the dry-run on Sunday. That gave the two of them a chance to be seen together on the town, which was expected on a Saturday night. Dolcé and Zimmerman returned to his place, put their glad rags on, and headed for the pub first and then to a dance club. Of course, Dolcé got all dolled up to go out, and Zimmerman couldn't help but be proud of the attention she always attracted. She played her part perfectly, and he knew he was a lucky man, even if it was only temporary.

Chapter 24

Zimmerman and Dolcé/Nancy were suddenly all business. They understood the importance of their actions over the next four days, both socially and professionally. Eyes were watching from both sides of the conflict. Interpol was watching, not only to assure Nancy's safety, to affirm Zimmerman wouldn't double-cross them. And then there was the gang and its members. Eyes were always on each other. Traitors were never tolerated, and the punishment for breeches was often death.

Sunday morning was overcast and drizzling when Zimmerman and Dolcé pulled out of the driveway. "Now, this is what I picture when I think of London weather; wet, gray, and miserable," stated Dolcé. Zimmerman nodded his agreement. "Berlin's weather can be just as cold and wet," he added. "It shouldn't affect our day, however. Normally we ignore the weather and do whatever we need to, just with a raincoat or umbrella. One good thing about the rain is that it makes CCTV less invasive. The umbrellas cover a person's identity pretty well. So, rain can be a good thing." Dolcé hadn't thought of things that way. Chicago had security cameras everywhere now, but not so pervasive as in London. She had always thought of the cameras as security, like a friendly chaperone, but now could see that they could and often did compromise a person's privacy. "Hmmm. That's an interesting way to think about it, and I'm not sure which side of the controversy I'm on," she said thoughtfully.

"Stansted Airport is about an hour's drive, so make yourself comfortable," Zimmerman said. "It's a smaller airport with less security. It's easier to keep track of people and things than at Heathrow. Ryan Air has cheap flights from Bucharest many times a day. We have the women come in on a flight that arrives just after noon. By the time they get through immigration and customs, they are exhausted, which is exactly what we want. We round them up, welcome them pleasantly and then collect their passports. We give them refreshments that are laced with a sedative in the van before beginning our journey. It is too late when they understand what is happening to them. They are already ours."

"It's that easy?" asked Dolcé with amazement in her voice.

"Well, not quite, but almost," replied Zimmerman.

"Wow, if they only knew," whispered Dolcé, primarily to herself.

Since they were not in a hurry to get to the airport, they stopped for breakfast on the way to Stansted. Dolcé read the menu carefully, then commented, "I don't even know what many of the things on the menu are."

Zimmerman smiled. "I can translate if you wish," he said gently.

"OK, what are kippers, for instance?" she asked. "And, do they really serve breakfast with baked beans and mushrooms? Beans just out of a can? That sounds pretty strange to me. I'm not criticizing, but the thought of beans on toast for breakfast sounds pretty unappetizing."

"Beans on toast is a British classic. Kippers are small herring fish and are very salty," he explained.

"English breakfasts are an acquired taste. Traditionally, everything is fried in lots of bacon grease, including the toast," he explained. "If you look at the small print on the menu, under the listing for an English breakfast, you will often see the name and phone number of a local cardiologist," he joked, making Dolcé laugh.

Dolcé decided to go the safe route and ordered the muesli with yogurt. Zimmerman went the whole hog and ordered The Big Breakfast with the works. "I'm a growing boy," he explained with a smirk, knowing Dolcé was cautious with her diet and body image.

As they ate their breakfasts and drank numerous cups of coffee each, they quietly discussed every possible detail of their mission, including possible contingencies if things went wrong, which was highly likely. As they talked, Nancy's personality surfaced slowly but firmly with her unwavering logic. Zimmerman observed the merging of the two forceful personalities into one powerful, capable, intelligent, and incredibly sexy woman. He was astonished when observing them up close and knew that she/they would be ready and able to handle just about anything thrown at her/them.

Even though Nancy didn't have a UK driver's license, Zimmerman asked her to drive the van for the rest of the day. She needed to know how the van worked and feel comfortable driving on the "wrong" side of the road. Staying to the left was against any American driver's instincts, and she needed to overcome them, especially in an emergency.

Nancy didn't mind the constant instructions to "stay to the left" from Zimmerman, especially on the roundabouts, and they seemed to be everywhere. Her instinct was to point the van to the right and go around it counterclockwise. Of course, that was absolutely the wrong thing to do. "Practice makes perfect," Nancy kept reminding herself after being reminded at least forty times.

The van had a manual transmission, which meant Nancy had to shift gears with her left hand, adding an extra dimension to the difficulty of driving. She found it extremely uncomfortable at first but slowly adjusted. "Watch out, mailboxes, here I come," she said once when she miscalculated the van's width and gently hit the left curb.

It took about an hour before she began to feel confident with her new driving style. Traffic was relatively light because it was Sunday morning. The challenge would increase as the day progressed. Thankfully, adapting to new environments and situations was easy for Nancy. She thrived on them; she embraced the new driving methods and quickly became proficient. Zimmerman was finally able to relax a bit and became the navigator. "It's important you know the route," he said to Nancy. "That's why I'm having you drive this yourself, just in case something happens to me." Nancy appreciated the logic in this and smiled assuredly.

They arrived at the airport, parked in the short-term car park, and then walked to the terminal. They checked out the arrivals hall and noted many cameras but no security officers. The eight women would be arriving all at the same time and were instructed to meet Zimmerman and associates outside the international arrivals exit after going through immigration and customs. "This seems very straightforward," said Nancy. "It's normal for people to be waiting with signs to identify themselves to travelers as they arrive."

"Yes, this is the easy part," said Zimmerman. "We welcome them, collect their documents and escort them to the van. That's all very pleasant and routine. The unpleasantness begins when they find out they do not have the jobs promised and are now obligated to us for their passage. It can get very unpleasant, but we manage. Things have become routine. Human nature doesn't vary much. We have dealt with all types over the years, and none have escaped…unfortunately."

"OK," said Nancy. "This all seems straightforward. Let's continue back and check out the route and timing." Nancy had to correct the direction she was walking around the van when she realized the driver's seat was now on the right side of the van instead of the left. "Oops," she said. "This is going to take some getting used to." Zimmerman nodded and climbed into the left-sided passenger seat.

The drive from the airport to the new location took more than an hour and a half. Zimmerman and Nancy used the time to brainstorm and come up with a list of items they might need and things to discuss with the Interpol team. They wanted to be as prepared as absolutely possible.

As they arrived at the unoccupied house, Nancy was struck by how "normal" it appeared. It was a three-story brick walk-up in a solidly middle-class neighborhood. They opened the front door and entered the hall with the stairs to the upper stories on the left, the entrance to the living room on the right, the kitchen behind the living room, and a laundry room at the back that led to the back garden. The bedrooms and bathrooms were upstairs. Nancy was reminded about the differences between the U.S. and Britain when she observed that the toilets were in a separate room from the bath and were located off the landings between the stories of the house. "So very strange," Nancy thought. "There must have been a reason, but it doesn't make sense to me." Zimmerman couldn't explain it. He was German, after all.

They spent the next hour thoroughly inspecting the house from top to bottom, including the basement, which was finished into a subterranean flat and used by the house mother and other staff members. Nancy noted that there were cameras strategically positioned in each room of the house where the women could be monitored at all times. It appeared that the monitoring system was located in an office in the basement, so Nancy assumed there might not be a central monitoring system. Each house had its own monitoring system, which was a good thing. Any discrepancy in one place would not automatically go to headquarters and make it easier to change courses if things did not go as expected on Wednesday.

The rooms were ready for occupants. Beds were made, the house was stocked with linens and other supplies, the kitchen with essentials and plenty of food, and Nancy noticed that every door had at least one deadbolt lock. Was it to keep people out or to keep people in? She assumed correctly that it was the latter. Nancy found a few possible "hidey-holes" on each level, took the provisions she had brought from the van, and hid them strategically. Zimmerman felt it was a safe thing to do and was impressed with Nancy's foresight. Over the years, things had become so routine for him that he hadn't thought of what might happen if something went wrong. And, of course, things could go very badly on Wednesday.

Once they were satisfied they had done everything they could to be prepared for Wednesday's pick-up and possible confrontation, Zimmerman and Nancy quietly left the neighborhood. They had not crossed paths with any of the neighbors, which was a plus. Perhaps the neighbors kept to themselves here. The less they knew, the better.

It was mid-afternoon as they finished. Zimmerman dropped Nancy off at a convenient tube station and then drove back to his place. He didn't want any possibility of being seen dropping her off at the hotel and definitely couldn't drive her to the Interpol office where Nancy was headed. Before she forgot any important details, she wanted to brief Agents Harris and O'Reilly on what they had found and planned.

She quickly called Jonathan and told him of her plans. He was at the office and told her he would look forward to seeing her as soon as she arrived. "I'm glad you're OK. I've been worried about you," he said. "Can you come into the office? There's a huge meeting just about to begin, and you should be here."

"Sure. I'll be there as soon as I can. And there's been nothing to worry about so far," Nancy replied. "Everything I've observed of Zimmerman assures me he is in with us one hundred percent and will not double-cross us. We do have a problem with Wednesday's pickup, however. There will be two extra men with us to act as bodyguards. They will need to be neutralized one way or another. We can talk when I get to the office in about 45 minutes," and she hung up the phone as she entered the tube station.

She was an old pro now and able to quickly figure out the best route to get to her destination. It was like a puzzle for her, and she loved puzzles. The excitement she felt riding the underground trains had not waned. She still loved people-watching. London was a cosmopolitan city with ethnic groups from all over the globe. As Nancy rode, she heard numerous unfamiliar languages and gawked at the fashions people wore. Each person's attire seemed to make a statement about them somehow. She saw the young mother with a hijab, and a baby in a stroller, an older Indian man with a Sikh turban, teenagers with pink and green hair and torn jeans, businessmen in their blue and white striped shirts with the white collars and their matching ties loosened. All types, ages, and sizes. It fascinated Nancy. She became so distracted that she almost forgot to get off at her stop. "Mind the gap," she kept hearing. "Minding the gap," she playfully replied to the recorded voice, and nobody else seemed to find it amusing.

Nancy suddenly realized she couldn't remember when she was happier than she was at that moment. Life was exciting, there were amazing things to learn and do, and she was thoroughly appreciated for her achievements and personality…not for her sexiness or appearance. The Dolcé in her always wanted to be admired for her beauty, but even she was surprised at how happy she was. Life was good!

Chapter 25

"What's going on?" asked Nancy as she entered the conference room with Agent Harris.

"It's an interagency briefing about Wednesday's raid," he answered quietly as they made their way toward the front of the gathering. "Everyone involved is here."

Nancy saw Agent Robinson in front of the crowd, but a fit fifty-ish female officer was beginning to speak to the group.

"Could I have your attention, please," she spoke clearly into the microphone on the podium, causing the many conversations to abruptly halt.

"I am Detective Inspector Sheila Thomas. I have been asked to give you a brief lecture on the subject of human trafficking in the UK. I apologize to those of you who are already experts on the topic. Still, we feel it is essential for everyone involved in Wednesday's raid to understand the victims and the perpetrators.

"Let's first define human trafficking. Some people define it as 'modern-day slavery,' and for a good reason. The dictionary defines it as the unlawful act of transporting or coercing people to benefit from their work or service, typically in the form of forced labor or sexual exploitation," she began. "Now that we know the definition, let's talk about the scope in the UK. Although the government reported ten thousand six hundred and thirteen potential victims in 2020, one NGO (Non-governmental organization) estimates the actual number of victims in the UK was closer to one hundred thousand. Not all of these victims are being used for the sex trade, but many are. Today we are concentrating on the young women trafficked from Eastern Europe, mainly from Romania. There are four stages to trafficking:

Stage 1. Luring: the victims are lured into the UK with promises of good jobs and modeling contracts. Some are aware of the dangers, but most are simply anxious for a new and better life. Of course, they never find that better life. Once they get off the plane, their traffickers take their passports and any money they might have, drug them and then tell the victims they need to work off their debts.

Stage 2: Grooming and Gaming: this happens more with individuals than groups of victims. This is when the trafficker makes the victim seem unique in some way, mostly when she obeys his orders to have sex with either him or a client. Her excellent work appears to make him happy, at least temporarily.

Stage 3: Coercion and manipulation. This is when the trafficker starts sending mixed messages. Some people call it gaslighting. Verbal abuse is very common at this stage. The pimp does what he can to confuse the victim, decrease her self-esteem, and break her down.

Stage 4: Exploitation: The trafficker can become violent if the victim does not comply with his demands. The traffickers we are going after on Wednesday use isolation, debt, drugs, sleep deprivation, and physical and sexual abuse as their tools to keep the victims submissive. They convince their victims they will never get out, so fighting is futile. If they get out of line or try to run away, punishments are doled out liberally and brutally.

To give you an idea of how lucrative this trafficking is: one brothel of six women can bring in over a million pounds of income annually. Multiply that by 15, which is our target on Wednesday. And then, take that money, launder it, use it to buy and sell street drugs and illegal firearms and you have an accurate picture of the organized crime gangs here in the London area. This is big business, and we need to stop it!"

DI Thomas had successfully rallied the troops. They broke into spontaneous applause and conversations. The noise was so deafening that Nancy had to cover her ears. Agent Robinson stepped up to the podium as DI Thomas found a seat.

"Any questions so far," bellowed Robinson. "Let's settle down! We have a lot of information still to cover."

It took nearly two minutes before the individual conversations decreased, and attention was once again focused on the front of the room.

"We will spend the next few minutes reviewing our mission for Wednesday and most of the details we have so far. First, I would like to introduce you to two people who have been instrumental in finding and confirming the information we needed to get this mission on its feet. Interpol Agent Jonathan Harris and private citizen extraordinaire Ms. Nancy Calloway from Chicago, Illinois." All of the Interpol Agents rose to their feet and, with thunderous applause, acknowledged the two unsuspecting souls for their accomplishments. The other officers joined in on the ovation. Nancy was speechless. She had never experienced anything like this. People were applauding her for just being her. Incredible!

"If you have questions for either Ms. Calloway or Agent Harris, please see them after the presentation," Robinson continued. "Now, let's get specific about the mission."

"This 'beast' is too large and too organized to bring down all at once. But how do you defeat a beast? You cut them off at the knees! And that is exactly what we intend to do! By raiding all of their homes/brothels at once, we will deprive them of their workforce, thus depriving them of their income. We will also confiscate anything of value, including homes, cars, firearms, and even fine art objects if we find them. Basically, by cutting off their income stream, and will cause great damage to their bottom line. It won't kill the organization, but hopefully, it will injure it severely."

"Our mission is relatively simple: There will be simultaneous raids on fifteen locations/brothels. This is primarily a search and rescue mission. The highest priority is to get the victims to safety. The second priority is to arrest and detain any traffickers we can. We will then go in and impound anything of value and restrict access for the foreseeable future. We are not going after the johns on this mission. Any questions so far?"

There were none.

"Each of you will be thoroughly briefed by your commanding officers in the next two days. I want to spend a few minutes going over the basics now so we are all on the same page."

"Number 1: This is to be kept confidential! I don't want you talking about the raid in the pub or at home. The only way this mission will work is if it is a surprise. Severe penalties will be dealt to anyone speaking out of turn and jeopardizing the mission.

Number 2: At 2 p.m. on Wednesday, each location will be raided by eight to ten agents/police simultaneously. This is when we believe most victims will be resting and passive. All officers will be armed. Your job is to go in, rescue the victims and transport them by van to your designated safe house, where a Social Worker will assist.

At the same time, any traffickers you arrest are to be transported by separate police vehicles to your precincts. We anticipate up to ten women per location. Be sure to arrest the house mother. Although she is also a victim, she is directly responsible for maintaining the compliance of her workers.

You may find some of the victims resistant to your help. This is normal. And this is why we have assigned at least one female officer to each location. It would be advisable to learn a few phrases of Romanian so you can instruct the victims in their language. Most speak little to no English. We will have translators available at the safe houses but not on the mission itself.

Number 3: Although you will be armed, lethal force should only be used as a last resort. Use caution. Chances are very high that at least one person at each location will be heavily armed and ready to defend themselves.

Number 4: Be sure to inform any arrestees of their rights.

Number 5: Get in and out quickly and as quietly as possible. There will be no sirens or lights going to the location. We want to make the impact on the neighborhood as minimal as possible.

Number 6: Hospital A and E departments will be on standby for anyone needing immediate medical attention. Likewise, an ambulance will be standing by two blocks away from each location for dire emergencies.

Number 7: The floor plans for each location are different, but the mission is the same. Be sure to inspect the basement and attic. Each site has a monitoring system that will need to be disabled.

Now, if you have questions, come see me or check with your commanding officer," concluded Robinson. The meeting mentioned nothing about Nancy and Zimmerman's mission but wasn't considered necessary at the time.

A roar of voices broke out, and the meeting concluded. Robinson knew the nearby pub would be full of pumped-up officers in just a few minutes. They had responded well to the mission. Robinson was also pumped about the prospects.

Nancy and Agents Harris and O'Reilly quietly slipped into a private office to continue the planning.

"If this all goes as planned, this could be one of the biggest raids in history," said Jonathan. "And much of the credit will go to you, Nancy!"

"I'm not here for the credit. I want to get those bastards so they can't hurt anyone else again!" replied Nancy emphatically. "There's something else I would like," she added.

"What's that," asked Jonathan.

"I'd like to find out who made the movie on the flash drive and who else was involved. Whoever it was, they are truly evil and need to be removed permanently," said Nancy.

"I will keep that in mind," interjected O'Reilly. "That is another mission but no less important. I will do my best to find some answers for you."

With their meeting concluded, they headed to the exit. "Are you hurrying to get back to your hotel?" asked Jonathan. "If not, I'd like to spend the rest of the afternoon or evening with you."

"I'd like that," replied Nancy. "My hotel has an indoor pool and a spa. How about we go and relax a little."

"That's a perfect idea," agreed Jonathan. "I think we can all use a little exercise and pampering."

Chapter 26

Nancy and Jonathan spent Sunday evening swimming and indulging in a couple's massage at the hotel spa. They loved the pampering but felt guilty for feeling so comfortable when others suffered so severely. "It won't be long now," reminded Jonathan. "You've done so much for the cause. You need to give yourself the credit you deserve and give yourself a break. We won't need you tomorrow. Take the day off and do something fun or educational. We have everything under control, and nothing needs to be done tomorrow. We'll finalize everything on Tuesday. If we need you, we'll call. Otherwise, go out and have some fun! I wish I could go with you, but I have to work. Otherwise, wild horses couldn't drag me away!"

"You're so sweet," Nancy commented. "Since I have most of tomorrow, I'm thinking of going to Hampton Court. I have heard so much about it. Do you think that's a good choice?"

"Absolutely," agreed Jonathan enthusiastically. "It is steeped with history and mystery. I think you'll love it.

"Done," said Nancy. "You can find me there tomorrow. Thanks, Jonathan; I needed your company this evening. It's always so nice to spend time with you," she added sincerely.

"I feel the same way. Get some rest, and I'll see you on Tuesday, if not before," Jonathan said as he hugged her.

Nancy was still in the robe she had worn to her massage. She was so mellow from her experience that she ordered a light dinner from Room Service and then went straight to bed...by herself. She slept deeply for ten hours without stirring.

"What a beautiful day," exclaimed Nancy as she peered out of her window while sipping her first morning coffee. "Gorgeous. Sunny, warmish with just a mild breeze," she continued. "A perfect day to head out of town. It's like the Sightseeing Angels are protecting me."

Nancy found that the sightseeing angels were fickle when she discovered that Hampton Court was closed on Mondays and Tuesdays. "Darn!" she exclaimed. "But at least I found out now instead of when I got there." Nancy always tried to be an optimist about things she could not control. Her disappointment lasted only a few minutes before she formulated another plan. "If I can't go to Hampton Court, I'll do the next best thing. I'll go to the Tower of London. It's full of history, mystery, and jewels. Who could ask for more!"

As usual, Nancy mapped out the day's activities logically. She wanted to fit in as many sights as possible since her remaining free time might be limited. She would start at the Tower of London, which opened at ten o'clock. She figured that would take about two hours. Next, she would go to St Paul's Cathedral and at least see it from the exterior. Then, across the bridge once again to the South Bank for a beautiful stroll along the Thames River, past the National Theater to the London Eye. "Maybe I'll spend the time and ride the eye," she thought. "It's such a beautiful day. I imagine the visibility is incredible today. And besides, I may not get back here again and should take every opportunity I can while I'm able." She planned to cross the river once more at the Houses of Parliament and visit Westminster Abbey. She also wanted to see St Martin-in-the-Fields and get to a casual concert they had almost daily, as well as have a snack in the lunch room in the crypt. She had heard from a friend that it was one of her favorite places. The cafeteria was terrific, and the gift shop there was amazing. And, afterward, make a trip through the National Gallery. "Whew, that's a LOT to do in one day!" she lectured herself. "Don't stretch yourself too thin!"

She would have also wanted to get to Leicester Square, where she could grab a last-minute ticket to a West End Theater performance but stopped herself. "Enough, already!" she scolded. "Save something for next time; if there is a next time."

It felt like the calm before the storm to Nancy. She was nervous about the upcoming raid but tried not to think about it and knew that keeping busy would help her stay calm. It wouldn't help to dwell on possibilities. She knew the experts were considering every aspect and contingency. It was difficult for her to let go, even for the day. But she knew it was necessary.

She donned her most comfortable walking shoes, jeans, and a sweater and set out on her sightseeing adventure. She hopped on the Circle Line at the Gloucester Road Tube Station and rode for twenty minutes until she arrived at Tower Hill. "This is so easy," she kept telling herself.

Her first view of Tower Hill was impressive. More impressive were the stories she had heard about the castle that was once a royal residence, a prison, a mint, an armory, and much more. Her imagination went wild when she spied Traitor's Gate. How many people had been taken into the Tower through that gate and never came out alive? Her thirst for history surprised her; everything was just so darn interesting. She joined a guided tour led by one of the Beefeaters (formally known as the Yeoman Warders). He told stories of queens, kings, traitors, innocent detainees, and of course, the crown jewels. As fascinating as the tour was to Nancy, she looked forward to the end when she could see the real Crown Jewels for herself. She was not disappointed. The jewels were more than magnificent.

The Dolcé in her was dazzled by the bling. It amazed her that just a thin sheet of glass protected the treasures. She knew better, of course. They had to be safeguarded by an incredibly sophisticated security system. Which reminded her to smile and wave up at the CCTV.

As Nancy made her way up to St Paul's, she wondered what it must have been like to live in a castle one thousand years ago. People romanticized it, but Nancy was practical enough to wonder how the occupants kept warm in the winter and how they managed simple hygiene habits we take for granted today. She made a note to herself to do some research when she got home. "No wonder there are so many historians in England," she said to herself. "The history is so rich and real here."

The dome of St Paul's came into view, and Nancy followed what she thought was the path of least resistance to get there. It was very impressive, but she suddenly realized that the day was passing quickly. She took a few pictures with her phone and decided to leave the interior tour for another time.

Then it was back to the South Bank and the London Eye via the Millennium Bridge. She had never been on an observation wheel before and decided to give it a try. She was in luck when she could purchase a ticket and board the passenger capsule without delay. "I guess it's a good thing I'm not afraid of heights," she said to herself when she read that the wheel is four hundred feet tall. She got her camera ready and took about twenty shots in the thirty minutes it took to complete the one revolution.

"That was fun," she said as she disembarked the capsule. "Now, on to St Martin-in-the-Fields for lunch! I'm famished, and there's nothing better than crypt food," she giggled. Arriving just before one o'clock, she was pleasantly surprised to find a notice board announcing a mid-day concert. It had just begun, and Nancy silently found a seat in the back of the sanctuary. The string quartet sounded heavenly to Nancy's ears. "How lucky I was to be able to experience this today!" she whispered her thanks. After twenty minutes, the music of her stomach rumbling threatened to drown out the musician's instruments, so she snuck out of the sanctuary as quietly as she had arrived, without disturbing anyone.

She found the steps down to the crypt and was astonished at the beauty of the brick arches in the basement. Locals and tourists alike enjoyed their very "British" lunches of steak and kidney pies with three veg. And, of course, the requisite pot of tea. She joined the queue, paid for her food, and found a table where she could people-watch.

"This is strange," Nancy told herself. "This is the first time I can remember where Dolcé and I have been out in public, and we weren't out hunting for men."

Maybe it was due to her improved self-image or she was just too busy to think about things. Whatever the reason, she liked it.

After lunch, she perused the gift shop and was fascinated that one of the featured items was a kit to do rubbings of gravestones. "Just what every kid wants, their own gravestone rubbing kit," she said sarcastically and laughed out loud.

She knew she still had time and the energy to make at least one more stop. She was already at Trafalgar Square and could see the entrance to the National Gallery across the street. "It would be a shame if I was so close but didn't go in," she told herself. Art had never been one of her interests, but she could still appreciate the sheer beauty and magnitude of the talent and history displayed. And, there was no admission charge, so she felt she could spend as little or as much time as she wished without obligation to "get her money's worth."

From the moment she stepped into the first gallery, she was "hooked." She stared in awe at the painting of an incredibly beautiful stallion named Whistlejacket, painted by George Stubbs in the 1760s. Not only was the painting incredibly beautiful, but it was also huge and took up most of the entire wall (nearly 9 X 8 feet). Her awe was boundless.

She needed to know more, so she bought a guide to the Gallery. She learned that the gallery has more than 2,300 works on display, painted from the 13th century to the early 20th century. The medieval paintings were primarily religious, which didn't interest Nancy much, so she concentrated on the more recent pictures.

She had a few favorites as she roamed aimlessly from room to room. The Gallery was so overwhelming that she didn't know where she was or where she had been, but it didn't matter. Each room was more incredible than the last.

She liked a painting called The Arnolfini Portrait, which was painted in 1434. "Wow, that painting is nearly six hundred years old, and it still looks great," she commented. She knew she was no art historian, but she knew what she liked. And what she liked about this picture was the realism. A man with his very pregnant wife was standing in a room of a wealthy person. "She looks about thirteen years old," Nancy commented again. "I hope that's not the case." She loved the rich colors of her dress and the detail of her scarf. She also liked the detail in the mirror. She looked closely and saw reflections of two other men coming into the room. "Amazing!" Nancy exclaimed. "It's like a picture of the past."

Dolcé especially liked the naked pictures! "Of course, you would," laughed Nancy. There were lots of naked pictures. Dolcé most appreciated the portrait called Rokeby Venus by Velazquez painted about 1650. She thought Venus was incredibly beautiful with her tiny waist and sensuous butt.

And, of course, they both liked Van Gogh's Sunflowers painting. Nancy would have wanted to see more of his work but knew many of his paintings were in the d'Orsay Museum in Paris. "I'll have to go there someday! Who knows, it might be sooner than anyone thinks! Anything is possible."

She continued to wander from one hall to the next, forgetting the time and everything except the exquisite art.

She was startled when she heard the announcement that the gallery would close in fifteen minutes. She looked at her phone. 5:45! Where did the day go? She reluctantly left the building and called Jonathan to check in with him.

"What a day I've had," she said excitedly. "You've heard of Afternoon Delight? Well, this has been pure tourist delight." It took Jonathan a few seconds to register the reference Nancy had made to the 1976 song by the Starland Vocal Band. When he finally got the connection, it made him laugh out loud. Only Nancy/Dolcé would find something sexual about sightseeing.

"I'm glad you enjoyed your day. You deserved a break!" Jonathan said encouragingly. "And, you didn't miss much. We will brief you tomorrow on the few additions, but there is nothing for you to do tonight, except you may want to contact Zimmerman. We were not able to get ahold of him today."

"I'll do that as soon as I get back to the hotel," she said. "I'm pooped and want to make it a quiet night by myself tonight. I guess this is the calm before the storm, and I want to be as strong as possible when the storm hits." She was impressed at how wise she sounded. Was that really her, or had the Brits exchanged her for a pod person? She laughed at the thought.

After returning to the hotel, Nancy called Zimmerman. There was no answer, so she left a message as if it was his frustrated girlfriend calling to check on him. "Strange," Nancy thought. "I hope everything is OK."

To top off her perfect day, she opened a bottle of very cold Pino Grigio, poured herself a glass, and made herself comfortable while opening the art book she purchased from the Gallery gift shop. "Yes, indeed. I am hooked," she said as she slowly flipped through the pages of her new precious possession.

Chapter 27

Nancy was startled awake by the sound of her phone chiming at 2:55 a.m. "Hello," said Nancy sleepily.

"It's Zimmerman."

Nancy sat up in bed, fully awake. "Is everything OK?" she asked. "People have been trying to get ahold of you."

"I'm OK, but there's been a lot going on," he said.

"Where are you?" Nancy asked. "Do you need me for something?"

"That's why I'm calling. Some of the guys have been asking questions about you. It would be good if we were seen together until Wednesday's raid. Can you come here?"

"Sure, but the tube isn't running now," answered Nancy wisely.

"I'll pick you up. Meet me in front of the Gloucester Road Tube Station in forty-five minutes. Plan on spending the duration away from the hotel. We want the guys to see your presence loud and clear for the next two days. So, come prepared," he said resolutely. "And Nancy, thank you."

"No problem," she interjected. "And it's Dolcé, not Nancy," she added in a sexy voice.

"Hmmm," Zimmerman hummed lustily. "See you in forty-five," and hung up.

Nancy texted Jonathan to let him know about the new developments. She didn't want to disturb him unnecessarily. Her phone rang again.

"So, what's going on?" asked Jonathan in a concerned voice.

"I'm not sure. Zimmerman just said that things have been going on, and some of the guys have been asking about me. He feels I must be seen with him over the next two days, so he's picking me up, and I'll probably be going to his place for the duration," she said.

"Thanks for letting me know. I am assigning two undercover agents to you from now on. They will be outside Zimmerman's flat when you arrive, and although you won't see them, they will be with you until after the raid on Wednesday. If you do see them, let me know. If you can see them, others can too," he added.

"I'll be in touch tomorrow whenever I can," said Nancy.

"Nancy, be careful. These are very dangerous people!" he said sincerely. "It's not too late for you to back out."

"Absolutely not!" she said too quickly and loudly. "Sorry, but you know how much I want to be a part of this!"

"Yes, I do. Remember, we still have the GPS tracking you, so we will always know where you are, even if we can't see you. Use your phone or whatever you can if you need immediate help. And Nancy, don't take unnecessary chances. I want you around for a long time to come."

"Thanks," she said. She was touched deeply by his sincere concern for her. She hung up the phone, began throwing things in her small duffel bag, and waited for Zimmerman to pick her up.

There were no effusive greetings when he arrived. Dolcé quickly and deftly climbed into the van, and they were gone in less than thirty seconds.

"Let's stop at an all-night coffee shop to talk before getting to the flat. Everyone is asleep, so they shouldn't see us arrive. We will need to be very quiet, though, so it's best if we get any business discussed before we get there," said Zimmerman.

Twenty minutes later, Zimmerman pulled the van into one of the many parking places available in front of the coffee shop. "That's the advantage of having coffee at three in the morning. Parking is easy," he said.

"Is that a joke?" asked Dolcé, astonished. "Good one!" She hadn't thought of Zimmerman as having any sense of humor, and it tickled her.

"Yes," he nodded with a shrug of his shoulders. "I tried."

They settled into a table away from any prying ears.

"So, tell me what's been going on," began Dolcé.

"They have been keeping me very busy," began Zimmerman. "I'm unsure whether it's because there's more shit going on than usual or if they're testing me. I've been driving all over town, overseeing the pimps. One of the girls disappeared, and everyone was told "not to worry about her." That's not a good sign. I doubt that she is still alive. I hope what happened to that other poor girl didn't happen to her."

"Speaking of which, have you found out more about who was there when the movie was made?" asked Dolcé.

"It's not something you ask. It could have been filmed anywhere there is a basement by anyone. But I will keep my ears and eyes open over the next two days. After Wednesday, I don't think I'll be welcomed into the gang's confidence anymore. Do you?"

"Yea, you're right. You'll be lucky to have your head attached come Thursday," she said sympathetically. "That brings me to ask, what are your plans after Wednesday?"

"I have been offered Witness Protection, but I'm not sure I will accept. I will probably return to Germany but not Berlin, and disappear for a while. I figure I will worry about that after Wednesday. What about you?" he asked.

"I have a life in Chicago I will go back to. There's no reason to believe I will be in danger there, so I'll go back to being Nurse Nancy by day and dangerous and mysterious Dolcé by night," she added with a sexy smile.

"Both roles you play so well!" he added with a wry smile. "We will miss you!"

"Let's just worry about Wednesday first, and then we can think about any future we may or may not have," Dolcé added.

They discussed several minor issues and decided it was best if Dolcé stayed with him or close by for the duration. Zimmerman now knew who the two guards would be accompanying them to the airport. "And they are ruthless sons of bitches," said Zimmerman disgustedly. "We are going to have to be very careful with them. I think it is important to make the run as routine as possible. That means arriving at the airport, picking up the girls, drugging them, driving to the house, and getting them settled in. Everything is as normal as possible. When we get to the house, I will try to get rid of them. If they refuse to leave, we must contain them and ask for backup, which should be right around the corner. The sweep will be taking place while we are on our way back from the airport. Let's hope it stays confidential and it is successful. Otherwise, it could be a bloody mess in more ways than one."

"Will they be in the van or a separate vehicle?" asked Dolcé.

"In a separate vehicle, but always right behind us. If anything seems suspicious, one of them will ride in the van. Otherwise, they will hang close enough to intervene with anything that doesn't appear to be right," he answered.

"Who do they think I am?" she asked.

"My girlfriend, whom I am training to manage the house mothers," he said. "It is not unheard of, so the sham has worked so far and should hold up for another two days. As long as Dolcé is here, the plan should work."

"She's always here," she added slyly. That made Zimmerman smile.

"OK, it's time to put on a show," said Dolcé as she stood up and began to leave the café.

"Coming," said Zimmerman, following her to the van. "Wanna drive?"

They arrived safely at the flat twenty-five minutes later. It wouldn't be long until the sun rose, so Zimmerman and Dolcé quietly crept into the flat and caught as much sleep as possible. Before dozing off, Dolcé wondered what was causing the sudden change in her. She would normally have jumped any man's bones she was this close to, no matter the time or her state of exhaustion. Was Dolcé being diluted by feelings of self-worth and maturity? As flattering as that may have been, it wasn't much fun, and she certainly hoped it wasn't a permanent change!

Chapter 28

Tuesday morning was business as usual at the flat; coffee brewing with loud cursing heard from the kitchen up the stairs and into Dolcé's consciousness. Dolcé just smiled at the macho bravado Zimmerman's flatmates feigned. She had known hundreds of losers like them, who believed that the more foul-mouthed they were, the more manly they became. "Let's see how macho you are tomorrow when you are all incarcerated."

When she had worked in the Emergency Department, she had seen the "toughest" gang members, the ones who would shoot someone in the face without blinking an eye, act like a five-year-old child, screaming and crying and carrying on after sustaining a minor cut. "They're all big men until they're not," she thought philosophically and again fell asleep.

It was noonish before Dolcé and Zimmerman appeared in the kitchen. Dolcé tried not to look around the flat too much because it totally grossed her out. "How can anyone stand to live in such self-imposed squalor?" she wondered. It also made her question Zimmerman a bit. Did he put up with it because he was just there temporarily, or was he a slob too? She told herself it didn't matter because he would leave her life in a couple of days. She had no desire to change any man, much less Zimmerman. "My talent is to love and leave them, not love and change them," she thought, making her giggle.

"What's so funny," inquired Zimmerman.

"Nothing, just an inside joke between us girls," she replied. "So, what are the plans?" she asked, changing the subject.

"I need to do rounds this afternoon. You are welcome to come with me if you wish," he said in a little louder voice than he would normally, so the other flatmates would hear. "This way, you will learn the ropes faster."

"Sure," Dolcé answered succinctly. She found a mug that didn't have anything floating in it and cleaned it off in the sink before pouring herself a cup of coffee. She wouldn't eat anything from the kitchen/fridge. "We need to go out and get something to eat. I just can't..." she shook her head and didn't finish her sentence.

"I understand," said Zimmerman. "I need to make a few phone calls; then we can go. Make yourself at home if you can stand to. I think it's safe to sit on the chairs. You shouldn't get any dread disease from them," he said with a teasing smile.

The flatmates came and went without paying much attention to Dolcé. She even saw a few unfamiliar females walking around the flat in all sorts of dress and undress. Dolcé looked at them carefully. They showed the classic signs of being trafficked, making Dolcé sad at first and then furious. "Not much longer," she said to herself and silently to the beleaguered women. "Just hang in there for another couple of days."

"Let's go," ordered Zimmerman once he finished the phone calls. Dolcé did not protest. She knew it was part of the act. She followed him out of the house without comment and automatically went to the van's passenger side.

They stopped at a local takeaway. Dolcé was craving a juicy American hamburger but knew better than to order one at the tacky little shop. They bought a pizza they could share, and it would be easy to eat in the van. "Hopefully, we'll have something a little more nutritious later," Dolcé hoped. "Oh well, at least it fills the hole for now," she said resignedly.

Over the next four hours, they drove to five of the houses/brothels. Not only was Zimmerman doing his job by collecting the weekly earnings and ensuring everyone was being appropriately controlled, but he was also scoping the properties for tomorrow's raids. Dolcé kept careful notes as she accompanied him into the houses. She mentally recorded the exact address, the floorplan, the number of women in each room and their locations, the number of guards, if any, and the general condition of the house, looking for any problem areas. She would then add the notes to her phone once they returned to the van. This information was then forwarded to the Interpol Agents to give them the latest intel.

Things went smoothly. Zimmerman didn't have to threaten anyone and didn't have to deal with any arrant behavior from the pimps or the women. Collections were ready and were within the acceptable range. It was a bit like the calm before the storm.

Zimmerman advised Dolcé to talk as little as possible while they were at their next stop. Surprisingly, he drove through a beautiful rod iron gate, up a very long driveway, and stopped in front of a two-story modern mansion. Two armed men greeted him as he exited the van with the duffel bag full of cash. They saw Dolcé, looked at her thoroughly, and signaled for her to get out of the van. Zimmerman assured her with a nod and a smile. They were invited inside for a drink, a reward for a job well done.

Dolcé slid out of the van and made herself as attractive as possible, which was not difficult. Looks of approval passed between the guards and Zimmerman as if to say, "prime meat, good going." Dolcé understood and shivered, although she didn't let her disgust show on her beautiful face.

Zimmerman wrapped his arm around her in a possessive gesture, stating to all around that she was his possession and he was proud of it.

They entered the open front door and were welcomed into a foyer of the impressive and expansive house. "And, who is this lovely thing," the owner of the house asked after looking her up and down at least four times lustfully.

"This is my girlfriend, Dolcé, Mr. Bingham. "I wanted her to meet you."

"I'm glad you did. Please, come in and have a drink by the pool," he instructed as he led them through the house to the back patio. Dolcé drew in her breath when she saw the opulence of the pool. It was huge, with a waterfall, a separate hot tub, and gold fixtures everywhere. She wanted to say, "Wow, I'm definitely in the wrong business," but she refrained and smiled without saying anything. She had wished Zimmerman would have warned her about this. She was caught off guard.

Although he was charming and gracious to Zimmerman and Dolcé, Bingham gave Dolcé the creeps in a significant way. Yes, she could believe this man was capable of anything, including murder. The hair at the back of her neck stood up from fright. This man was evil personified. She felt it with every cell of her body. She squeezed Zimmerman's hand to signal that she wanted to leave. He understood and said, "We'll pass on the drinks tonight, Mr. Bingham, but thank you," and guided Dolcé back into the house toward the front door.

"I hope you will come back soon, Dolcé," she heard Bingham say. "I'd like to get to know you better. Much better."

Dolcé had never before felt the sheer terror of a man, but she did with Bingham. Although she kept calm and pretended to be flattered by his attention, she wanted to scream and run out to the van. Thankfully, Zimmerman interpreted her feelings and offered his goodbyes to his boss without hesitation. Within thirty seconds, they were both in the van and exiting the property.

It took a couple of minutes for Dolcé to control her emotions. When she did, she said, "He is the most evil person I have ever met. Really and truly evil!"

"Yes, he is. I have worked for him for over two years and have seen what he is capable of. I hope we can bring him down tomorrow, but I doubt it. He is too well insulated with his bodyguards and his legion of lawyers. For now, we have to play his game."

"You did well," he added. "Thank you. I'm sorry for throwing you into this. I didn't know I would deliver the goods myself."

Dolcé had a thought. "Could it have been him that produced the movie?"

"Who's to say?" responded Zimmerman. "He is certainly capable of it. I don't know if he had the motivation to do something that despicable. I wouldn't put it past him."

"Oh my god, those poor women!" Dolcé exclaimed. "It is like the devil himself owns their bodies and souls! Let's get far away from here!"

Zimmerman obliged. Once they were out of range, Zimmerman pulled the van over so Dolcé could calm down. She took a few deep breaths and appeared to be meditating for five minutes before she was once again able to communicate coherently. "I'm sorry," she said. "I've never reacted so strongly to anyone like that before."

"No worries. I feel the same way. That is why I am doing what I am. I couldn't tolerate seeing the devastation to human life any longer. It just has to stop!"

Dolcé needed to report her findings to Agents Harris and O'Reilly. She called Jonathan's number and was very relieved to hear his voice. "Jonathan, I need to talk with you in person as soon as possible. Are you available," she asked shakily.

"I'm always available for you," he replied. "Can you come to the office, or should I meet you?"

"I'll meet you at the office," she said. "I'm with Zimmerman. He cannot be seen anywhere near the office but can drop me off at a tube station, and I will find my way to you." Zimmerman nodded his head in agreement. "I'll be there as soon as I can."

Dolcé had no idea where they were, but Zimmerman ensured she was thoroughly oriented before he dropped her off. "Are you going to be OK?" he asked thoughtfully.

"Yes, I'll be fine," she bravely assured him. "It will take a few hours, but I plan to spend the night with you to keep the charade intact. I'll meet you at your pub later. I will either call or text you and let you know," she added as she left the van and entered the tube station.

It took about forty minutes, but she made it safely to the office. Jonathan was in the lobby to greet her. "Thank goodness you're here and fine," he said sincerely. "When agents Davis and Smith saw you drive into the Bingham estate, they were really worried!"

Dolcé had utterly forgotten that she had protection with her at all times now. Nancy collapsed into Jonathan's arms and embraced him hungrily. "Oh, Jonathan, I was so terrified by that man! I could tell he wanted me for his new toy, and it paralyzed me with fright!"

"You're safe now. Come, let me get you a drink to help calm your incredibly strong nerves!" he said with admiration in his voice.

Nancy thought it strange that alcohol would be allowed in the office, but this was Britain, after all. She recalled that on every British cop show, nearly everyone had a bottle of whiskey stashed in their desk drawer for such occasions. Did drama mimic reality? She thought it might be so and didn't question Jonathan when he pulled a bottle of Jack Daniels from his bottom drawer along with two glasses. Nancy noticed the clean glasses and silently appreciated Jonathan even more than she had before. She only wished there was an ice cube or two to go with the whiskey. "You can't have everything," she chastised herself gently.

After a few minutes and two hefty drinks, Dolcé was calm and ready to talk. And talk she did. She described everything she had seen and heard in detail as Jonathan took notes. He was totally in awe of Nancy's chutzpah (he wasn't Jewish, but the Yiddish word described her best to Jonathan). Agent O'Reilly was also present and asked several questions that Nancy answered in great detail. This last-minute information was deemed very valuable, and other agents in the office were invited to join in. Before too long, twenty people crowded around Jonathan's desk, all anxious for answers and a swig of whiskey.

Two hours later, Nancy was talked out and exhausted. "Ok, guys, let's give Nancy a break," Jonathan announced to the small crowd. They dispersed without complaint, and most of the guys waved to Nancy before they left. It was clear that she had the respect of every person in the room.

After everyone but Jonathan and Nancy were gone, he gently wrapped his arms around her and held her close for over a minute, more like a protective older brother than a lover. Nancy felt the warmth and leaned into him. He felt like a welcome security blanket that had been misplaced and was just found. She didn't want to break the spell but knew it couldn't last forever. And it didn't.

Jonathan gently pulled away and looked Nancy deeply in the eyes. "You don't have to do this," he said sincerely. "You don't need to go back."

"Yes, I do!" she said, nearly crying. "Those poor women are depending on me to help them, whether they realize it or not. I cannot disappoint them or myself simply because I saw the face of evil personified today."

"You are one of the bravest person, man or woman, I have ever known," injected Jonathan.

"I'm not brave," said Nancy. "I'm furious. And you know what they say about a woman scorned. Well, I'm scorned big time!"

"How about some dinner?" asked Jonathan. "I think you've earned a nice meal."

"Oh, yes, please!" said Nancy excitedly. "The grub at the flat is horrible, and the neighborhood takeout isn't much better."

"There's a very nice place practically across the street called the Holborn Dining Room. Would you like to go there?" asked Jonathan.

"Again, yes, please!" she giggled, mimicking a little girl.

The restaurant couldn't have been more different from the tacky takeaway from earlier in the day. It was elegant, with lots of oak and antique mirrors, but with a modern twist. The menu looked absolutely delicious. Although the restaurant specializes in traditional British pies, Nancy didn't want all the crust and ordered grilled halibut with sprouting broccoli and mashed potatoes. She craved a healthy meal, and it appeared that she would finally have one. Jonathan went the more traditional route by ordering the curried mutton pie with a green salad.

Nancy didn't say anything, but she always thought of mutton as something tough and full of fat. She was hoping she would be pleasantly surprised.

The pie took twenty-five minutes to bake, so they had leisure time to have a pre-dinner cocktail. Nancy ordered a Manhattan on the rocks with some cherry juice, and Jonathan had a double Jack Daniels, also on the rocks. They sipped their drinks and chatted amicably, avoiding talking shop. That had talked enough shop for the evening and knew the next day would be filled with 'everything shop.'

Jonathan didn't want the answer but asked the question anyway. "When will you be going back to Chicago?"

The question startled Nancy. She looked at Jonathan with a confused look and replied, "I haven't even thought about it. Not once! So, my answer is, I don't know. I need to go back to work. I have patients who need me. I suppose I'll return on Saturday if I can get a reservation. That way, I can be available to begin work again on Monday," she added sensibly. "I guess it all depends on how things go tomorrow."

They spent the next two hours enjoying a truly memorably delicious meal. Nancy couldn't resist and ended dinner with a cup of coffee and the Blackberry and Apple Crumble with Vanilla Chantilly, which she shared with Jonathan. It was a perfect ending to a not-so-perfect day.

Nancy remembered that she had promised to call Zimmerman, so she did and explained that she would meet him at the pub in about an hour. That gave her enough time to finish the wine and the coffee before slumming it in Camden. Suddenly, going back to the hovel that was Zimmerman's home was not so appealing.

She did not share her feelings, though, because she knew that if she did, Jonathan would encourage her to quit, and she knew she couldn't even think about that.

"Thank you for everything," she said to Jonathan as she stepped out of his car two blocks from the Camden pub. Jonathan had refused to let her take the tube and insisted on driving her.

"No, thank *you* for everything!" he said decisively. "You have rocked my world in so many ways."

"Oh, Jonathan…" was all she could say.

"Please stay safe and call me in the morning. I'll be waiting for your call," he said through the open window. Then he drove away, and Nancy, now Dolcé, went to meet Zimmerman at the pub.

Chapter 29

The novelty of the English pub had worn thin with Dolcé, especially the Camden Town scene, with Zimmerman's cronies seeming to be everywhere. She hated their condescension toward women and their ignorant, brutish ways. An ironic thought came to Dolcé. "They will never be half the men I am," she thought glibly. To anyone else, the statement would seem strange. But anyone who knew Dolcé would understand completely.

Dolcé played her part of the adoring and submissive but very sexy and alluring girlfriend to the max. It was evident that if Zimmerman were no longer in the picture for some reason, the other flatmates would have pounced on her. But Zimmerman was careful not to leave her alone tonight, not even for a minute. It was too important that everything went well, that the charade continued for one more day.

Zimmerman joked with the guys while downing pint after pint of bitter, all the while carefully watching and listening for warning signs. He perceived none. Dolcé agreed later that she did not see anything out of the ordinary. They are just a bunch of gross overgrown bullies bellowing at each other.

They stayed until the usual closing time and then walked back to the flat arm-in-arm. They had a show to put on, but each also enjoyed the feel of the other's body against theirs. "Shall we do it one more time?" asked Dolcé. "For old time's sake? And for therapeutic reasons?"

Zimmerman knew he would have been a fool to resist, so he didn't. Although their sex was not frantic, it was satisfying for both parties and helpful in releasing some of the pent-up tensions they were feeling.

"Just what the doctor ordered," sighed Dolcé before she drifted off.

The morning began just like the morning before. Curses came from the filthy kitchen, and nearly naked men and women mingled in and out of the common rooms and bathrooms. It reminded Dolcé of some fraternity houses she had experienced in college. "Some boys never grow up," thought Dolcé as she searched for her coffee mug from the day before.

She continued to play the part of the beautiful but dumb and submissive girlfriend, even though it made her want to vomit. "It won't be long now," she kept telling herself.

She was able to go outside for some privacy and check in with the office. She was relieved to hear that all the plans were proceeding on schedule and everything was set to happen that afternoon. "One last time," said Jonathan. "You can bow out; nobody would think any less of you."

"Only I would," explained Dolcé. "No matter what happens, I want you to know how much your friendship has and will always mean to me, Jonathan. You have opened up a new life for me, and I appreciate it very much."

Jonathan was stunned because he would have said the exact words to Nancy/Dolcé if he had thought of them. "Ditto," was all he could mutter. Dolcé knew what he meant and was touched.

"OK, we'll try to keep in touch. We have our mission. I'll be safe and sound in my hotel later this evening if all goes well. If things don't go well, we'll all have to fake it until we make it. Don't worry about me. I can take care of myself. That is unless Bingham is anywhere near me. I think I'll lose it if I see him again!" Dolcé adamantly said.

"Well, we'll do our best to keep Bingham away," replied Jonathan.

"Thanks," said Dolcé and hung up.

Zimmerman had been loading the van while Dolcé was on the phone. "Be sure to get your stuff," he instructed Dolcé. "You may wish to leave something so it looks like you'll be back. Just in case someone is curious."

"Good thinking. When do you want to leave? I can be ready any time," said Dolcé. "

"That's what I like, a low-maintenance woman!" Zimmerman smiled and continued loading the van. "We need to be at the airport at one o'clock. The plane arrives at The plane arrives at 1:20, and it will take and it will take some time for the girls to clear immigration and customs. We can stop for breakfast if we leave here between ten thirty and eleven. We must eat soon because we can't be sure when our next opportunity will be."

Dolcé went into the flat and returned with her packed duffel bag that she had been careful to conceal from the others. She didn't want them to ask questions. Not that they would care enough to ask questions. She was just chattel and was not significant in their eyes.

"Chattel, indeed," she whispered. "We'll see about that!"

The time to leave came quickly, and with an increased heart rate and minimally shaking hands, Dolcé climbed into the van and into her future.

They stopped on the way to Stansted Airport, and each had a hardy breakfast with multiple cups of strong coffee. While eating, they reviewed the details one last time. The plan was to meet the new arrivals, drug them, transport them to the new location and then let Interpol raid the house and "save" the victims while arresting all others involved, which might include Zimmerman and Dolcé if it was necessary to keep their covers intact. The raids on the other houses were timed to occur while Zimmerman and the company were driving back from the airport. Zimmerman would not be involved in the other raids and would have an alibi in case there were questions from the gang at a later time.

Dolcé noticed the two extra guards were nowhere to be seen. "They will meet us at the airport," explained Zimmerman. He wasn't aware of the Interpol chaperones, but Dolcé appreciated the extra backup.

Their trip to the airport was uneventful. Traffic was light, and the day was overcast but without rain. They arrived at the short-term parking lot at precisely one o'clock, and the plane was due to land in twenty minutes. Zimmerman retrieved the handwritten sign saying "Bine ati venit," "welcome" in Romanian.

The sign reminded Dolcé that she had intended to learn a few Romanian phrases but had been distracted and forgot.

The two brutish bodyguards arrived and joined Zimmerman. They exchanged a few words and then stood quietly behind the van. Nobody would escape them! Dolcé also looked around to see if she could spot the Interpol agents. She couldn't. "I guess that's a good thing," she said to herself. "If they are here." The thought of them not being around frightened her, but she knew she needed to focus on the mission ahead and not worry about things she could not control.

Zimmerman and Dolcé joined the crowd in the International Arrivals Hall, watching for the arrival of their prey. Zimmerman straightened, signaled Dolcé to join him with a big smile, and held up the sign. Six women, mostly in their early to mid-twenties, were grouped together, shyly progressing into the Hall. It was like Zimmerman was a Tour Director for a prestigious tour company, meeting the new guests. The women saw his smiling face and sign, perked up, and willingly followed him to the waiting van. Dolcé offered each "guest" a glass of cold punch and some pastries, which each girl thankfully accepted and consumed.

Still smiling, Zimmerman collected their passports as if it was the most natural thing in the world to do and invited each of them into the van. "Buckle up," he said pleasantly after the luggage had been successfully stowed and everyone comfortably seated in the back. The atmosphere was still happy and congenial. Dolcé rode shotgun in the front passenger seat. She saw the two bodyguards in an SUV directly behind the van.

Unsuspecting, the women relaxed, and most fell asleep within twenty minutes of leaving the airport. So far, the mission was going perfectly. "Better not tempt fate," said Dolcé to herself. "The mission isn't successful until it is done."

Her words were prophetic. Fifteen minutes later, Zimmerman received a call. One of the bodyguards reported that something was happening in town. He didn't know what, but it wasn't good. Their instructions had not changed, and Zimmerman was to proceed to the house as planned. They just wanted him to know that things may change quickly.

Zimmerman hung up the phone. "The raids have begun," he said, returning to his driving.

Their arrival at the house was calm and controlled since the women were still asleep in a drugged stupor. The front door was opened, and the women were gently escorted inside and placed on a bed to sleep things off. The bodyguards were called to an emergency at another location and left quickly. Zimmerman and Dolcé were then ordered to stay until the "managers" arrived to take over. This would be the perfect time for the raid on this location. Dolcé phoned Agent Robinson to report their status and was told to stand by while he checked with the team that was assigned to them.

Dolcé's phone rang ten minutes later. It was Agent Robinson following up as promised. "We're having some issues in your area, and the team won't be available for another forty-five minutes to an hour. You do have your two undercover men standing by, just in case. I would recommend you call them now and give them a status report. That will save me from having to do it. As you can imagine, I'm a little busy right now."

Dolcé thanked him and proceeded to call Agents Smith and Davis to provide them with the update. She told them all was well but that things could change at any moment. The delay of the raiders was concerning because Zimmerman had been told to expect the two pimp managers to show up at any moment. Zimmerman and Dolcé had agreed they would not allow the pimps to enter the house, even if it meant using excessive force. If there was to be a confrontation, Dolcé wanted to be sure that Agents Smith and Davis were ready and able to respond. She felt somewhat relieved when they confirmed they were close by and in position.

Ten tense minutes later, an SUV pulled into the driveway. Two burly men got out and headed up the sidewalk to the front door. Zimmerman recognized them as Bingham's personal bodyguards and was instantly concerned. These were not the regular pimps that were supposed to be here. He understood that something was very wrong!

Zimmerman immediately slammed and locked the multiple deadbolts on the door. He called to Dolce and instructed her to retreat upstairs to one of the bedrooms and to be ready for trouble. She obeyed instantly, hesitating only long enough to retrieve the pistol she had hidden the day before and quickly texting an SOS to Agents Smith and Davis.

Dolcé's senses were on high alert. The hairs on the back of her neck were erect with tension. She found a strategically advantageous hiding place behind a bunk bed in one of the first-floor bedrooms, where she had a clear sight line to the closed door. She checked the pistol to make sure it was loaded and ready to fire. She was hoping not to use it, of course, but wanted to be prepared for the worst. Luckily, the women continued their peaceful, drugged slumber without stirring.

Dolcé listened intently, but couldn't hear much from the upstairs bedroom. Then she heard knocking on the front door, followed by insistent pounding and muffled shouting. She checked her phone to see if Agents Smith and Davis had responded to her SOS. They had but hadn't arrived at the house, so she signaled once again to call for help.

Zimmerman had no choice but to react by yelling back at the two men. Obscenities from both sides of the door echoed throughout the neighborhood. "This is not good," said Dolcé to herself. "Not good at all!"

"These women are my responsibility," Dolcé heard Zimmerman yell, "I am not going to let you molest them."

"We're not here for the Romanians," shouted one of the goons. "We are here to take your pretty little morsel of a girlfriend and present her to Mr. Bingham."

Dolcé's blood ran cold. If she were to be captured, she knew exactly what was going to happen to her. She had to do whatever was necessary to prevent that, even if it meant defending herself alone.

The shouting and obscenities increased to a feverish level. Suddenly a gunshot rang out and Zimmerman screamed in pain. Dolcé wanted to run to him but knew that would be a fatal mistake. Instead, she sank even lower into her hiding place. One hundred percent of her focus was now on the door to the room. She trembled with fear and adrenaline, and her heart was nearly pounding out of her chest. "Calm down, and breathe," she told herself. She took five deep breaths in through her nose and then exhaled from her mouth, which helped to calm her. She braced the pistol against the post of the bed and aimed it steadily at the closed door. She was ready for whatever might happen next.

Dolcé heard heavy footsteps...first on the ground floor, then on the stairs, and finally coming down the hall to the bedrooms.

She knew that her actions in the next few moments might be the difference between life and death for her and possibly the sleeping women.

The doorknob of the bedroom turned silently and the door began to open slowly. "What do you want?" shouted Dolcé to the unseen assailant. She knew that by calling out she had given away her location, but also knew that it was just a matter of time until she was discovered. This way she was in charge. "You can't have me, or any of the women. Go away," she insisted.

"Not on your life. We have a job to do and we're not leaving until we have you safely in our custody," one goon replied.

"What does Bingham want with me? I only met him once," cried Dolcé.

She wanted to add that she was armed and would shoot if they came any closer, but refrained because they would then have the advantage.

"You may have only met him once, but he's had his eyes on you for weeks. He wants you to be the star of his next film production. Don't you want to be a star?" the voice asked menacingly as he began to advance through the bedroom door.

"No, not at all. Please tell Mr. Bingham I respectfully refuse," replied Dolcé sarcastically.

"Mr. Bingham wouldn't like that. We don't want to make him angry. This is your last chance," warned the goon. "Come voluntarily or we will have to use force," said the second voice.

Dolcé now understood that Bingham's two men had come upstairs together, and could imagine just what kind of force they would use. The fear left her. What remained was sheer fury and hatred.

A gun began to protrude through the opening door. It was pointed at the center of the bedroom, ready to sweep to the corners to find Dolcé. She saw the gun, realized the imminent danger, and did not hesitate.

Aiming carefully at the hand that held the gun, Dolcé pulled the trigger. A scream filled the air, the gun dropped to the floor, and the goon stumbled and fell into the hallway. Dolcé instinctively pumped two more shots through the open door, straight and low to the floor. She heard another scream of pain, and suddenly the second man burst through the door. Once again, Dolcé did not hesitate. She pulled the trigger, hitting him squarely between the eyes, killing him instantly.

Dolcé did not move. She needed to evaluate the situation and overcome her initial shock. She had never killed anyone before. The second bodyguard was clearly dead. He was lying on the floor motionless with blood gushing from his head wound. Shaken and a bit confused, she continued to point her pistol toward the door, not knowing whether the first bodyguard was dead or merely wounded.

Suddenly there were more voices coming up from the ground floor, and Dolcé readied herself for another onslaught from Bingham's men. She lowered her gun only after hearing Agents Smith and Davis identify themselves and recognizing their voices. They had barged into the house after hearing the gunshots, ready to assist Dolce in any way necessary.

With great relief, Dolcé yelled, "I shot Bingham's men and I think they're dead. I'm upstairs in the first room to the left."

As Agents Smith and Davis entered the room, they found Dolce crouching in her hiding place, perfectly still. "Are you injured?" Agent Davis asked. "You were right. Bingham's men are both dead," he added gently.

I'm not hurt," she answered quickly, "just in shock. And, all the women are untouched and safe," she answered. "How is Zimmerman?

"We don't know," said Agent Smith. "We were so intent on saving you that we didn't check on him. He was lying on the floor, unconscious as we hurried in to help you."

Since Dolcé knew she was safe, she quickly ran to Zimmerman, who was critically injured but not dead. Agent Davis called for an ambulance while Nancy instinctively went into her nursing mode and knelt down to apply pressure to the hemorrhaging wound in his left shoulder.

"Stay alive," she pleaded to him quietly while keeping pressure on his wound. "We need you," she added sincerely.

Within five minutes, it seemed like half of the police force of London had descended on the house. EMS had patched Zimmerman up and transported him to the ambulance, IV already running full bore. They also assessed Dolcé, who was fine physically, except for some mild shock from the incident. She accompanied Zimmerman to the hospital, and Agent Smith attended to them both. There would be many questions to ask and answer.

Female officers were escorting the unconscious and groggy women to a mini-bus, and officers were already marking the crime scene and covering the two dead bodyguards.

The street was filled with flashing lights and curious neighbors. "So much for getting in and out without much commotion," said Agent Davis to another officer.

Chapter 30

By the time they reached the hospital, Zimmerman was stable, and Dolcé was a mess. She had been in combat before, but as a healer, not a killer. The gravity of her having killed two people seeped into her consciousness like the water in a live cave, one drop at a time. Rationally, she knew that she had done the only thing possible. She was defending herself and all six of the women from those monsters. Irrationally, she wondered if she could have done it without ending their lives.

Then rationally again, she realized the possible consequences if she hadn't defended herself. The two goons were on assignment from Bingham to bring her in, so he could do to her what had been done to that poor girl in the flash drive video. She was sure of it. She was also convinced that Bingham was the one who filmed the snuff video. Probably in his home. He was rich enough to lure any innocent, unsuspecting girl into his web and evil enough to play with her like a cat would with a mouse until he tired of the game and ended it and her. The evil she perceived in him was pervasive and palpable. She had wanted to shower in holy water just thinking about him, and she was not religious.

As Zimmerman was wheeled into the hospital Emergency Department, Dolcé was escorted into a private waiting room by Agent Smith, who was to keep her company until Agents Harris and O'Reilly could make an appearance. Agent Smith did not ask any questions. That would be left to someone else. He was there primarily to ensure she was mentally and physically safe and did not need a thorough medical evaluation and treatment.

Dolcé was at the hospital for an hour before Agents Harris and O'Reilly arrived. When she saw him, she ran into Jonathan's arms like a small child. She even cried a bit, which she hadn't done in years. Agent Smith was excused to perform other duties, and the three sat around a hardwood table and chairs to recap precisely what had occurred.

Dolcé went into great detail about every aspect of the successful transfer of the women to the house. It had gone perfectly. The women were completely oblivious to their fates and made no effort to escape. Until Bingham's goons had shown up, everything had gone according to plan. Dolcé did say that the raid team had been late to arrive, but if they had arrived on time, there may have been many more casualties.

She also went into great detail about when Zimmerman answered the door. How she hid in a bedroom, the yelling, the gunshot and scream, the stalking her with a pointed gun, defending herself and the women, shooting the two men trying to break into the bedroom, and having Agents Smith and Davis arrive on the scene.

"Please don't take this the wrong way," said O'Reilly. "But, why did you shoot them so quickly? Was there any other choice you could have made?"

"I shot to defend the women in the bedroom where I hid. And no, they had already shot Zimmerman, and whoever it was led with the gun pointed towards me. I felt and still feel that if I hadn't fired, he would have done bodily harm to all the women in the room and me. I had no choice." Dolcé said decisively.

O'Reilly asked Dolcé a thought-provoking question, "And why did you shoot to kill instead of just shoot to injure."

"That's a fascinating question," Dolcé began. "One that doesn't have a simple answer. But I will say that I was trained to kill if I had to use a weapon of this sort. Training like that stays with a person for a lifetime. And everything happened so fast. There was no time for decisions. Instinct took over, and I got off some lucky shots. They would have killed me in a heartbeat if they had a split second opportunity," she ended. "Did I answer your question to your satisfaction?"

"Yes, thank you," said O'Reilly quietly.

Dolcé shared the terror she felt when she met Bingham. "Nobody has ever made me feel so vulnerable. The evil permeated from his pores."

Dolcé had no idea who Bingham was before they were introduced at his house, and she certainly wasn't aware that he knew her identity. Dolcé also believed that Zimmerman had not known that Bingham had recognized her.

"And I am sure Bingham had something to do with that snuff film on the flash drive. When his goons were after me, I asked them what they wanted. They said they were sent to get me because Bingham wanted me as his special guest and recognized me from Berlin even with my new look. A few days ago, Zimmerman told me I had been chosen as the next film star. I am now putting the pieces together and seeing Bingham's face."

"How is Zimmerman?" she asked, remembering where they were.

"He is in surgery. The nurse said he is going to be fine," Jonathan explained.

"Oh, thank goodness!" sighed Dolcé.

"We will take you back to the hotel, where I want you to get a good night's sleep. We will pick you up in the morning," said Jonathan. "No arguments," he added when he saw she was getting ready to protest.

"How did everything else go?" she asked.

"Well, things are still going on right now, but so far, so good. We hit all fifteen houses. We'll hear the reports tomorrow morning. If you're up for it, you are welcome to join in," O'Reilly remarked.

"I'll see how I feel," she replied. "Jonathan, will I be prosecuted for shooting those goons?"

"You will need to answer questions, but there is no doubt in anybody's mind that you acted in self-defense. Any legal proceedings will be a formality only. Please don't be concerned about that," said Jonathan assuringly. "I am more concerned with your mental well-being."

"Please don't worry about that. I am not upset that the goons are dead. It was either them or me…and I prefer them," she said.

"Hmmm," hummed Jonathan. It seemed like a firm answer. That didn't sound like Nancy. She had been through a lot over the last few days. The stress was bound to have given her strong emotions.

"We realize that Bingham is still out there. We want to keep you protected until he is arrested and cannot get to you. We will escort you in and out of the hotel but don't feel you have to have a guard outside your door. Hopefully, after tonight we will have enough evidence against Bigham to get him to put away for decades. We have always had trouble getting the hard evidence against him in the past," continued O'Reilly.

"And Zimmerman?" she asked. "What is to become of him?"

"He will be in the hospital for a few days. We will have a twenty-four-hour guard on him. After he is discharged, he has many options we haven't discussed with him yet," said O'Reilly. "But be assured, he will be treated fairly."

Jonathan offered to take Nancy back to the hotel and Nancy thanked him gratefully. There was no reason for her to hang around the hospital. Zimmerman would be unconscious until tomorrow at least. She was feeling well enough not to need to be babysat overnight. She just appreciated having Jonathan there for her.

Once they reached her room and were finally alone, he gave Nancy a long and warm hug. "I was so worried about you," he said. "When we heard that shots had been fired, I had mental images of you being injured, lying on the floor bleeding. Boy, was I wrong!" he chuckled.

"The moral of that story is to never underestimate Nurse Nancy!" she chimed in.

"I promise I never will again," said Jonathan as he raised his right hand in the Boy Scouts pledge salute.

"You'd better not," she added. Suddenly she became serious. "Really, Jonathan, I don't know what I would have done without you these two weeks."

"Well, I'd better get back to the office," Jonathan said weakly. "I am sure the stories will be rich and numerous after today's raid."

"I understand," she whispered. "But, could you stay with me until I fall asleep? I don't want to be alone tonight."

"Of course," he said and sat in the chair.

Nancy went into the bathroom and came out in her comfy pajamas. "I'm very tired, but I'm not sure I can get to sleep right now. Will you just hold me for a while?"

They crawled onto the bed and under the sheets, Jonathan fully clothed after he managed to quickly remove his shoes. Nancy cuddled up spoon-like in his warm embrace and was asleep almost immediately. Jonathan felt so profoundly moved by her innocent gesture that he stayed longer and also fell asleep. He awoke two hours later, slightly panicked knowing he was expected at the office. Gently, slowly and quietly he extricated himself from her embrace without waking her.

Jonathan looked down on his sleeping Nancy. "What an angel she appears to be right now," wistfully, but then after his expression changed, "but what a little devil she can be at times," this time smiling at the irony.

He kissed her lightly on the forehead before he turned out the lights and made sure the door was tightly closed and locked before he headed for the elevator.

Chapter 31

Nancy was astonished at the noise level when she entered the Interpol building late Thursday morning. What seemed like hundreds of variously uniformed officers were milling about, congregating in huddles, meeting around desks, and slapping each other on the back in congratulatory celebrations. Obviously, Wednesday's raids were highly successful, which made Nancy very proud and extremely happy.

"You look like the Cheshire cat that just ate the canary," one of Interpol's agents said to Nancy as she passed him by. "Why are you grinning so broadly?"

"No reason, except the atmosphere in here is contagious. It makes me smile just seeing how happy everybody is!" Nancy explained as she continued down the hall to Agent Harris' office.

He smiled brightly when he realized Nancy was standing next to him. "Good morning!" he said musically. "It's good to see you looking so well," he added in a professional voice. "You should have let us pick you up. I thought we had agreed that you would be guarded at least for a few days."

"Please don't scold me," she said sincerely. "You don't have to fuss. I'm fine."

"Well then, since you are here, Agent Robinson requested to see you the moment you arrived. I will take you to him now," he stated in his most concise agent voice.

Agent Robinson was surrounded by very important-looking people as Nancy entered the conference room. They all looked up to stare at her when Agent Harris announced her arrival. As if on cue, everyone broke into thunderous applause for Nancy. Someone shouted, "Three cheers for Nurse Nancy!"

"Hip hip hurray. Hip hip hurray. Hip hip hurray!" shouted everyone in the British tradition.

Nancy was nearly knocked off her feet by the sheer noise of it all.

Agent Robinson worked his way through the crowd to her, shook her hand enthusiastically, and finally decided he would go in for the big bear hug, which he did. Nancy loved it. Someone in the back of the crowd shouted, "Speech!"

Nancy was shuffled to the front of the room and encouraged to say something.

"Well," she started. "I'm not sure what all the fuss is about. I just started the ball rolling. The mission was only successful because every person did their job, kept things quiet, and worked as one large team. I have never seen different agencies work so well together! You all should be very proud of yourselves and everyone on your team. Hopefully, London and maybe even the world will hear of what we have done by saving those one hundred women from an endless life of slavery and addiction. I want to thank the Interpol team who listened to my story and included me in their family, especially Agents Robinson, Harris, and O'Reilly." Applause for the team was loud and generous. "I cannot wait to hear the results of yesterday's raids. I understand that the mission isn't over until we reunite the victims with their country and family, and convince them of their freedom. Our mission was to cut the beast off at the knees. We accomplished that. To what extent? Only time will tell. There are other parts of the beast we need to attack and defeat. The person that comes to mind more than anyone is Mr. Bingham. His evilness is too dangerous to be tolerated. We need to exterminate his type of vermin...legally, of course," she added quickly.

Her little extemporaneous speech was well received. She spent the next few minutes shaking hands, although she didn't understand why they were making such a fuss over her.

"Nancy, if you could take a seat, we are just about ready to call everyone in for announcements and a summary of yesterday's raids."

"Gladly," she said and took the nearest empty seat as the rest of the room filled quickly, and all the remaining empty chairs disappeared.

"Ladies and Gentlemen," began Agent Robinson. "We should all be congratulated for a job extremely well done yesterday!" A cheer rose, and people settled to hear the good news.

"As you know, our mission was to raid fifteen known houses/brothels where human trafficking victims were being kept, rescue the victims, arrest any traffickers we may encounter, and confiscate anything of value that could have been purchased with illegal earnings."

"I am happy to announce that all fifteen houses were raided successfully. From the fifteen houses, we recovered ninety-eight females and saved six more females from certain slavery directly from Stansted Airport. All the women are now in safe houses and are getting medical evaluations and treatment as needed as well as special services of social workers to discover what is best for these women's futures. Some will be transported home, mainly to Romania. Some will wish to stay in the UK, and each case will be evaluated separately. And some have agreed to testify against their captors.

We also arrested forty-nine suspected traffickers, including mostly lower-ranking pimps, house managers, and a few middle management workers. We could not arrest any of what we consider the higher echelon executives, but hopefully, that will come shortly.

We also confiscated ten late-model vehicles, five kilos of cocaine, and more than one thousand Fentanyl pills.

And I am very pleased to announce there was only one significant injury of one of our people and two fatalities, along with several minor injuries of the suspected traffickers. The one injured undercover informer had surgery last night and is expected to make a full recovery in a few weeks.

"We succeeded in seriously injuring the cartel, hopefully critically. Now, the attorneys and the legal system will hopefully do their jobs and shut these places down for good."

The entire crowd jumped to their feet and spontaneously yelled a victory cheer to celebrate their outstanding achievement. It took nearly five minutes for the group to finally settle so Robinson could continue his talk.

"We have temporarily cut off the income source for this cartel, but they will be back like rats in the sewers if we don't continue to clean out our city. We will work towards a city-wide interagency campaign to keep the vermin out. Please look for further announcements about this in the upcoming weeks. You are dismissed, and thank you all!"

Nancy was swept up into a group of unfamiliar officers until Jonathan rescued her.

"Oh, my hero," Nancy swooned and batted her eyelashes, which made Jonathan laugh.

"I'm glad to see you're doing well today. Sometimes the day after can be emotionally difficult," he said with sincerity.

"I slept well, thanks to you. Normally that's all I need to recharge the batteries. And yes, I am fine psychologically. I have no regrets about my actions," she added.

Jonathan was amazed at how easily Nancy/Dolcé could compartmentalize her life and the people in it. How easily she shifted from a caring and involved "girlfriend" to being able to walk away without a backward glance. It was something he didn't understand about her, but he realized there were many things he would probably never understand, and that was OK.

Nancy patiently answered the same questions over and over at the many interrogations she was required to attend regarding her involvement with the rescue of the victims from the airport and the shooting in the house.

She understood that a formal inquest was needed and knew the officers were doing their jobs. The more thorough they were now, the less chance she would have to relive the incident later. After the fifth interview, she was officially cleared to leave the office and the country if she wished.

Although Nancy knew that she had done nothing wrong, it was a relief for her to be formally exonerated for her actions. At least by the police. A wave of dread came over her. The police had only wounded Bingham, and his hierarchy of monsters had not been destroyed. Nancy knew all too well that a wounded animal was much more dangerous than a healthy one. She realized he would come for her in one way or another. Maybe not today or this week, but next month or next year. She was sure of it. She would never feel a hundred percent safe from his wrath until he was eliminated.

The question she kept asking over and over again to anybody who would listen was what could be done to put Bingham out of commission forever. That was her only goal at this point. Nobody had an answer for her, but they promised to find a solution. She was told that they were doing all they could. That may be true, but she could also work to protect herself without their help. She had proven to herself and everyone else that she was capable of almost anything once she put her mind to it. She was not going to let Bingham and company get away literally with murder if she had anything to do about it!

Nancy asked permission to visit Zimmerman in the hospital, which was granted without hesitation, then asked Jonathan if he would drive her to see him and then drop her off at the hotel, which he readily agreed to do.

"Before that, however, I need to make a quick trip to the infirmary. I almost forgot that I won't need the GPS anymore." Twenty minutes later, she was ready to go. The only evidence of her minor procedure was a tiny Band-Aid attached to the back of her neck.

Zimmerman smiled when he saw Nancy approach his bed. He had thick bandages seemingly everywhere, and his left arm was in a sling, but he was breathing without supplemental oxygen and looked a lot better overall than she expected.

Nancy spent a few minutes whispering to Zimmerman, telling him how thankful she was for everything he had done and that she was glad he was going to be OK. She also planted the seed about helping her bring Bingham down if the authorities couldn't or wouldn't do it themselves. He agreed to help her in any way he could. There was no talk about seeing each other again socially. Their mission was complete, and there was no point.

Jonathan observed Nancy's lack of emotional bond with Zimmerman, even though they had spent much intimate time together. It was neither good nor bad; it just was. And it was an observation he stored away in the farthest recesses of his brain. An observation that might come in handy in the future…or not.

"Where to?" asked Jonathan as they left the hospital.

"Back to the hotel for now, but I'd like to spend the rest of the day with you if you are available," she said.

"I have the rest of the day off, so your wish is my command," replied Jonathan gallantly.

Jonathan understood Nancy's need for privacy and offered to leave and come back. She waved that idea away with her hand and invited him to her room despite her need to regroup after the morning's excitement. He patiently and quietly made himself comfortable and nearly invisible by drinking a beer and checking his official correspondence while she gathered her thoughts privately on the balcony.

Nancy suddenly realized it was time to go home to her real life in Chicago. She called the airline and made a reservation to fly home on Saturday afternoon. That would give her almost two more days to tie up loose ends and do a bit more sightseeing. Nancy felt relieved once the reservations were made and an "end time" was set.

"Look," Jonathan began. "It's been a rough few days for both of us. We could use some good old escapism. How about I give you a few hours to regroup and pick you up later? How would you like to see a West End show? I know you haven't seen one before, and it would be a great way to finish your unforgettable trip to London."

"Gosh, I hadn't thought of it, but it sounds great! You choose whatever performance you like, and I'm sure I'll love it," she said. "You always know just the right thing to say and do. Thank you."

"OK, I'll see you around six thirty. We can grab something quick to eat and walk around the theater district before the performance starts at eight. You don't have to dress up. It's more important that you are warm and comfortable tonight," he added.

"See you then," Nancy said.

Jonathan left the room and stopped by the front desk on his way out. He arranged for Nancy's hotel bill to be paid in full by Interpol so she would not have any problems checking out on Saturday. "Just one less thing to think about," said Jonathan to himself. He was looking forward to a nap this afternoon and headed home with a smile.

Chapter 32

Nancy spent the afternoon trying to wrap her mind around the events of the last two weeks. It had been fourteen days since she left Chicago, but it seemed like a lifetime ago. So much had happened, both positive and negative. She was happy with how things concluded, except that Bingham was at large and above the law for all intents and purposes. Someone high up was protecting him; she didn't know who or why. She tried not to obsess but wasn't very successful. She could feel his malevolence every minute of the day. He would always be a danger to her as long as he wasn't in prison or dead. She understood that, but she felt helpless to change the circumstances. She wasn't, nor would she ever be a vigilante, and that is what it would take to rid her of his menace.

She was able to get a power nap in before getting ready to go to the theater. She was excited about the prospects of attending a real professional show and wondered what play or musical Jonathan picked for her. She was hoping for something funny and entertaining. After the few days she had had, she didn't need heavy drama or tragedy. She had seen plenty of that in real life.

Jonathan was right on time. He explained they would be taking public transport tonight because driving in the theater district is a huge hassle, and parking would be nearly impossible. Nancy didn't mind one little bit and told him so.

She squealed with delight when Jonathan announced that they would see 'Kinky Boots' and gave her a brief synopsis of the show. "Charlie inherits a failing shoe factory from his father. He forms an unlikely partnership with a drag queen named Lola and saves the factory by producing high-heeled boots for men described as two feet of irresistible tubular sex." Jonathan continued, "The show has great music and incredible choreography and is just about the best night I have ever experienced in a theater."

"Oh, you've seen it before?" asked Nancy. "Wouldn't you prefer to see something new?"

"No way!" replied Jonathan with gusto. "I would see it again and again if I could. It's that good!"

"I can't wait," said Nancy enthusiastically. Nancy knew Dolcé would adore the performance and might even get some make-up ideas from the drag queens! It would be an evening of pure joy and delight, just what the doctor ordered.

She grabbed her coat, and they made their way to the tube station, hand in hand. Being with Jonathan had become the most comfortable thing in the world for both Nancy and Dolcé. He had become a big brother, best friend, confidant, and protector. Nancy did not care if there was no romance in their relationship. She had had plenty of empty romance. She would take this feeling over romance any day!

They had a pub dinner and the requisite pint before joining the queue to get into the theater. As they entered, Nancy was awestruck by the architecture, the beautiful décor, and the old-fashioned wooden seats upholstered with red velvet. "This is exquisite!" she whispered to Jonathan with wonder in her voice. Even the ceiling is incredible! And the chandeliers are magnificent! If the performance is half as impressive as the theater, it will be an evening to remember for the rest of my life," she exclaimed sincerely.

And they weren't disappointed. It was a fantastic show! Full of laughter, gorgeous costumes (and that's on the men, for heaven's sake!), fun songs, outstanding choreography, and even some life lessons. Nancy was able to forget herself completely and was totally absorbed in each minute of the performance. "Is this what the theater is all about? Goodness, what I have been missing," was all she could say.

Jonathan just laughed at the innocent joy on Nancy's face. He did not want that expression to fade, so he suggested they walk to Piccadilly Circus and have a drink at an outdoor café. That way, they could absorb the bling of the area and do some significant people-watching. Nancy loved the idea and agreed eagerly.

Piccadilly Circus was filled with the usual spectacle. The one-hundred-foot billboards were blazing with thousands of LED lights, street performers everywhere trying to make a few pounds by playing an instrument or pretending to be a statue, and thousands of pedestrians milling back and forth, just enjoying the party atmosphere.

Despite the cold, Jonathan and Nancy spent two hours sipping their drinks, gayly chatting about fun topics, and just enjoying life. They huddled together to keep warm, which was only an excuse. They just liked the feeling of the other person close to them. Comfortable, safe, and easy with no expectations. Just perfect!

At 1 a.m., they were ready to head back. The evening had been charming. Nancy was sure she would remember it fondly for the rest of her life.

"Once again, thank you, Jonathan," she said sincerely. "Words cannot express how you have made my world so much better," she added as she opened the door to her room.

It had been decided that Jonathan needed his beauty sleep and would be heading home because tonight was a "school night," and he would be expected at work in the morning.

"You are more than welcome," was all he said before turning to leave. "Sweet dreams, and I'll see you tomorrow."

Nancy slept within twenty minutes, dreaming of drag queens in high-heeled boots. If anyone had been there to see her, they would have witnessed the big grin on her slumbering face. She was happy and content, if only for a fleeting moment.

Chapter 33

Nancy was rudely torn from her deep and dreamless sleep by something that sounded like thunder but from inside the hotel. "What the heck?" asked Nancy as she slowly regained consciousness. When she did, she realized that the "thunder" was someone pounding on her door. She looked at the clock: 5:23 a.m. She called to the visitors, "give me just a minute. I'll be right there," reaching for the robe the hotel had provided. She stopped in front of the door and looked through the peephole. She was surprised to see at least eight uniformed police officers looking back at her. She unlocked the security bolt and opened the door.

"Nancy Calloway?" asked the officer who was closest to her.

"Yes, I am she," she said formally. She recognized a few of the officers. They are the same ones who had congratulated her on a job well done less than 18 hours ago.

"May we come in?" asked the office once again.

"Yes, of course, if there is room for all of you," she added to break the tension.

Two officers stayed outside in the hall while all the others fanned out in the room, surreptitiously looking for anything incriminating.

"What is this all about?" she asked, truly confused.

"Where were you this morning from midnight to 3 a.m.?" the officer asked without preamble.

Nancy knew that this kind of question was never good. She suddenly panicked, wondering if Jonathan had been injured or worse on his way home. "Is it Agent Harris?" she squeaked suddenly on the brink of tears.

"No, Agent Harris is fine and on his way," the officer said. "Now, please answer the question."

"Well, last evening, I was with Agent Harris. We went to the musical "Kinky Boots," then had drinks in Piccadilly Circus until 1 a.m.. Then we took the tube back to Gloucester Road station. That would have been about 1:30 a.m., and then he walked me to my hotel, where I went straight to bed, by myself, and slept soundly until your pounding awakened me."

"Can Agent Harris corroborate that?"

"Yes, of course," Nancy answered, relieved but still confused. "I did not leave my hotel room after he dropped me off. Hotel CCTV should be able to verify it," she added.

The officers visibly relaxed but were still in their "police" mode.

"Will somebody please tell me what is going on?' she pleaded.

"Ms. Calloway. Are you acquainted with a man named Samuel Bingham?" the officer asked.

"I had met him once in his home. At the time, I did not know who he was, but he gave me the impression of being pure evil. I later found out that he is one of the high-echelon executives of the cartel we just brought down on Wednesday," she added. She knew that she shouldn't say more than she was asked. That was an excellent way to get in trouble even when you had done nothing wrong.

"Do you have any reason to want to see him dead?" he continued.

"Of all the people I have ever known, he deserved death more than anyone for what he did to hundreds of innocent women and probably children," she said earnestly. "Why do you ask?"

"Because Samuel Bingham was discovered dead in his home this morning. He had been shot numerous times," the officer confided.

Nancy was shocked but delighted and couldn't hide the glee on her face. "That's probably not the best reaction to the news you could give to a bunch of on-duty cops," she chastised herself.

Nancy couldn't control herself and knew she might regret it later, but she said, "It couldn't have happened to a more deserving, thoroughly evil deviant! But I didn't kill him," she added quickly.

"Do you know a man named Wolfgang Zimmerman?" he continued.

"Yes. Zimmerman and I worked together. He is the person who introduced me to Bingham just a couple of days ago. He is the informant who made Wednesday's raid possible. He and I were the ones who met and escorted the new Romanian arrivals to their new house and liberated them. He was one of Bingham's trusted deputies until he was exposed as a traitor and seriously injured during the confrontation with Bingham's goons. He was trying to protect me when he was shot. Again, why do you ask?"

"I think you should sit down," he instructed, which she did.

"Wolfgang Zimmerman was also found shot dead in Bingham's home."

Nancy gasped with disbelief. "But he was in the hospital. I saw him yesterday afternoon. Agent Harris and I visited him at about 2 p.m."

"Apparently, he removed his own IVs, borrowed some scrubs from a linen closet, and just walked out of the hospital during the shift change. We are unsure how he got by the guard outside his room, but that is a moot point."

"Did he have any reason to want Bingham dead?" the officer continued his questioning.

"Well, yes," said Nancy. "He hated what Bingham was doing to innocent women and children. He couldn't stand by any longer. That is why he produced the flash drive of evidence. But the straw that broke the camel's back was the snuff film. He realized that it was Bingham who had made the film and was probably the one in the mask who murdered that poor girl on camera. He couldn't stand it anymore. He wanted Bingham dead almost as much as I did."

She hesitated and then continued. "He didn't have much of a future with Bingham alive. He knew that Bingham would find and kill him eventually. Zimmerman didn't want to go into witness protection. It wasn't his style. He must have thought he had very little to lose and the world would have much to gain if Bingham was eliminated once and for all."

She didn't say she felt guilty for possibly pushing him into doing such a brave and stupid thing. She remembered their last conversation and how she had been so frustrated that Bingham would get away with everything. "Am I responsible indirectly?" she thought to herself but did not vocalize her concern. There was no need to muddy the waters.

It was then that Jonathan and Agent O'Reilly entered through the door. Nancy's first instinct was to run into his arms, but he was clearly in Agent Harris mode, and it would have been inappropriate.

"Ms. Calloway," Agent O'Reilly said conversationally, "Perhaps you would like to get dressed and accompany us to the office."

Nancy silently thanked him. She had felt very vulnerable in her robe and pajamas when everyone else was in full combat attire, Kevlar vests and all.

The officer in charge turned to Jonathan and asked him to corroborate that he and Nancy had been together at all times until approximately 1:30 a.m., which Jonathan did. "We went to 'Kinky Boots,' then walked to Piccadilly Circus and spent about two hours there having a drink and people-watching. Then at one o'clock, we returned to the hotel via the tube."

The stories matched precisely. Nancy's alibi was solid, but that didn't mean she wouldn't be helpful in the investigation.

Nancy dressed quickly in the bathroom and was ready to be escorted to whichever office/police station they decided to take her to. Jonathan signaled to her that he would be following right behind them and would be with her to answer questions. That made her feel better.

"You are not under arrest," stated the officer to Nancy. "You are not required to go to the station with us, but we would appreciate your presence."

"Of course, I will come with you. I have nothing to hide," she said with a bravado that she wasn't feeling very strongly. The shock of hearing that Zimmerman was dead hadn't sunk in yet, but it would, and soon.

Chapter 34

Nancy was once again the center of everyone's attention. "This is getting old," she said to herself. "I can do with a little less attention, thank you very much." She was now inside the Kensington police station on Earls Court Road. It was closest to the hotel and had a large enough conference room to hold the twenty officers present.

"Ms. Calloway, please tell us about your encounter with Mr. Bingham."

"I believe it was Tuesday evening, but it may have been Monday. I rode along with Zimmerman while he did his rounds, as they call it. He had several regular visits to a designated number of houses/brothels. That day we visited five of them. I posed as his girlfriend and as a trainee. At each house, he would collect the earnings from the previous week and count them carefully. If something didn't add up, it was his responsibility to find out why and dole out any punishments to anyone caught skimming off the top. He was also in charge of discipline when the pimps didn't feel they could handle a situation with the women. There were times when he had to be violent, and he hated it. On Tuesday there were no problems.

I tagged along to get as much information about each house as possible and passed it on to the raid team so they could have up-to-the-minute intel. I said very little; for the most part, I was entirely ignored by the pimps. Or so I thought!"

"What do you mean by that?" asked the head officer.

"I first encountered Zimmerman in Berlin at a nightclub. Someone had slipped some Ecstasy into my drink, so I was feeling no pain when he began dancing with me and put the infamous flash drive into my handbag without my knowledge. We snogged for a couple of minutes, and then he disappeared. It wasn't until the next day, when I was with Agent Harris, that I realized what had happened. The Berlin Interpol office was able to open the files on the flash drive, which eventually led to Wednesday's raid."

"Please continue," encouraged the officer.

"Not only was there a wealth of information on the flash drive, but there was also a graphic snuff film on it. Interpol made a copy, and I took the original into theU.S.and mailed it according to the instructions I found in my purse."

"I had not seen Zimmerman again until my first or second night here in London. He tried to approach me but was quickly arrested. The unique tattoo on his left neck had given him away. He offered his services to be an informer because he was tired of seeing so much suffering simply for greed's sake. Once Interpol felt he could be trusted, a plan was put into place to find and release approximately one hundred women who had been trafficked in the London area."

"All of this is in the report," Nancy finally said. "What is not in the report was Zimmerman's ignorance that Bingham had spotted me at the Berlin club that night and wanted me as his next "film star." So, he had seen me and had requested I be kidnapped and brought to him. That never happened, thank goodness!"

"What did happen is that the evening that Zimmerman had done his rounds so efficiently, Mr. Bingham had invited him to his home. We thought it was to reward a job well done. That was not the case. It turns out that despite me changing my appearance almost entirely, Mr. Bingham recognized me from before. He wanted me and only me. If he had succeeded in capturing me, I probably wouldn't be alive right now. We went into the house and out the back to the pool area. I paid close attention and still have a clear picture of the house's interior. We didn't stay long, just long enough to get a glance at how the other half lives."

"He recognized me, yes, but didn't let on to either myself or Zimmerman. He sent his goons to pick me up at the house where we had taken the arrivals. Fortunately, unbeknownst to anyone but me, I had two Interpol agents watching my every movement. They broke into the house to rescue me once they heard the gunshot that injured Zimmerman. Fortunately, I had already rescued myself. While the goons were stalking me, one of them said that Mr. Bingham was inviting me to be his new special guest. Of course, I was the next to be snuffed on camera. Thankfully, I shot first and straight."

"Yes," said the officer, breaking a smile. "We heard that Annie Oakley was among us," he added. His comment helped to break the tension in the room.

Changing the subject a little, Nancy said, "I strongly believe that if you look hard enough, you will find the "studio" where the snuff film was made."

"Would you be willing to come to the house with us?" asked the head officer. "It could help us a lot with our investigation."

"Sure, whatever I can do to help is my highest priority!" stated Nancy with conviction. "I can easily recognize the house's interior. I don't have any idea of its location. I was not driving at the time and was unfamiliar with the area."

"That is fine. We have the location along with the two bodies," the officer reminded her.

"Oops," injected Nancy. "I'm still in shock, I guess, and not thinking completely clearly." That was a bit of an understatement. Most people who had been through what Nancy had would have been halfway to a nervous breakdown. But not Nancy. She seemed to be made of pure steel; that's how strong she appeared.

Jonathan was assigned to accompany Nancy to Bingham's home, as both officer/agent and as comforter and friend. After hearing her story, it was clear that Nancy could have easily been Bingham's next victim. Instead, she had become the Crown's most valued witness. Almost instantly, she was treated like a queen instead of an alleged murderer.

Nancy and Jonathan sat in the back of one of the police squad cars on their way to Bingham's. Even though he was on duty, he held both of Nancy's hands in his as a caregiver and as a beloved companion. Nancy felt the connection and was slightly startled by the intimacy.

"Intimacy without lust," thought Nancy/Dolcé. "Hmmm. I wasn't aware that was even possible. Live and learn." Whatever it was she was feeling, she liked it!

"Nancy, if any of this is too much for you, just let one of the officers know," the head officer Billings said with compassion as they pulled up into Bingham's driveway.

"Hopefully, I'll be fine," she replied as they walked the short distance from the parking lot to the front door, which was slightly ajar.

Not knowing what to expect, Nancy grasped Jonathan's hand tightly, lowered her eyes, and entered the living room. Seeing nothing unusual, her confidence returned, and she was able to inspect the space thoroughly. There were no blood stains on the floor, but instinctively her feet headed for the back door and the pool area. "Come with me," she whispered to Jonathan. "Bingham liked showing off his opulence."

The pool area was anything but pristine. Furniture had been overturned; miscellaneous items were floating in the pool, and broken glass was strewn everywhere. Bingham's body was slumped near the diving board, swimming in a deep pool of coagulating blood. Had it not been for Nancy/Dolcé's sheer hatred, the sight would have made her instantly sick. Instead, she reveled in his miserable little death.

Seeing Zimmerman lying on the ground near the outdoor bar gave Nancy different emotions, and sorrow wasn't one of them. Sure, she was sorry for a life lost too soon. But more than grief, she felt pride and gratitude. Pride in Zimmerman for choosing to protect her no matter the cost, and the deepest gratitude for knowing that Zimmerman made the ultimate sacrifice for her. She knew it without having to be told. Zimmerman was a hero even if nobody else knew it.

Nancy stood silently for a few minutes, silently giving her thanks to the dead Zimmerman and offering her blessing for his life given so valiantly. She was not religious but said a silent prayer for his soul anyway. It just seemed like the right thing to do.

Jonathan was still there holding her hand. It had felt so much like an extension of her arm that she was startled a little when she saw his facial expression full of compassion. "I'm OK, Jonathan, really I am. I was just saying goodbye to Zimmerman."

When Nancy returned to the real world from her deep thoughts, she saw so many officers milling around that she couldn't count them all. She wondered where they had all come from. A clown car flashed across Nancy's mind, and she giggled but instantly stifled it. This was not the place for frivolity.

Officer Billings was approaching her. "Are you well enough to accompany me while I inspect the house?"

"Yes, of course," she said immediately. "Would it be OK if Agent Harris stays with me? I'm still a bit shaky." Officer Billings nodded.

"Now, if you were a door to a basement, where would you be?" questioned Billings, more to himself than to Nancy, but she answered anyway.

"It depends on what the basement is used for. A typical basement door would be off the kitchen, where it would be easy to access for storage. However, if the basement were used for more nefarious purposes, access would most likely be from the garage. That way, cargos could be unloaded from a vehicle and taken directly underground without neighbor's prying eyes," stated Nancy logically.

"We need to put this woman on the payroll!" Billings exclaimed.

"We already did," explained Jonathan. "At least temporarily," he said, looking at her with evident admiration.

Billings ordered his men to inspect the garage, and within two minutes, there was a call for Billings to join them.

They had found a solid metal door they suspected would lead to a basement. It was locked, but it didn't take long for a specialist to open the door and turn the lights on in the corridor.

"Nancy, stay here until we clear the area. Your safety must be our deepest concern." She did not argue and stood back while five other officers followed Billings down the stairs, pistols drawn and flashlights blazing.

Nancy stood for what seemed like hours, waiting to hear anything indicating that the officers had found something of interest. It had been less than five minutes when she heard an officer shout, "We need an ambulance here!" An officer at Nancy's side was using his radio to dispatch the EMS staff. They had been standing by and were in the basement in less than a minute. "We're going to need two more vehicles," Nancy heard the EMS call over her radio.

"What do you think is going on?" asked Nancy to Jonathan.

"I think they found someone down there. It appears that Zimmerman may have saved more lives than yours!" said Jonathan.

Billings emerged from the basement, slightly green but focused on managing the crime scene.

"It's pretty bad down there," he said before moving into the living room to bark out new orders.

Over the next half hour, three girls, all less than seventeen years old, were brought up from the basement on stretchers and immediately transported to the nearest hospital.

"They are all alive," stated Billings to the shell-shocked Nancy. "But barely. If Zimmerman hadn't caused this bloody scene, we would have never found the girls in time. I guess we should all call him a hero."

Nancy nodded weakly. "You may go downstairs if you wish," speaking to both Nancy and Agent Harris. "But don't touch anything," he added unnecessarily.

Jonathan searched Nancy's eyes, silently asking if she wanted to view the basement or not. She nodded, and they slowly started down the stairs. Upon reaching the bottom, Nancy observed a normal-appearing basement with relief. It wasn't until she heard "in here" that the dread overtook her. "Courage, my dear," she told herself as she took small steps toward the disembodied voice.

When Nancy and Jonathan entered the strongly reinforced false walled room, Nancy just about vomited, but she controlled the urge. The stench was as overwhelming as the sight of the "film studio." Instruments of torture covered in gore and blood were carelessly tossed on tabletops. Professional appearing cameras and lighting were positioned as if a crew would be arriving any minute to make sure that the one last take was perfect before putting the film in the can. And just out of camera view was a cage consisting of heavy bars (like a prison cell), a concrete floor with a drain, chains with handcuffs attached to the wall, and little else.

They had found the room that was on the flash drive. Jonathan saw Nancy's violent reaction to the unspeakably horrible scene and quickly helped her upstairs and out into the fresh air by the pool.

Nancy vomited into the bushes, and her body gyrated with the great sobs she had finally allowed to escape.

Jonathan held Nancy's hair back while she vomited and held her close until the howling sobs and convulsions calmed into barely audible whimpers and fine tremors. And then he continued to hold her. Nancy perceived the change and welcomed it. Jonathan's embrace had morphed from protective to passionate, although it had not tangibly changed to anyone but the two of them. Nancy deeply explored Jonathan's eyes. There was panic, sorrow, and relief in them. There was also undisguised love.

The mood was broken when Billings approached Nancy to ask her if she needed medical attention. "No, thank you," she replied. "I'm fine, or at least I will be in a couple of minutes." She gently extricated herself from Jonathan's arms.

"If it's not too much for you, I would appreciate it if you would identify both of the bodies while they are still here. It will save us and your time if it is done now instead of later at the morgue," Billings said almost apologetically.

Jonathan began to protest, but Nancy gently placed a hand on his chest and whispered, "It's OK. Thanks to you, I am fine now," and let Officer Billings lead her to the bodies that were now on gurneys covered in sheets.

Nancy pulled the sheet from Zimmerman's head and looked into his serene face. She looked carefully and acknowledged his identity. Before replacing the sheet, she bent down, kissed him on the forehead, and whispered her sincere thanks. "You are truly my hero, and I thank you more than you can ever know for saving and changing my life. You made mistakes, yes, but you have more than atoned for them with this selfless act of bravery. I will praise your name forever and will never forget you. Goodbye."

Dolcé had to say her goodbyes too. "I hope all the female angels are looking out for themselves because you're going to be very popular, you sexy thing," as she kissed him passionately.

Nancy then moved to the other gurney and not so gently removed the sheet. A gunshot had partially blown off Bingham's face. It seemed like poetic justice to Nancy. She formally identified him and bent down to say a few words over his lifeless body. "Good riddance, you evil son of a bitch! I hope there is a special corner in hell for you. May you rot painfully and eternally." She flicked the sheet back with a rude gesture that Billing couldn't help but witness and secretly approve of.

"She's got balls the size of Texas," he said only to himself. Then to the group, he announced, "The major work has been done.

The clean-up crews will be here for the next few hours. The rest of you should return to the station, where we will continue our investigation. Good work, everyone!" The room quickly emptied, and quiet was restored at last.

"As for you, Nancy, we cannot thank you enough. You once again have helped to save the day." Then changing the subject, "We will need to continue our questions when you feel up to it."

"I will be leaving London tomorrow afternoon. We will need to finish sometime today," she said. "When do you want me to be at the station?"

"Would one o'clock work? That way, you can go back to the hotel, clean up, have a meal, and have some time to unwind before the questioning begins. You do not need to worry about anything. You have done nothing wrong, and we know it. On the contrary, if it hadn't been for you, we would still be running around in the dark, and those poor girls would probably have died."

"I'll be there at one," and she turned to Jonathan. "Will you please take me back to the hotel?"

He answered so quietly that she could barely hear his response. "Of course, I will," was all he said.

As they walked out to the police car, Nancy turned to Jonathan and quietly asked him, "Did he leave a note?"

"Who?" asked Jonathan, genuinely puzzled.

"Zimmerman," she answered.

"I haven't heard, but I will check. If he did leave a note, it would probably be in his hospital room. I will ask the hospital staff and the officers who inspected his room. If there was a note I will make sure you get a chance to read it. It's the least we can do for you," said Jonathan.

"Thanks. It would mean a lot to me," said Nancy quietly. She was surprised that sadness swept over her, thinking of how Zimmerman planned his escape from the hospital and his revenge on Bingham. It didn't turn out as he had hoped, but on the other hand, Nancy would have been surprised if he hadn't figured he'd be killed if he went after Bingham. Was it suicide then, or revenge against evil? "I guess we'll never know," said Nancy, this time to herself.

Chapter 35

"Can we stop on the way to the hotel and get some breakfast?" asked Nancy of Jonathan and the officer in the front seat that was driving them back into town. "I'm famished!"

"I can drop you anywhere you want, but I need to get back to the station. Is that acceptable to you?" he asked politely.

Nancy looked at Jonathan, who nodded silently. "Sure, just drop us off near Harrod's, and we'll find our way back from there," she said.

"Your wish is my command," added the officer tipping his cap in a partial salute.

Nancy and Jonathan only attracted a small amount of attention as they departed the back of the police car in front of Harrod's Department store. "I wonder if they think we're criminals being let loose on an unsuspecting public," Nancy quipped.

"Wow, your imagination is something else," was all Jonathan could say, shaking his head.

It was only 9 a.m.when they arrived, and Harrod's hadn't opened yet. "We've had a full day already, and other people's day hasn't even begun," commented Nancy, disappointed that the famous department store was not yet available.

"Let's find a small café, have some breakfast and come back," suggested Jonathan.

"That sounds like a plan," replied Nancy cheerily.

The ride back into town had given both Nancy and Jonathan a chance to clear their heads and regain their strength and humor and begin to deal with the horror they had witnessed in the last few days. Not being able to get into Harrod's was hardly a tragedy, and both laughed at the irony.

They found a local dive and ordered breakfast with abandon. "Screw healthy eating this morning! We are alive and should celebrate!" Nancy whooped a little too loudly, and curious faces turned her way. "Oh, sorry, but not really."

Both Jonathan and Nancy ordered the Big English Breakfast, but Jonathan attacked it with a bit more gusto than Nancy once she saw the plate filled with fried eggs, half-cooked bacon, baked beans, mushrooms, tomatoes, and toast swimming in bacon grease.

"Just don't look at it," suggested Jonathan, making Nancy giggle.

"Well, that was quite something Nancy admitted when they left the restaurant. "To say it was interesting is, to put it mildly, an understatement. I guess I've now experienced almost everything British. Except Harrod's." The store still wasn't open. "I think I'd better pass and go back to the hotel. I have a lot to do before returning to the police station this afternoon."

"Do you want me to stay?" asked Jonathan.

"No, thank you. You have been more than wonderful, but I need some alone time to regroup," she added sincerely.

"I certainly understand," Jonathan replied. The short walk back to the hotel was filled with quiet contemplation and comfortable companionship. "OK, I'll see you at the station later, " Jonathan said as he dropped Nancy off at the hotel's front door and headed toward the tube station.

Finally, Nancy was alone. Alone with Dolcé, who had been hiding in the background. Dolcé had not been given a chance to participate actively this morning, but she had been there, and she grieved for Zimmerman. They each suffered in their own ways.

Instead of going back to bed or taking a long hot bath, Nancy changed into her exercise clothes and went for a five-mile run. The exercise was her way of exorcizing her demons, and plenty of them needed banishing. Once she hit her stride, she felt a sense of freedom and well-being envelop her. "I am going to be just fine," she said to herself repeatedly.

An hour later, she was returning to the hotel, feeling refreshed and ready to face the future. But before she reported to the police station, she had an overwhelming need to make a not-so-quick stop. She couldn't leave London without seeing Harrod's. It had always been at the top of her "bucket list," and it would have broken her heart just a little bit to leave town without at least saying hello."

So, instead of being a good girl and returning to the hotel as she had initially intended, she jogged to the entrance of Harrod's, took a selfie in front of the famous department store, and went in…jogging clothes and all. She had heard about an infamous "Harrod's Dress Code" but decided to try to get in anyway. To her delight, she was welcomed through the door the same as someone dressed in a Chanel suit would have been.

She headed directly to the very famous Food Halls on the ground floor. She had heard from many of her friends that you could get ANYTHING there…anything…and once she was standing in the middle of the new Chocolate Hall, she understood that her friends had not exaggerated. There was chocolate in beautiful boxes and tins wherever she looked, from the floor to the ceiling. She didn't know how anyone could make a decision.

The temptation was too great, and she bought three different types of chocolate truffles. "I'll take them home to the girls in the office," she said, knowing that all three boxes would never reach their original destination intact.

Then to the cheese hall. Hundreds of wheels of cheese were on display. Nancy knew she could not take it home with her, so she just admired the variety with a watering mouth and finally tore herself away and went to the meat hall.

"OMG!" she practically yelled in delight. "This is truly incredible! And so are the prices!" She had never paid almost $50/pound for a steak, but she imagined the ones in the case would be spectacular.

She spent nearly half an hour in the grocery section, especially with the tinned foods. There were sauces from all over the world, at least forty types of olives, dozens of jams, preserves, and marmalades, and just about anything that Nancy could imagine.

She had heard about the shrine to Princess Di at the foot of the Egyptian escalator in the basement and headed there next. Nancy was too young to remember Princess Di, but she had heard of her over the years and admired her kindness and beauty. The shrine made her sad at the life that was ended way too soon. Even the Egyptian escalator was so impressive. Nancy felt like she had stepped back in time three thousand years, but then she realized they didn't have escalators back then. "You idiot," she chuckled. "But still, it's very impressive!"

"Maybe someday I will be able to see the real thing," she thought. "Egypt is so steeped in history. And chaos. Perhaps they will need stem cells. I would love to go there sometime," she whispered to herself as she stepped onto the moving stairs.

So, up the escalators she went to the first floor. Everything in the store was so overwhelming that she didn't know where to begin. She found the shoe department, and her breath was taken away, not only by the variety and how incredibly gorgeous they were, but also by the price tags. "How many catheters would I need to change to afford just one of those shoes, much less a pair?" she laughed at herself. The pair she liked was over 1,300 pounds sterling, which was equal to about $1,500 American. "Look, but don't touch," was her mantra today.

She found the women's fashions and had the same ethereal feeling. She was in heaven and a little bit of hell since she couldn't afford to buy any of the items she coveted.

Eventually, the longing became too much for her. She also realized she had been in the store for over two hours and was due back at the police station soon.

Reluctantly, she pulled herself away, exited the building, and made the short walk back to her hotel in record time.

"What an incredible place," she gushed. "That would be worth a trip across the pond by itself!" As she walked to the hotel, she couldn't keep herself from turning around and blowing a kiss to Harrod's, the great institution. "I hope to see you again real soon and with some real money," she added, laughing. She was happy, really happy!

Nancy called Jonathan and told him of her little detour and that she would be late. "Take your time. We'll be here for another five hours easily," he said, letting her off the hook a bit. "Was Harrods nice?"

"Nice doesn't begin to describe it! It was wonderful! It makes every store in Chicago feel like Walmart in comparison, and those are nice stores!" she said excitedly. "OK, I have things to do. I'll see you later."

Nancy had a couple more stops before settling into the hotel. She bought two bottles of Pinot Grigio at the bottle shop and quickly stopped at a nearby Boots pharmacy.

Two and a half hours later, as promised, Nancy appeared at the local police station, but nobody recognized her. She was no longer Dolcé, the blonde bombshell with henna tattoos and wild sexy hippie outfits. She was brunette Nancy in attractive but sensible autumnal clothes. Everyone but Jonathan took a double take when she walked into the conference room.

Jonathan said, "welcome back, Nancy," and she knew exactly what he meant.

The late afternoon passed quickly, if not easily. Nancy was questioned over and over again until her head spun. The same questions were asked in a hundred different ways. Nancy understood that the officers were trying to understand what had happened between Bingham and Zimmerman last night, but Nancy didn't know anything more than they did.

She assumed that Zimmerman had walked out of the hospital, found some transportation to Bingham's house, and probably gained access from the pool area to murder him. He may have been surprised to find Bingham on the back patio bar as he arrived. Zimmerman confronted Bingham. A fight broke out, and Zimmerman took the first shots. Shots meant to kill. Bingham must have only gotten off one shot, but it had found its mark, killing Zimmerman as he was dying.

Nancy shared her theory with the police, who felt it was logical. There were many more questions, but Nancy could not answer them. She had not been involved with that aspect of the investigation, and she reminded everyone of that fact. They finally ceased their endless questions and thanked her profusely before allowing her to once again return to her hotel.

But before she did, Agent Robinson asked to see her privately in his office. That startled Nancy slightly, and she sat in front of his desk, wondering what she had done wrong. The insecure little girl was sitting in front of this powerful man instead of the strong, capable woman she was. She looked at him with a questioning facial expression.

"Nancy, I called you in to ask you a question, and you can take your time answering it. Take as much time as you need," Robinson began.

Nancy was wondering what question he could ask her that would put on her guard so readily. "What is it?" she asked a little meekly.

"The men and I have been talking about you, and everyone is very impressed with how you handled yourself during and after the raid."

Nancy smiled humbly and didn't say anything. She just listened.

"We were wondering if you would consider coming to work with us at Interpol?" he continued. "You have the skills, courage, intelligence, and have demonstrated great loyalty to your cause and partners. We would be honored to have you become one of us."

Nancy was flabbergasted. Never in a million years had she seen that coming. At first, she was speechless, but she was never silent for long. Her voice came to her in just a few moments.

"Thank you so much for the huge compliment. I haven't loved every minute of the adventure, but I have loved working with everyone knowing we put away a lot of bad guys for a very long time. It could become addictive," she said. "I'd have to think about it very seriously when I get home. I can't imagine moving to London because my life is in Chicago."

And after thinking about things for a couple of minutes, she asked, "Would you consider hiring me as a special agent on specific projects? I could work with you when you need my unique skill set. You know I'd love to go just about anywhere at any time. That way, I could still live in Chicago and travel to my assigned job in London, Paris, Cairo…or anywhere! My new mantra would be, 'Have passport, will travel'."

Robinson thought about her proposal for a moment and replied, "I think that could be arranged. Let me talk to the higher-ups and get back to you. Please don't talk about this to anybody, not even Agent Harris, until we can work out the details."

"Of course," she said and stood to shake Agent Robinson's hand. "I'll be looking forward to hearing from you very soon," and left the room giddy with happiness. "This could be the beginning of something incredible!" she admitted.

Nancy ran into Jonathan as she was leaving Agent Robinson's office. He hadn't had a private moment to share with her since she had arrived at the station.

"So, how is Dolcé holding up through all of this? Dolcé did all the work, and Nancy got all the glory," said Jonathan wisely.

"We're both fine. Dolcé and I are one, remember?" she said.

"Of course, I remember," he said, a little hurt. "I always remember."

"I'm sorry, Jonathan. I didn't mean to snap. It's all been a lot to absorb."

"That's OK, I understand," he said.

"Do you?" asked Nancy pointedly. "How can you? I don't even understand it myself. What I do understand is that you have been phenomenal to me through this whole ordeal. You have been my keeper, caregiver, comforter, and protector, and I cannot tell you how much that means to me. It also frightens me terribly. I have never been as close to anyone as I am to you. I have never been able to depend on anyone but myself, and then you show up."

Jonathan began to fidget, and Nancy continued. "You have opened up a whole new world to me. One of stability and calm caring and even love."

Jonathan began to speak, and Nancy once again stopped him and continued. "But I am not capable of anything more than who and what I am right now. I am not ready to receive your nonjudgmental nonconditional love. And neither should you be offering it. You think you know me, but you don't know all of me, and I'm not sure I want you to know the rest at this time."

"I need to go home, and you need to go back to your life. I thank you more than you'll ever know for everything you have done for me over the last two weeks. It's been the best time of my life in so many ways!" she said with genuine sincerity.

"I think you should stay here at work, and I will go back to the hotel where I need to be alone. I will be in touch as soon as I get home. It's better this way," she said determinedly.

What could Jonathan do or say? Nothing. With a hurt and confused expression, he turned and retreated into the conference room, where the officers were loudly debating their theories. He didn't look back, and neither did Nancy.

After returning to her room, Nancy opened the first bottle of wine and poured herself a large glass, which was emptied in less than a minute. She poured herself another glass that she drank more slowly since she was beginning to feel the effects of the first glass. She enjoyed the calming warmth the wine gave her. She needed it!

The bottle was almost empty when Nancy decided she needed a nap more than anything else. She removed her clothes, put the "do not disturb" sign on the door, pulled the black-out curtains closed tightly and drifted into an alcohol-induced slumber.

She woke up at 9 p.m., disoriented but refreshed. "Wow, I guess I needed that," she said to herself before crawling out of bed. She was surprised that it was dark outside and checked the clock. "What!" she exclaimed. "How long have I been asleep? And boy, my mouth is parched," she said before getting a cold bottle of water out of the fridge and emptying it in one long swallow.

She checked her phone. There were no calls or messages, and she was a bit relieved.

"I have fifteen hours before I must be at Heathrow Airport, and I am wide awake. Dolcé wants to get in one last night of fun before going home. I think she deserves it!" said Nancy to herself.

Nancy went to the lobby and picked up a copy of "Time Out" to see where a good place to go would be. She had to be sure she would find someplace wholly new where the possibility of running into someone she knew would be negligible. It was a Friday night, so the options were endless.

A superb place appeared immediately. Nancy laughed at the perfection of it. The nightclub was in Kensington, within walking distance, and called, of all things, Dolcé London! It was advertised as "a unique playground for the extravagant, designed for affable debauchery and indulgent fun without pretentiousness." That fit Dolcé and Nancy to a tee. The club didn't open until 10 p.m., so Dolcé had plenty of time to change into her finest clubbing ensemble. "You deserve a great night out," said Nancy to Dolcé. And she truly meant it.

Two hours later, Dolcé appeared at the door of Dolcé London, still amused at the serendipity of the name. The doorman took one look at her and gestured for her to enter with a gallant bow. She fit the image they were trying to portray beautifully. Young, sexy, elegant, mysterious, and playful, all wrapped into one package. That was Dolcé tonight!

The manager waived her membership fee, and she was given her first drink, a Cosmopolitan on the house. It was just a matter of a couple of minutes before the men started schooling around her, like sharks in the ocean. "I think Jimmy Buffet had a song about that," she thought and hummed, "sharks to the left, sharks to the right, and you're the only bait in town." She felt totally free for the first time in weeks.

At first, she wondered why, but then it came to her. She no longer had any tracker on her. Not Interpol's, not Travis'…nothing. And the feeling was beautiful. Bingham was dead, so his threat was obliterated. Sure, he still had goons, but the organization had temporarily been paralyzed. And she was sure they wouldn't be coming to Kensington, where they would stand out like a sore thumb. She was free!

Her happiness and excitement were contagious. She didn't wait to be asked to dance. She joined anybody on the dance floor and showed them what happy dancing was all about. She wasn't naïve, though, and was very careful about not leaving her drink unattended. She didn't want a repeat of what had happened in Berlin.

Many men offered to buy her drinks and asked her to dance. She obliged but did not stay with any one man for more than fifteen minutes. She didn't want to pick someone up tonight. She just wanted to let loose, and that's precisely what she did!

Just before closing time at 2:45, she ran out of steam. She heard protests when she announced she would be leaving but ignored them. She knew instinctively it was time to go. Without much ado, she reclaimed her coat, left the building, and made the short walk back to her hotel alone and unimpeded.

She needed to leave for the airport at noon, so she finished most of her packing before taking a shower and once again slipping between the luxurious sheets, where she fell into a peaceful and happy sleep. Dolcé was back, and Nancy was glad!

Chapter 36

Dolcé's euphoria continued through the morning while Nancy got packed, checked in online with the airlines, and checked out of the hotel in person. She was pleased to find that her bill had already been paid in full. She hadn't expected such generosity but appreciated it greatly.

She didn't call Jonathan or anyone else. It was time to look forward, not backward. She texted her bosses at home, telling them she would return to work on Monday. She decided one last time to take the train to the airport. It was silly, she believed, to take a taxi when the train to Heathrow was so easy and convenient, even with luggage. Besides, she wanted to hear "mind the gap" just one more time before departing jolly old England. "Minding the gap," she whispered to herself when she exited the train for the last time.

"This adventure is done, but the next one is just around the corner." It became her mantra over the next few months and years. "If everyone thought that way, we would have a lot happier world!" she told herself repeatedly.

Heathrow was busy and a bit confusing, but Nancy navigated the airport well by following the signs carefully. She successfully passed through security without a problem after dropping her checked bag at the airline's designated spot. She even had some time to spare, and suddenly realized that she had not purchased anything to take home to her co-workers. "How could I be so inconsiderate!" she told herself and quickly headed to the largest souvenir shop in the terminal. "Thank goodness for tacky shops," she said sincerely, but it sounded sarcastic.

Nancy spent the next thirty minutes and over a hundred dollars on refrigerator magnets, coffee mugs, Union Jack tea towels , and even a solar-powered statue of the queen that waved to her subjects. She wondered how she would get all her loot home without breaking before the clerk was kind enough to wrap each gift in bubble wrap and place it gently into the shopping bag. "That is so nice," thought Nancy. She skipped the Duty-Free, especially after having consumed two bottles of wine in the room and numerous but watered-down drinks at the club last night. She didn't want to look at a bottle of alcohol this morning and knew that if she bought it, she would have to carry it when she arrived at O'Hare.

Oh, my goodness. I forgot about my car. It had been sitting in the parking lot for two weeks now. I imagine it will be filthy.

I hope the battery didn't go dead. Crazy thoughts swam through her head until she told herself to cool it. "Everything will be fine. People leave their cars at O'Hare for weeks and months sometimes. That is the definition of Long-Term Parking!" she laughed at herself.

She boarded the plane without a single glance backward. Her future was beginning now. That corny but nice saying from the seventies came to her mind. "This is the first day of the rest of your life," she quoted. "And I am going to make the most of it!"

She wasn't in a very talkative mood, so she silently settled into her window seat, smiled at her row mates, and feigned sleep. She found that was an excellent way to discourage unwanted conversations.

The plane took off without delay or incident, and Nancy watched England disappear as they flew through the low cloud cover that hovered over London. "Goodbye, old girl," Nancy whispered. "I hope we see each other again!"

Her usual nine-hour sleep was interrupted by her thoughts of the last two weeks. As hard as she tried, she couldn't put it all aside. Her brain chose the highlights one by one and dissected each before allowing her to move on to the next, beginning with her close call at the Car Wash nightclub. Seeing Zimmerman had frightened her to her very core, and for good reason. He could just as easily have been a really bad guy as the good guy he proved to be in the end. And she exposed herself recklessly to him and his gang of mobsters. Would she never learn that picking up strange men could be dangerous, especially in a foreign city she wasn't familiar with? Even meeting Officer Mathews in front of Buckingham Palace. Despite looking relatively innocuous, he could have been a serial killer for all she knew. Are her days of Dolcé picking up guys on the weekends over because it was now just too dangerous? She hoped not!

Dolcé had been allowed to run wild for two weeks, and Nancy loved the freedom and spunk she felt when she was running the show. Changing her appearance to a blonde hippie biker chick was like putting on new skin. It fit well, but she knew she would have to give it back to its rightful owner at one point or another. She had loved the henna tattoos but still wasn't ready to get a real one. Was changing her appearance a way of hiding or a way of expressing herself? Nancy couldn't answer that question now. Maybe the answer would come sometime in the future.

And Zimmerman, what a trip that was! At first, being terrified of him then became physically attracted to him without feeling any more profound feelings. Even though they had some pretty good athletic sex, it was just that, athletic sex. They worked well together, but there was no bond between them. Was it strange that they could spend so much time together and she not feel profound grief when she found out he was dead? Did she really think he wasn't actually a good guy, but that he had just decided to do one decent thing for the world? Is that why he committed suicide by going after Bingham? Was it to save her or because he didn't feel worthy of living? Perhaps, perhaps not.

And what about working with the Interpol team? Did she love it as much as she thought she had? Or was it just the adrenaline of getting back into combat mode again? Or, was it the adulation she received from the guys when they were pleasantly surprised to realize she was better at their job than they were?

And there were the women, those poor women. Nancy closed her eyes and could still see their defeated and hopeless look when she inspected the houses. It made her skin crawl thinking how each of those women was once happy and free. And what kind of long-term psychological damage had been done. Would those women ever recover? Now that they had been liberated from their captors, would they ever be truly free?

And the instant hatred she felt for Bingham, even before she knew his real intentions. At least his pure evil was stopped. Or was it? He couldn't have been the only one participating in his cruel and demonic obsessions. There would always be more to fill the void Bingham left. Nancy knew this was a very cynical way of thinking, but unfortunately, she believed it to be true.

And then there was Jonathan. Kind, caring, handsome, intelligent, dedicated, loyal Jonathan. What was she going to do about him? She was becoming very fond of him for a good reason. He was perfect! Too perfect. For the first time in her life, Nancy felt she could fall in love with a man, which terrified her. She had shared the "real" Nancy/Dolcé with him but wasn't sure he understood how deeply that relationship went between the alter egos. And when he did, would he leave her? Would he be able to accept her and be nonjudgmental when they were together as a couple? She doubted that anyone could be that understanding. Nancy did not want to lose Dolcé, and she felt the only way a real relationship with a man would work would be to do just that. Lose Dolcé. It would be like cutting off an arm. It just wasn't possible.

And finally, how would she balance her hospice job, the courier job, and a job with Interpol simultaneously? She wanted to do all of them. Her hospice job gave her the joy of helping others when they couldn't help themselves. The courier job was easy and enabled her to travel to places she had only dreamed of seeing. And the Interpol job would be exciting, dangerous, and possibly the best job ever! How could she possibly choose? Maybe she didn't have to.

It was all too much for her brain to handle, so she asked the flight attendant for a glass of red wine to help relax her. It did the trick.

She fell asleep two hours into the flight, and that slumber lasted until her plane landed safely at O'Hare Airport.

After effortlessly passing through immigration, she had nearly half an hour of waiting for her luggage to arrive. She had bought so much stuff during her two weeks in London that she needed to buy another suitcase to carry it all. "Now I remember why I don't ever want to check a bag," she told herself. "I'd nearly be home by now if I only had my carry-on. Oh well, I'll enjoy the new clothes when I finally get home!" she said, trying to put a positive spin on something she couldn't control.

"Now, where did I park my car?" she asked when she finally arrived at the long-term parking. She panicked for a split second, then remembered she had taken a photo of her parking place when she arrived. "What a great hack that is! I'll have to thank whoever gave me the recommendation…if I can remember who that was," she said, smiling. She took a deep breath, coughed deeply, then realized she inhaled nothing but car fumes from the parking garage. She just laughed at her silliness. She was very happy to be home!

The drive from the airport took most of an hour, and Nancy did not have time to reminisce about her time in England. Traffic was unusually heavy, and she needed to focus on her driving, especially now that she was driving on the "right" side of the road again.

Her apartment was just as she had left it, giving Nancy a comfortable feeling. She loved her little home, and as much as she enjoyed getting away, she loved coming home. "There's no place like home," she quoted Dorothy from the Wizard of Oz. "And, that's the truth," blowing a strawberry and quoting little Edith Ann from the Laugh-in TV show.

She unpacked and put everything away carefully before taking a long hot shower and washing her hair. The normalcy of everything seemed like heaven to her. Even being alone felt good. She knew she had all day Sunday to prepare for work on Monday and allow the events of the last two weeks to sink in. But, for now, she poured herself a glass of wine, turned on the TV, and allowed herself to revel in her happiness of being safely home.

Chapter 37

Nancy awoke to a dreary gray overcast morning with light rain forecast for most of the day. She took one look out the window and decided she could afford another two hours in bed. She quickly fell back asleep after setting her alarm.

When she finally regained consciousness, the first thing Nancy did was check for messages. There was one from Jonathan.

"Hi, Nancy. I hope your flight home was smooth and easy. I'm calling to let you know that Zimmerman did leave a message. One of the nurses who cared for him in the hospital found the note. She had given it to the officer who inspected his room after the incident. He turned it in to us just this morning. It was addressed to you, and I thought you'd want to read it as soon as possible. Check your Email. I have sent you a photocopy of the letter. We can talk about it later or not. It's up to you. You know I'm always available if you need or want to talk," Jonathan said. He wanted to make his tone businesslike since he instinctively understood that Nancy would not need nor want sympathy or overt understanding at this point.

Nancy scrambled to her laptop and opened her Email account. Over four hundred messages were waiting for her, but she was only interested in the one Jonathan had just sent.

The note was handwritten and barely legible. It read: "Dear Dolcé, As long as Bingham is alive, neither one of us is safe. I cannot allow that. Thanks for everything. It's been nice knowing you. Zimmerman

"That isn't much of a note," said Nancy. "But it said everything he wanted to say, I guess." Nancy now knew that her theory had been correct. Zimmerman needed closure and wouldn't stop until Bingham was out of the picture.

Nancy also knew that Zimmerman had done what he did for her, and she was thankful to him. Very thankful. She was now safe. Strangely, she did not feel any more sorrow than she had the days before. It was more relief than anything.

She texted Jonathan. "Thank you for the note. I'll be in touch very soon." She didn't want to speak with him directly today. It felt too intimate, and she needed some space. She would call him later. Maybe in a few days. That would give her time to think more rationally, with her logical head instead of her screwed-up heart.

She put on her jogging clothes. Despite the nasty weather, she was determined to put in her usual three miles. She knew it would help to clear the cobwebs out of her head. The endorphins she produced with the exertion would help too. She needed a natural high today, knowing that any "unnatural" high was out of the question. It was Sunday. She needed to prepare herself for work tomorrow, Monday.

When she returned to the apartment, she was soaked to the skin and freezing cold on the outside but burning hot on the inside. Her run had allowed her to free her mind enough to be able to recap the events of the last week, both good and bad.

Strangely enough, most of the memories were good. Especially when she was Dolcé. Nancy loved the freedom of thought and spirit that Dolcé brought to her life. Her alter ego was adventurous without restraints. She was wild and happy without reservations, something that her true self could never be. "Never leave me, Dolcé," Nancy whispered. It was a little like Peter Pan never wanting to grow up. Dolcé was her youth, her wild abandon, and a beloved part of her.

The rest of Nancy's day was pretty routine. She took a long hot shower to warm up, did three loads of laundry, vacuumed and dusted the apartment, replenished the fridge with fresh groceries, and prepared herself for the "normal" week to come. She did not doubt that the week ahead would be just that.

When Monday morning arrived, she woke up at the regular time, jogged her usual route, and returned to the apartment as her routine dictated. Everything felt ordinary until she checked her emails.

There was another one from Jonathan. It simply said: see the attached. She opened the attachment and was astonished to find an article in "The Times" newspaper in London. The headline read: "Big Interagency bust frees over 100 trafficked Romanian Women".

There was a picture of the Mayor of London presenting a framed Certificate of Achievement to Agent Robinson with his "army" flanking him, all with big smiles on their faces. Nancy recognized most of the men in the picture and also smiled. They were so much like an extended family.

The article reported many of the highlights of the mission, mainly including the successes they had: the rescuing of the women; recovering cash, drugs, and illegal firearms; shutting down the cartel, to name a few. It also reported that Interpol was especially thanking two undercover agents who were instrumental in the mission's success but would not be named for security reasons. One was fatally injured during the operation. Nancy knew whom they were talking about and didn't need nor want to be identified. Nancy was just happy to have been a part of such a significant undertaking. She didn't need public recognition. On the contrary, she would have hated it.

She printed out the article and pinned it up to the cork board she had in her "office space," where she could see it whenever she desired.

She also responded to Jonathan's Email, thanking him for sending the article and explaining that she would get back to him in a few days when she had time.

Smiling and happy, she hopped into her car and drove to the hospice office. She left checking in with the Courier Service until later in the day since she didn't feel it was urgent. She did text the office and explained that she would be in after she finished her hospice work in the late afternoon. Maria greeted Nancy as she entered the office.

"Welcome, intrepid traveler!" she chirped. "I just know your trip was memorable, and I want to hear all about it when you have a chance."

Nancy remembered to bring the gift of chocolates and presented them to Maria. "For everyone," she said. "Please enjoy them. They are from Harrod's world-famous department store and cost a fortune…but you all are worth it! And I also brought you other things as she presented the souvenirs, she had bought specially for them. "Take your favorite memento from London and please enjoy!" she announced. Magically, all the women in the office appeared when they heard the words chocolate and souvenirs. They squealed with delight and thanked Nancy profusely before returning to their chores.

"That was very nice of you, Nancy, thank you," said Maria fondly. "Now, are you ready to get back to work? Your patients have missed you terribly," as she handed Nancy her schedule for the day. "And so have we."

Remarkably, the day went well. It was almost as if she had not been away for two weeks. Two of her patients had passed away during her absence, and two were added, but otherwise, her duties were unchanged. She was as happy to see her patients as they were to see her.

It wasn't until after four o'clock that she could break away and stop by the courier service office. When she arrived, Nancy was greeted warmly and asked to join the head administrator, Maureen Adams, in her office. "Strange," she thought as she followed the receptionist down the hall.

"Hi, Nancy," she heard Maureen call as she entered the office, and the receptionist closed the door behind them. "It's great to have you back. We appreciate your good and reliable work," she started to help ease any tension.

"It's my pleasure, and I appreciate the company being so flexible with me. I had a very remarkable trip to London," Nancy replied.

"Nancy, I've called you into my office because of a very sensitive issue," Maureen said, sounding quite serious. Nancy couldn't imagine what she was talking about.

"I don't want you to be upset, but we have had to fire Travis," Maureen began. "Although we did a thorough background check on him when he was hired, we found out that he was part of the cartel in London and that he had been spying on you before and during much of your trip."

Nancy was shocked and showed it.

Maureen continued. "We found out he knows you from some nightclub you both frequent. Your personal life is your business, but Travis made it ours when he involved you. We believe he purposely hired you to expose you to the cartel members. He knew you would be a perfect specimen for them and assigned you accordingly." Nancy was again shocked. She had worked so hard to separate her regular life and her "Dolcé life" and hadn't realized they had overlapped.

"Here at the Courier Service, we never give GPS to our staff to track them. That is against everything we stand for. Didn't you think it was unusual?" Maureen asked.

"Yes, I did. But I thought since I would be traveling out of the country, you would want to be able to know where I was, just in case something went wrong," Nancy explained, now feeling very foolish. No wonder she had felt that she was being stalked; she was.

"He had also confessed to entering your apartment without your knowledge when you were in Berlin," Maureen continued.

"I knew something was not right when I got home!" asked Nancy, truly confused.

"If you want to press charges against him, I will stand behind you. He has already been arrested for his association with the cartel. When they searched his apartment, the FBI found a copy of the film you have probably seen, as well as $50,000 in cash, numerous handguns, and a small amount of cocaine and Ecstasy. He has been denied bail, so he is in jail and should not be a threat to you."

Again, Nancy was so shocked she could barely breathe. It took a few moments before she could process everything Maureen had said.

"Everything is beginning to make sense," said Nancy, disbelieving. "It will take me some time to put all the pieces together, but I'm glad to know I wasn't imagining things."

"That's a good way of seeing things," added Maureen. "Considering these factors, I question whether you want to continue working with us or not."

"Yes, I do." Nancy said enthusiastically. "I love the opportunities the job gives me. As long as you can be flexible, I would love to keep working with you."

"Then, we will be happy to keep you on the payroll. You have done a great job for us, and we would hate to lose you." Maureen stated. "When can you be ready for your next assignment?"

"I will need some time to recharge, and I don't want to lose my "day" job, so I think it best if I wait a month before heading out again. Even though you had nothing to do with it, the assignment to London was anything but uncomplicated. I'm just happy to be home alive and in one piece, no thanks to Travis."

"Great. I'll take your expense sheet now and will be sure there is extra in your paycheck for your inconvenience," said Maureen. "Just let me know when you can be ready, and we'll have a new assignment for you. Thanks for being so understanding. And Nancy, destroy that GPS!" she said with a sincere expression of concern on her face. "Oh, and Nancy, change the locks in your apartment and send the bill to me."

"Thanks, I will," Nancy replied and left the office, more confused than relieved. "No wonder I was a trouble magnet. I was set up from the beginning."

Her confusion transformed into anger. "It's a good thing that Zimmerman is dead because I think he would come to Chicago to do some major damage to Travis," she said to herself. "Travis is one lucky dude. That is unless I get my hands on him!"

After some time to cool down, Nancy called Maureen and explained that she probably wouldn't press charges against Travis because he was already in a heap of trouble, and her complaint, in comparison, would be minimal. Besides, she didn't want the hassle and possible publicity going to court would cause. Her privacy was still paramount to her. Maureen said she understood, but if Nancy ever changed her mind, all she had to do was call.

"I don't remember ever seeing Travis at a club, but the idea isn't out of the realm of possibility. He did seem somewhat familiar to me when I first saw him, but the memory is vague at best," she thought.

She drove home, took a long hot bath, had two glasses of wine, and attempted to make her life "normal" again. How could anything be normal after all of this? She especially felt betrayed by Travis. "Shame on him, serving me up like a prime piece of steak," she said. "That reminds me, I didn't have lunch, and I'm hungry!" Nancy knew she was back to "normal" when her appetite was robust. "Thank goodness," she sighed.

She went to the kitchen and grilled herself a nice steak. Nancy realized it wasn't a "Harrod's quality" steak, but it would do just fine!

After the meal and the two glasses of wine, Nancy was feeling very mellow. Instead of fighting it, she surrendered to relaxation and slipped into bed. She knew it would be just a couple of minutes before she was fast asleep, and she was right.

Chapter 38

At first, Nancy's routine life at home in Chicago had consoled and nurtured her. Through her work, she was able to come to terms with the events in London, both good and bad. As usual, Nancy could compartmentalize those events and store them away where they didn't constantly remind her of the trauma she had seen and experienced. She would have seemed completely unaffected, even normal, to anyone observing her.

But there was nothing ordinary about Nancy or Dolcé, nor did they desire to be normal. They wanted to be extraordinary, always. By Thursday, her "normal" life was downright dull. Yes, she still loved her patients. They hadn't changed; she had. They were still needing her exceptional compassion and skills. They were still as appreciative as ever. She still received recognition and gratitude from her coworkers at the hospice. But that wasn't enough.

She had lived on high levels of adrenaline for nearly two weeks, and that adrenaline was like a drug to her. She needed another fix. She understood how dangerous these feelings were. High levels of adrenaline couldn't and shouldn't be sustained forever. It was like lighting a candle with a blow torch. It was just too much. But she missed the fire, the excitement, and the extreme emotions she did not feel at home. She missed feeling truly alive, not just living.

She missed the guys at the office. She missed the combination of their adoration for her skills, bravery, and protectiveness. It was like having thirty older brothers looking after her and giving her shit more often than not. She missed their comradery and their terrible jokes. She even missed the warm beer! And, as much as she hated to admit it, she also missed Jonathan very very much.

By Friday, she had to do something about it. As much as she wanted to call Agent Robinson and accept his offer of a full-time position with Interpol, she instinctively knew she wasn't ready for that. She understood that most of the time, an agent's work was just as routine as hers, and she wasn't prepared to give up one routine job for another.

Instead, she called Maureen and told her she was ready for another courier assignment. It might not be "over-the-top" excitement, but at least she would be getting out of town, and there was always the possibility of seeing and learning something new.

"I don't have anything right this minute," she heard Maureen say, "but something should be coming up in a few days. I'll call you the minute I know anything."

Nancy was a little disappointed, but she knew that patience wouldn't kill her…or would it! "No," she told herself. "It just feels that way," she said resignedly.

She was so desperate for a small fix that she waited until after work, poured herself a large glass of wine, and called Jonathan. She had been home almost a week, and it was time to call him. She dreaded talking to him, especially with the way she had left things, but she ached to hear his voice.

"Hi, stranger," she said into the phone when he answered her call. "What are you up to?"

"Hi," he replied. "I didn't know whether you'd be calling, but I'm glad to hear from you," he said stiffly. Nancy heard the hesitation in his voice and wondered if she had blown it with him.

"Stupid, stupid, stupid!" she said silently, away from the phone. She hadn't realized how she would feel if there was doubt that Jonathan would always be there for her. Suddenly, she did know, and it didn't feel good.

"How are you?" he continued.

"I'm all right. I've been able to partially process everything that happened in London, and I've come to understand many things," she replied.

"Oh yes, and what is that?" asked Jonathan, continuing in his "all business" voice.

"First of all, I miss all the guys at the office," she said honestly. "Will you please say hi to them and give them a little hell for me," she said.

"I can do that," Jonathan replied. "I know they miss you too, especially your hippie outfits with the exposed tattoos," he added, breaking the tension. "So, what's the second thing?"

Nancy laughed and knew that things would be OK and Jonathan needed some assurance.

"That I really miss you," she said with complete sincerity.

"Do you now? That wasn't the impression I got when you left so abruptly," he added.

"I'm sorry about that. Truly I am. It's just that you came as a great surprise to me. You caught me off guard, and I felt, no feel, things for you I have tried to avoid my whole adult life," she explained.

"Like what?" Jonathan wasn't going to let her off easy.

"Like, you showed me how someone could care for me. I never felt worthy before, but you taught me that I deserve caring, affection, friendship, and respect. You showed me all of those things, and it frightened me. It terrified me!" she admitted. "And I ran. It's funny; I can stand up to a killer wielding a loaded gun without a moment's hesitation. But, to have someone show me unconditional love (or even just like) paralyzed me."

"It was the first time I felt a real connection with a man, and as much as I wanted the feeling to last forever, I knew it wouldn't, and I had to pull away," she continued. "And, I could see how you were feeling about me, and I didn't and don't want you to get hurt. Not just now, but also in the future. I am a really fucked up woman, and you deserve better!"

"Is there a third thing? For instance, you miss and can't wait for another one of our famous Big English Breakfasts?" Nancy heard him say and completely cracked up laughing. It was the perfect thing to say to break the extreme seriousness and tension of the conversation.

"Hey, look, Nancy," he started. "Yes, I admit I was a little hurt and angry about how things ended, but we are big boys and girls, not junior high schoolers. We can agree to disagree on anything and still have a connection. We don't need to make this a big deal. Let's just enjoy each other as much as possible and leave it at that. Remember, no judgment and no commitments. Just a great friendship."

Nancy was relieved. "You are my best friend; I need you to know that. And the thought of losing your friendship made me very sad."

"Don't worry about it. We are good," said Jonathan. "Now, if you don't mind, I'd like to get back to sleep. It's one in the morning here."

"Oh, I'm sorry. I completely forgot about the time difference. OK, good buddy, get back to sleep, and let's talk soon. And Jonathan, thank you!" she added with a tenderness in her voice.

"You are welcome, now good night," he said with finality.

Nancy hung up the phone, relieved. Suddenly, Chicago didn't seem so bad. And normal wasn't too bad either. Her overwhelming desire to get out of town dissolved like sugar in a cup of coffee. It was there but no longer visible.

Could she find contentment? Probably not. Would Dolcé keep doing her thing? Definitely yes! Would she and Jonathan continue to grow together? Probably and hopefully definitely. Would Nancy look forward to her next assignment? Definitely, yes, whether with the courier company or with Interpol.

Once again, life was good!